GOOD GIRLS DIE FIRST

KATHRYN FOXFIELD

Content Warning

This book contains depictions of eating disorders, suicide, drunk driving, date rape, and drug and alcohol misuse.

Cover design by Nicole Hower/Sourcebooks
Cover images © Ivan Bignami/Arcangel; Sergey Ryumin/Getty Images
Internal design by Ashley Holstrom/Sourcebooks

Published by Sourcebooks Fire, an imprint of Sourcebooks
P.O. Box 4410, Naperville, Illinois 60567-4410
(630) 961-3900
sourcebooks.com

Originally published in 2020 in the United Kingdom by Scholastic.

Library of Congress Cataloging-in-Publication data is on file with the publisher.

Printed and bound in Canada.
MBP 10 9 8 7 6 5 4 3 2 1

You know who you are.

ONE

On nights when the winds blew wrong, distorted music seemed to drift inland from Allhallows Rock. Sunset cast the island in foggy shades of red and orange, and for a moment, it appeared as if it was still burning.

Then tar-dark waters swallowed the lights, and the people of Portgrave once again looked away. Any questions they had about the abandoned carnival and its mile-long pier vanished. Most of the time, Ava forgot the island was even there.

Nothing like blackmail to refresh the memory.

Up and down the shadowy beach, silence stretched on and on. In one direction, an expanse of shingle and seaweed paved the way toward the grubby neon lights of Portgrave seafront. In the other, a concrete seawall followed the curve of the shore, making the dilapidated huts and boarded-up shops look like a prison complex.

Ava saw no potential blackmailers, or anyone else, for that matter.

Eight o'clock. Portgrave Pier.

Can you keep a secret?

That was what her invite said. Earlier that week, a pristine white envelope had dropped onto her doormat. Inside, a photo Ava thought no one but her had ever seen. Someone had used an old typewriter to print that day's date and the cryptic instructions on the back. Nothing else. It had to be blackmail. Why else would someone have sent Ava evidence that they knew her biggest secret?

She turned her attention to the pier. Beyond the padlocked gates, it stretched out to sea like a matchstick bridge left out in the rain. Rotting wooden boards hid a perilous drop into foaming water. Forty-year-old scaffolding dangled at awkward angles. For anyone unconvinced, a hand-painted sign read DEATH LIES THIS WAY.

Once, the island had been a pleasure pier. Carnival attractions. Fairground rides. An arcade and a nightclub. The Magnificent Baldo had been its king until his kingdom was destroyed in an unexplained blaze. The fire department and the coast guard had dutifully put out the flames. Someone had erected emergency scaffolding to save the pier. Then everyone had returned to the mainland and locked the gates.

That was as much of the story as Ava knew. The adults in town didn't talk about Portgrave Pier. They didn't talk about Baldo. It was almost like they'd forgotten. Ava had asked her grandma a few times, but she had replied with warnings to stay away, then couldn't explain further when pressed. The strange aura of forgetfulness surrounding the pier meant Ava *had* stayed away until blackmail had brought her to the pier's gates.

Out of habit, Ava raised her DSLR and framed a shot. There was a strange beauty in the rusty turnstiles and collapsed doughnut booths. But Ava wanted her photos to be more than dramatic natural light and washed-out colors. She wanted them to say something. She wanted to capture the ghosts of capitalism and disinvestment that still lingered on the pier four decades after the people had vanished. At least, that's what she wrote in her Instagram captions.

She held the camera at arm's length and half-heartedly snapped a selfie. She immediately viewed the photo. Dusk gave her face a pixelated appearance. Dark waves cut blunt below her jawline. Olive skin made flawless by the low light. Lips slightly parted and unsmiling. Ava never smiled in pictures; smiling made her look sixteen.

"That camera will steal your soul," a voice called.

Ava's stomach tightened. She didn't need to turn around

to know it was her best friend, Jolie, approaching over the breakers. Ava and Jolie were rarely apart, like fries and ketchup or those creepy twins from *The Shining*.

One time, Jolie had broken her arm falling off the seawall, and Ava's own arm had ached for weeks. Another time, a dye-based disaster had left Ava's hair a garish shade of orange, so Jolie had colored hers to match. Everyone had called Jolie "Bozo" for weeks, and Ava's own mistake had been obscured by Jolie's larger-than-life, ginger-hued shadow.

Sure, there were times when Ava found Jolie's friendship claustrophobic and stifling. But most of the time, there was no one she'd rather have in her corner. Only this was different. The blackmail was something Ava needed to fix by herself, without Jolie's interference or judgment. Jolie wasn't meant to know she was here right now.

Ava switched the camera off. When she finally looked up, her friend had circled her to lean against graffitied boards, glaring out from beneath the hood of a giant panda onesie. Frizzy blond curls, ends still dyed orange, escaped in every direction.

"Fancy seeing you here. I thought you had a hot date with Photoshop tonight," Jolie said.

A definite *tone*, but Ava let it go. "You can't talk. You told me you were revising. You were going to switch off your phone."

Jolie narrowed her eyes, clearly unsure whether it was

worth staying mad at Ava when she'd also lied. "So what are you doing here?"

"Urban decay is my thing," Ava said, nodding to the pier.

"I'm sure all fourteen of your followers will be delighted."

"Nineteen thousand, but who's counting?" She paused. "Did you follow me here?"

Jolie continued to glare. "Um, no? I got an invite in the mail." She pulled a face, wrinkling her freckled nose. "Who even sends things through the mail anymore?"

Old people and blackmailers. Emphasis on the blackmailers. So Jolie was here because she had a secret of her own.

"What did it say?" Ava asked.

Jolie eyed her suspiciously. Eventually, she pulled a piece of crumpled-up paper from inside the onesie and practically threw it at Ava. "Take a look if you want."

Ava smoothed out the creases. It was a mock-up of a nineteenth-century circus poster. A bearded lady sat primly in a high-backed chair with a tiny woman standing on her knee. At their side was a boy who looked more wolf than person and a man with elephantiasis. WELCOME TO THE FREAK SHOW, read the banner above their heads.

Ava flipped it over. On the back were typed instructions identical to those on her own summons.

Eight o'clock. Portgrave Pier.

Can you keep a secret?

In Ava's opinion, there were two kinds of secrets in the world: secrets that lost their power when you told them, and secrets that changed everything. The second kind of secret turned a person inside out and showed who they really were. Ava knew what kind of secret her own was, but what about Jolie's?

"Does the picture mean something to you?" Ava said.

"Mean something?" Jolie said.

"It's just that my invite was...personalized," she said.

Jolie's hard expression cracked a little. "I figured it was someone messing with me. Trying to be funny, you know? Because of Max. Some of the dead ends on the estate call him freak show when he leaves the house."

"Oh," Ava said.

Jolie's older brother had almost been killed in an accidental house fire the previous summer. A cigarette left unattended. Flames that spread too fast for him to escape. He was probably going to spend the next five years undergoing painful skin grafts and plastic surgery to repair the damage to his face.

Ava scrubbed her fingers through her hair, already sticky with ocean spray. "That's harsh."

Jolie took her invite back from Ava. "That's why I'm going to find out who sent this to me and knee them in the bojangles. Yours isn't the same, I take it? Hand it over, then."

Ava tried to decide how much to reveal. One person—the mysterious blackmailer—knowing her secret was already too many. She pulled the invite from her pocket and toyed with it.

"Is that the car park at the Oracle?" Jolie snatched the photo and examined it. "Why has someone sent you a picture of a multi-story car park?"

Ava opened and closed her mouth, unsure what to say.

"Um, what happened at the car park?" Jolie said.

"Nothing."

"Liar! I can tell when you're hiding something from me. You go all pink and sweaty."

"And I can tell when *you're* hiding something from *me*. Like what that freak show poster really means."

They stared at each other. Once upon a time, Ava had believed there could never be any secrets between her and Jolie. Ava wasn't the only one who'd been hiding things.

In the end, it was Jolie who broke the standoff. "Isn't the Oracle a hookup spot?"

"Why would you even know that?"

"I don't know. You're the one with a thing for photographing concrete bollards or whatever, you weirdo."

Ava forced a smile. She almost managed a laugh, but then a distant church clock struck the hour. Each chime vibrated in the pit of her stomach. She faced the pier. A lamp flickered. One by one, the pier lights buzzed on, shining grubby orange through the fog. Ava had never seen the island lit up; she hadn't realized it still had power. "Someone's gone to a lot of effort for a Thursday night," she said.

"I won't lie," Jolie said, "this is basically the opening

to every horror film I've ever seen. Teenagers mysteriously summoned to a derelict pier, and *then the murders begin.*"

Ava peered through the fence. "You're screwed in that case. In the films, the bad girls always die first."

"Balls, you're right. Especially when they're dressed as a comedy panda."

"Which brings me on to my next question..."

Jolie shrugged. "All my other clothes are in the wash."

Ava rested her back against the fence. Jolie ambled over to join her. She stuck a hand down the neck of her costume and pulled out a battered metal lighter. She flicked it on and off, staring at the flame until the wind breathed it out. *Flick, click, flame*, start again.

She snapped the lid closed. "I keep trying to work out why we're here. Whoever's behind this thinks they're being Hawking clever with those invites."

Ava stood up straighter as she spotted a dark shape approaching along the deserted embankment. She squinted at the figure, recognizing the familiar slouch of his shoulders. "Talking of someone who thinks they're clever..."

"Is that Skanky Clem?" Jolie said.

Ava rolled her eyes. Jolie hated everything popular, be it fashion, music, or people. Clem embodied all three. "That's mean. But yes, I think so."

Clem stepped into the glow of a streetlamp. He saw them and stopped in his tracks. The way the shadows fell turned him into a silhouette, sinking into a puddle of light. It reminded Ava of an album cover, all mysterious and artsy. She couldn't resist lifting her camera. He covered his face with a hand before crossing the road to join them. Red-rimmed glasses, vintage suspenders over a torn Kraftwerk T-shirt, fair skin with pink cheeks.

"What are you two doing here?" he said too loudly, then removed the headphones from his ears. They hung around his neck, spewing out something electronic and full of discordant notes.

Ava stared at him. His woolly hat was pulled low. His full lips were curled into an almost-smirk. Full lips Ava could still remember tugging on with her teeth. Shame crept up her cheeks.

"You two? Doing here?" he repeated.

"Just out for a nice evening stroll," she said, then instantly regretted how dorky it made her sound. She clamped her mouth shut and made a mental note to avoid talking at all costs.

He shot a confused glance at Jolie's panda costume. "All right, then."

"Did you get an invite too?" Jolie said. "Hand it over."

"Wow, you're bossy." He reluctantly took out a piece of paper and held it out to Jolie. Three people. Three secrets.

Ava leaned close to take a look. It was a gig flyer printed on cheap paper, like the ones littering the pavement outside

Black Box on South Street. The artwork was the silhouette of a naked woman, her head thrown back in ecstasy.

APPEARING LIVE TONIGHT, the print read. WHITE FLAG.

White Flag was the name Clem went by on the sites he used to promote his music. Was someone trying to blackmail Clem over his music? That didn't explain the woman's silhouette.

"Classy." Jolie shot Clem a *look*. She'd deliberately plucked her eyebrows so one was permanently quirked in an expression of disbelief. Ava knew how disconcerting one of her looks could be.

Clem glared back at Jolie, teeth clenched. "It's not a real flyer."

"Obviously," Jolie said. "We all know you only play music in your bedroom and use Ava's pictures to make your album covers look less basic."

"He did ask permission," Ava said quietly. This was the closest Jolie had come to complimenting her photos in a long time.

"Whatever. So, are we going in or what?" Jolie shook the security fence like a caged monster.

"You think we're meant to walk over to the island?" Clem said.

"Tap-dance across if you want, I don't care," Jolie said. "Come on."

She heaved herself up the fence and jumped over. The

boardwalk creaked ominously as she landed on the opposite side, and two rats scuttled for the safety of a children's helicopter ride. Ava shuddered.

"Ladies first?" Clem said hopefully.

Ava shook her head and stared silently as he reluctantly climbed. She was being weird and awkward. They'd kissed. So what? There was no reason why she couldn't speak to him like a normal human. She could tell him to watch out for the rats. Or she could tell him to be careful.

"Be the rats," was what came out. God.

"That's handy advice. Thanks." He swung himself over the top.

"Be the rats?" Ava whispered to herself, pushing her camera through a hole in the fence before following him over. "What's wrong with you?"

She landed on the other side and scooped up her camera. The three of them picked their way along the pier, stepping over gaps in the boards. Waves crashed in the darkness below. Clem walked ahead, Ava and Jolie behind.

"What's going on?" Jolie whispered to Ava. "You're being odd. Even odder than usual."

Ava's eyes flicked over to Clem, then away again. "It's nothing."

"Clem?" Jolie's mouth fell open. "*You* and Clem?"

"It was a one-time thing, and now it's super awkward. Can we leave it?"

"Nope, definitely not. I can't believe you never said."

"It was hardly something I wanted spread around the whole school. He's so—"

"Skanky? Too right. He's slept with half of the girls in our year. *Oh, Clem, your music is so wonderfuuuullll,*" Jolie drawled. "He's as pretentious as a peacock without the peas."

Ava fought a smile. "You know," she whispered, "he did tell me straight-faced that major seven chords are the music of love. Then he played a harmonica for me. He keeps one up his sleeve."

"And you found that attractive why?" Jolie said flatly.

Ava tried to come up with an answer. Clem wasn't the sort of boy who would ever make sense to someone like Jolie. He didn't make much sense to Ava either. At school, he swaggered around, flashing a lopsided smile at all the girls. And every few weeks, like clockwork, the girl waiting at his locker morphed into a new model.

Ava would be lying if she said she hadn't spent the last few years *looking*. Indulging in the odd daydream. But that was all; she needed more than hipster glasses and a famous wink. Only then she'd got talking to Clem online. Through the screen, he'd been an entirely different person, and it was *that* version of Clem whom Ava had fallen for.

So they'd started swapping photos and music, and Clem had used some of Ava's artwork for his album covers. The next logical step was to meet up one night after school, but it had been a disaster. Once they were face-to-face, Ava had found herself possessed by awkwardness and could barely string a sentence together, which hadn't mattered, as Clem had talked nonstop about himself. Kissing him had been the only way to make the pain stop, but it had also been nothing like her daydreams. Wet and slightly bitey.

"Urgh, what were you thinking?" Jolie continued.

"I wasn't thinking," Ava admitted.

"Not with your brain, anyway."

Ava playfully elbowed Jolie in the side. "Shut it."

"Hey, Clem," Jolie called out. "Ava was telling me she thinks you—"

Ava clamped a hand over Jolie's mouth. "I'm going to throw you in the sea if you don't stop."

Jolie nodded meekly, and Ava removed her hand. "Ava loves you!"

Ava glared at her. "I don't," she said weakly.

Clem watched them with narrowed eyes. "Right," he said slowly, then walked on with a shake of his head. If Ava hadn't known better, she'd have thought he looked hurt. But she did know better.

"Have I told you lately that I hate you?" Ava sang at Jolie.

Jolie grabbed her by the sides of the head and planted a wet kiss on her lips. She pulled away, laughing, and continued down the pier. Ava wiped her mouth and watched Jolie's self-assured swagger with narrowed eyes. Jolie wasn't acting like someone worried about blackmail. Then again, it was hard to read Jolie these days. Things had become strained between them, and Ava wasn't sure if it was Max's accident or the Oracle that had changed things.

"Stop being a pussy and hurry up!" Jolie called over her shoulder. Ava jogged to catch up.

They all stepped through a grand iron archway onto Allhallows Rock. Everything stank of abandonment, like slimy wood and rancid seaweed. The estuary at the height of summer. THE MAGNIFICENT BALDO WELCOMES YOU, a faded billboard read. An image of Baldo showed him to be a middle-aged white man in an old-fashioned black suit. Chains glinted at his waist, trussing him up like he was a criminal or a monster.

It wasn't Baldo that held Ava's attention, though. Just behind him, hidden in the background, was another man. Younger, with black face paint smeared across his eyes like a mask and a wicked grin. Ava shuddered.

"What a dump," Jolie said.

Ava pulled her gaze away from the billboard. Jolie and Clem were looking up at a circular building perched at the highest point of the small island: a video arcade topped with a nightclub. It had survived the fire intact and looked as tacky as it had the day the island was abandoned forty years ago.

To the right of the arcade were the viewing decks and

fairground rides, including a gigantic wooden roller coaster that had been almost completely destroyed by the fire. To the left, a path between stone buildings led to the stairs down to the lower half of the island. Ava could just see the tents and shacks of the carnival at the bottom, arranged along the island's craggy shoreline, half swallowed by the sea.

"I was imagining something more…" Ava tried to think of the right word. "Romantic," she went for, although it didn't quite fit.

"What did you have in mind for tonight?" Clem said, smirking.

Her mouth dried up. All she could think about was how they'd kissed, and it wasn't a good memory.

Jolie threw an arm around Ava's neck. "Ava is going to document the moment when I work out who invited us here and punch their dick off."

"You have such a lovely way with words," Clem said.

"I'll write you some lyrics, if you want."

"Thanks," he said, "but my tracks don't have vocals."

"Would it detract from those major seven chords?" Jolie said, biting her lip.

Clem's gaze flicked back to Ava. She died a tiny bit inside. To avoid the awkwardness, she crossed a wide-open square, heading toward the arcade and club. She wasn't there to obsess over boys. She was supposed to be finding out who was trying to blackmail her.

She stopped at a signpost in the center of the square. All but one of the arrows were broken off. The sole remaining arrow, which just said WHISPERS, pointed to the left of the arcade, to the path that led to the shoreline carnival. Ava went over to peer down a staircase cut into the cliff face.

At the bottom, she could see the outlines of old fabric tents, the material hanging in wind-shredded strips. Forty years of tides had eroded the rocky shore and partially flooded the carnival. Water lapped at the bases of the old fairground shacks.

Something moved.

At first, Ava thought it was just the wind blowing through the tents. And then it emerged into view.

It was a figure made of shadows, human but also not. Its limbs were oddly articulated, as if every joint had been broken. Its eyes were black holes. With awful, jerky movements, it passed through the empty space between tents, staggering across the mirrored surface of the water.

And then it was gone.

Ava breathed out with a shudder. *Stay calm, stay calm, stay calm.* "Did you…did you see that?" she stammered.

"You saw someone?" Jolie cracked her knuckles and marched over.

"No. Maybe."

Now that she couldn't see the figure, Ava was no longer convinced it hadn't been a figment of her imagination. Or, a fleeting thought whispered, maybe that *thing* had been her reflection. All the tar-like guilt filling her heart, brought to life as the monster Ava was inside. She shoved the thought back down.

"I thought I saw something," she said. "Down there. But I don't think it—"

"Right, time to get some answers." Jolie headed for the steps without waiting for Ava to finish.

"What happened to this being the opening of basically every horror film ever?" Ava called after her.

"This is the real world," Jolie said, "and bad girls always win."

TWO

Ava stepped down into ankle-deep water, disturbing a thick carpet of silt. Vintage bell-bottoms in heavy corduroy had seemed like a good idea when she'd gotten dressed, but they immediately soaked up half the ocean and suckered wetly to her calves. Jolie's panda costume didn't fare much better, but she didn't appear to care.

"The Magnificent Baldo's Carnival," Jolie said. "Not so magnificent these days."

Ava snapped a quick series of pictures. Over the years, waves had eaten away at the rocky shoreline, and the carnival now swirled in the swash. The main square and the pier had been striking in their desolation. But the carnival, with unforgiving cliffs on three sides and the equally unforgiving ocean on the fourth? Ava struggled to find the beauty in this stinking swamp.

Clem and Jolie began to explore the dark passageways between the ragged tents and rotten shacks. Ava approached a fishing game, a hexagonal hut with a counter on each side. Yellow ducks lay in a thick puddle of green liquid. Buckets of prizes spilled out their contents, the potato guns and tiaras still as vibrant as the day they were manufactured. Five hundred years could pass, and the ducks and toys would still be patiently waiting for someone to return.

Ava photographed prizes suspended from the ceiling of the hut with fishing wire, stuffed toys hanging like moldy piñatas. The carnival, like the arcade, had suffered only smoke damage during the fire that had destroyed the funfair. It could have been salvaged. The island could have reopened. So why had the Magnificent Baldo abandoned everything as it stood?

"We live in a disposable world," she said, remembering the title of Clem's latest track. She'd created the artwork, a photo of some unemployed teenagers sitting on a litter-strewn beach.

In the reflection of the camera's screen, she saw something shift behind her. She spun around with a gasp, lifting the camera up like it might protect her, her finger reflexively pressing down on the shutter.

It was only Clem, a silhouette against the pinks and

purples of the sky. They stared at each other, a question on his face.

His lips parted like the words he wanted to say were stuck to his tongue.

"Hey, losers," Jolie interrupted. "Get over here."

"What is it?" Thankful for the rescue, Ava splashed over to where her friend was peering out from behind a giant teacup ride.

"Do you hear that?" Jolie said.

A distorted beeping sounded from behind the next row of tents. It reminded Ava of an old-fashioned video game—alien spacecrafts firing on Earth, or something like that.

"Someone's there," Ava whispered. "I can hear voices."

"I'll cover your rear," Jolie said, smacking her on the bum hard enough to send her stumbling into the open.

Ava crept between the tents toward the source of the sound. There was something around the next corner. Multicolored lights bled their garish colors into the water. Voices. Laughter. A heavy thud sent ripples toward her. She glanced back at Jolie, who gestured for her to continue. Taking a deep breath, she crept over to the tent blocking her view. She tentatively peered around it.

A high striker game flashed brightly among the unlit attractions, making the beeping noise she'd heard. Someone stood with his back to Ava, wielding a rubber mallet in one hand. He swung it high above his head and slammed it down on the target. The lights rose to the top and exploded into electronic fireworks and music.

"Hell yeah!"

He tossed the mallet aside and thrust his arms in the air, his top riding up to flash his deep brown six-pack. Olly Okeke, Portgrave's answer to Captain America. The winner of the Mr. Junior Portgrave bodybuilding title three years in a row. Unbranded tracksuit, nine-carat gold chains from the market. Ava breathed out slowly. Olly was all right, even if he did strut around school with his arms tensed like he was carrying hot coals in each armpit. Maybe that was a normal consequence of having muscles so big you resembled a balloon animal.

She edged farther around the tent. There were two girls there as well, watching Olly show off. Scarlett Matthews and Livia Holt. Ava frowned. There were *six* of them on the pier? Ava barely spoke to Livia these days, and Scarlett was just a fake-tanned face from the corridor. School royalty who mixed with popular people like Olly and Clem, not the Avas of the world. What kind of blackmailer invited six seemingly random people to a derelict carnival a mile out to sea?

"Good job, Dora the Explorer," Jolie said loudly. The three new additions turned to look.

"Olly, Olly, Olly!" Clem called happily, squeezing past Ava. Clem and Olly were best friends. At school, you could always tell when they were together by the eruptions of laughter that carried down the corridors. A bromance, Clem called it.

"Lad!" Olly said, punching Clem on the arm hard enough to nearly knock him over.

"Ouch," Clem said, rubbing his arm. "What's this all about?"

"I'm being epic, and the girls are wishing I wasn't quite so gay," Olly said. He rolled up one sleeve and flexed his oversize biceps.

"All right, all right, put it away," Clem said. "You're making me feel inadequate here. And slightly confused about my sexuality, if I'm entirely honest."

"Anytime," Olly laughed, winking at Clem. He picked up the mallet and shoved it against his friend's chest. "Let's see what you've got."

"Not much," Clem said.

"That's what she said," Olly retorted.

He held up a hand to high-five Clem. When he was met with raised eyebrows, he high-fived himself instead.

"When you've finished with the misogyny..." Jolie snatched the mallet from Clem. "Stand back, children, and marvel at my panda bear strength."

"I thought pandas were known for being rubbish at sex, not their strength," Scarlett said.

The prettiest and meanest girl in school. A walking cliché. Scarlett had painted dramatic flicks at the corners of her eyes and was wearing a tight T-shirt dress with a skull and crossbones on the front. It must have been a right pain to climb the security fence. Although Scarlett spent most evenings at the AliKatz Dance School, so Ava supposed she was even fitter than Olly. Her dress clung to every lean muscle.

"Can I help you with something?" Scarlett said, glaring at Ava.

Ava quickly looked away. "Actually, pandas have one of the strongest bites of any carnivore," she babbled. "Polar bear, tiger, brown bear, lion, then giant panda."

Everyone stared at her.

"I read it online," she finished, mentally kicking herself. The old Ava said stuff like that. The new Ava was cool and calm and, if she had nothing sensible to say, quiet.

Livia laughed abruptly. "Is a panda a carnivore? No way. I always thought they were, like, mythical. And they do kung fu in their spare time."

"What are you on?" Scarlett muttered.

"All the things," Livia said, grinning at Scarlett and blinking rapidly. Eight thirty, and she was already high. Not that Ava was surprised. Each one of them was known for something. Scarlett was the hot dancer, Jolie the angry loudmouth. Clem was the musician, Olly the sporty one. Ava took photos, and Livia did drugs.

They'd been friends once, Ava and Livia. Not friends like Ava and Jolie were. More like the sort of friends who'd make each other friendship bracelets but then go days without actually talking. Only at some point, the days had become weeks and then months. Nowadays, Ava only saw Livia from a distance, wearing that oversize purple leather coat that smelled of ammonia. Smoking with people whom Ava didn't want to know. Livia still wore Ava's bracelet, though.

Jolie swung the mallet at the target. Ava jumped at the bang. The puck made it less than halfway up, labeling Jolie as a daisy. She didn't appear to care and danced smugly at Olly. He grinned crookedly at her and took a swat at her panda hood, knocking it off her head. She grabbed him, and they tussled, laughing, each of them playfully trying to trip the other. Ava watched through her camera, always watching.

She envied Jolie's fearlessness. The way she could leap into any situation, even with near strangers, not caring what anyone thought of her. Jolie could be intimidating and sharp around the edges, but she was never boring.

Online, Ava tried to be more like her. Unapologetic about the things she loved, confident in her opinions, open and funny. In the real world, though, this version of Ava morphed into a turtle and retracted back into its shell.

"Get off me," Jolie said. The tone of her voice made Ava's head snap up. Jolie was still smiling, but it was an angry sort of smile. Olly, oblivious, had hold of her sleeve and was dragging her in a circle. He didn't know how much Jolie hated not being in charge.

"Ow," Olly said, letting go abruptly and rubbing his arm. "Did you just pinch me? What did you do that for?"

"Because you were being a dick," Jolie said, straightening out her sleeve.

"Come on, you two, let's keep this friendly, all right?" Clem said, stepping between them.

"Just relax," Livia said. She rooted around in the pockets of her purple jacket. "Have a pick-me-up. I came prepared for every eventuality."

Ava snapped a photo of Livia. Her pupils remained dilated despite the flash, black holes against the paleness of her skin and the red streaks in her dark hair. She hadn't always been that way. A little over a year ago, Livia had been up for a laugh, but not a self-destructive screwup. It had seemed funny back then, the way Livia was always the first to light up a joint or swallow a pill. Something had changed.

Jolie looked Livia up and down. "Quit trying to sell us drugs. This isn't a party."

"Then what is it?" Olly said.

"Of course it's a party," Scarlett said. "What else would it be?"

The uncomfortable shuffles from the rest of the group hinted that, like Ava, they hadn't come to the pier for a good time.

"Can I see your invite?" Ava said.

Scarlett handed over an expensive-looking gold-embossed

card. The curling script invited her to an evening soiree on a yacht. On the back, though, were the same typed words as the other invites.

Eight o'clock. Portgrave Pier.
Can you keep a secret?

"You don't think this part about a secret is weird?" Ava said.

"Nope. Yacht parties are very exclusive, you know? Oh my god, last weekend, I was on the Stumpff-Montjoy boat, and it was a-maz-ing. Seriously, I've never seen so many rich men in the same place before."

"Rich *old* men," Olly said, shaking his head. "You're shameless."

"And you're surprised?" Jolie said. "Scarlett's as shallow as a puddle in the Sahara."

"But I do have a lot of nice things." Scarlett jangled the men's Rolex hanging loosely on her wrist. "And one day, I'm going to sail out of this dump and move to Monaco. I'll send a postcard to the crappy social flat-share you'll be living in, Jolie."

The two girls stared at each other. They'd grown up on the same run-down street. They both came from families who were barely getting by. But whereas Jolie acted like those things were a badge of honor, Scarlett had always seemed ashamed of her roots. She never invited anyone to her house, and she never looked anything less than polished and perfect.

Clem cleared his throat. "Where's the boat?"

"Maybe it saw you lot and turned around." Scarlett angrily crossed her arms. "It's not like I can call the coast guard and find out. There's no phone reception."

Ava checked her own phone. Scarlett was right. "Why's there no signal?" she said.

"Why's there still power?" Olly said, shrugging. "Everything's standing in ten centimeters of water."

Livia raised her hand. "Magic!" Her grin faded. "I think it might be all the dead people."

Jolie's mouth fell open. "Uh, say what?"

Livia tilted her head to one side as if thinking. "All the ghosts."

Ava wanted to tell Livia there was no such thing, but the words dissolved on her tongue. When she blinked, she could see the outline of that shadow thing and sense those empty pits staring off at a world hidden from view.

"You're freaky when you're high," Olly said nervously.

Livia narrowed her eyes at him. "My granddad worked on the pier, back before the fire that closed it. After he'd been drinking, he'd tell me stories."

"Your granddad who hangs around with those homeless beardo-weirdos on the beach?" Scarlett said. "Ewww."

Ava's heart skipped a beat. She'd followed the beach

sleepers for a while. Some evenings, they made their way to the industrial estate car parks, where they pummeled each other with their fists until they were bruised and bleeding. Ava had never found out why, but the pictures she'd taken had been some of her best. Those pictures had also gotten Ava into all sorts of trouble. She tried to not think about them.

"Yeah," Livia said. "Well, no. Not anymore. He died. Over a year ago."

Scarlett shrugged. No condolences.

"What did he say about the pier?" Ava asked.

"That this whole island is built on top of bones."

"We weren't invited here by bones," Clem said wearily. "Bones don't craft personalized invites and use post offices, and neither do ghosts."

"Aren't you the cleverest boy in the band," Jolie snapped.

"You're so touchy today, Big Jo," Scarlett said. "Why don't you tell us what's bothering you? We can keep a secret."

Can you keep a secret?

Scarlett's phrasing felt like more than a coincidence. Briefly, Ava wondered if Scarlett knew more than she was letting on. She couldn't be behind their invitations, right?

"Say that again," Jolie hissed dangerously.

Ava's attention returned to the here and now. Jolie and Scarlett were squaring up to each other, Scarlett was licking the tips of her teeth, and Jolie had her panda hood pulled low.

Ava sighed. Jolie and Scarlett had despised each other for as long as Ava could remember, unconditionally and without reason. Arguing with each other was just what they did.

"Go on, I dare you." Jolie took a step toward Scarlett. "Say it again."

"Shall I spell it out?" Scarlett said. "*H-o-r—*"

Jolie slammed Scarlett against the side of a candy floss stall. Plastic bags full of dirty pink liquid swayed dangerously. The two girls wrestled in a whirl of pushes and scratches. Scarlett tried to rake her boot heel down Jolie's calf, but Jolie grabbed her by the hair and dragged her in a circle. The other four watched with wide eyes and open mouths.

"This isn't as hot as I thought it would be," Clem said.

"Make them stop!" Livia squealed. "Before someone gets hurt!"

"I'm not getting involved," Olly said. "Scarlett's nails are fricking claws, man. This face is all I've got going for me."

"Hey," Ava said, her voice coming out small. She cleared her throat. "You two, stop that!"

"Get off me!" Scarlett screeched. She aimed one boot sharply at Jolie's stomach and shoved her away.

Jolie snatched the Rolex off Scarlett's wrist and hurled it over the tents.

Scarlett wiped her eyes with the back of her hand. "Bitch," she spat.

"Whatever." Jolie walked away. "We're done here."

"Where are you going?" Ava called after her.

"I'm bored of this crap," she said. "I'm going to find out what's going on."

Scarlett waited until Jolie had taken a few steps to shove her hard in the back. Jolie went flying, arms outstretched. She smashed into the side of a carnival shack, wet splinters and rotten shards of wood exploding in every direction. The gaping hole in the wall exuded the stench of mold and something like pickled onions.

Ava rushed over to Jolie, hauling her to her feet.

"Are you okay?" she asked. But it was a struggle to keep her attention on her friend and not the hole in the wall. There was something inside—Ava could feel it. Feel it like she had felt electricity crackling in the air when Clem's first message had popped up on her laptop. It drew her in and scared her in equal measure.

"Crap, that was my favorite hand," Jolie muttered.

Ava glanced at the graze along Jolie's forearm and her bleeding knuckles. It wasn't so bad. She'd seen her hurt herself worse by jumping off the seawall for a twenty-pence bet.

"Someone find an ax, I think we're going to have to amputate," Ava said.

Jolie raised a bloodied middle finger at Ava. "Oh, wait, hang on—it still works. Thank god."

"Look, there's something through the hole," Olly said, coming over.

"Is it the rest of my arm?" Jolie muttered.

The fight temporarily forgotten, they jostled to peer into a small, dark room. There was no window or hatch, only dirty fairy lights that barely lit the space. There *was* something inside, but Ava couldn't make it out. She circled the shack, looking for the door. The building stood right at the edge of the carnival, separate from all the other attractions. It was almost as if driftwood had washed up against the island and somehow formed itself into a hut. Black tendrils of fungus snaked up the walls like they were holding the structure together.

Ava found the door, but before she could touch the handle, it swung open on the wind. Her eyes slowly adjusted to the gloom. There was a table in the middle of the room. And along the walls, she could see portraits. Some were oil paintings of stern-faced men. Others had been painted on pieces of wood and looked like they were hundreds of years old. A few were photographs, ranging from nineteenth-century sepia images to a more recent one: the Magnificent Baldo.

The one constant in all the pictures was a gold-framed mirror. It hung behind the subject of every portrait, half hidden by shadows. And in every mirror, there was the same face. Black paint smeared across his eyes like a mask and a wicked grin.

The man from the billboard.

Out of the corner of her eye, Ava caught sight of something golden hanging among all the portraits: that same mirror.

No grinning man, though.

"What's that?" Olly said, craning to look over Ava's shoulder and gesturing at the table.

Ava stepped farther inside. Swallowing her unease, she approached the table. "It's a jar," she said.

She stooped down to take a closer look. The jar was large and filled with murky liquid. The yellowing label read, *Can you keep a secret?*

More secrets.

"What's inside?" Scarlett said.

She shoved past Ava to lift it, holding it in the crook of her arm and wiping the dirt away from the glass with her hand. The dirty liquid inside clouded when she picked it up, and the oniony stench intensified.

"Formaldehyde, I think," murmured Ava.

They all watched the sediment settle. What looked a bit like fat snakes were coiled up in the jar.

"Um, guys?" Olly stammered. "Are those tongues?"

"Of course they're not," Clem said, laughing nervously. "They're just…fat worms. Or slugs."

"Because a jar of slugs is totally normal," murmured Scarlett.

"My whole life, I never knew my granddad to be scared of anything," Livia said, backing away. "Except for whispers."

"What whispers?" Scarlett said.

"Not what. *Who.* Whispers. The thing in the mirrors.

That jar is his." Livia turned, pushing past the others crowded in the doorway. Her footsteps splashed away outside.

Scarlett shook the jar again and pulled a face. "So disgusting." She shoved the jar at Ava and went to look in the gold-framed mirror. She smoothed her hair and wiped away smudges of mascara.

"What do worms have to do with secrets?" Ava said quietly.

"I don't know, but I've had enough." Jolie turned and left, slamming the door so hard that the Magnificent Baldo's photo thudded to the ground.

THREE

"Wait up." Ava quickly put the jar down and hurried outside after Jolie. "Where are you going?"

"To find the sicko who masterminded this nightmare." The loose feet of her panda costume slopped through the puddles as she walked. "Nobody messes with me like this and lives."

Ava couldn't tell if Jolie meant this literally, which was worrying in itself. She'd always thought she knew Jolie better than she knew herself. Their hands always used to end up intertwined as they walked; their texts always crossed. They could talk without either needing to speak a word. But that had been *before*. Something had changed during the last year. *You're the one who's changed*, a voice in Ava's head whispered. She silenced it.

"What's going on, Jolie?" Ava said, more wearily than she intended.

"Um, someone has tricked us all into coming here and is trying to freak us out?"

"I meant that thing with Scarlett."

"Scarlett had it coming."

"She's had it coming for the last ten years but you never hit her before. Why now?" Ava knew Jolie wouldn't answer even as she asked.

Jolie heaved herself up onto the counter of a Western-themed target range. She pulled out her phone.

"No reception, remember?" Ava said, sitting next to her.

"How will you survive two hours without posting a selfie?"

Ava bit back a reply, but only for a moment. "Why do you hate me having a life outside of you?"

"I don't hate it," Jolie said. "And it's not a life—not a real one, anyway. Pretending to be someone else on the internet doesn't make you better than me."

"I never said I was better than you!"

"You insinuate it with every contrived photo and virtue-signaling post about how much you care about the environment, or social inequality, or whatever other activist bullshit bandwagon you've jumped on that week."

Ava's mouth fell open. "It's not fake! Those things matter to me. Online, I feel like the real me for the first time in my whole life. That's who I am, and if you don't like it—"

"I *don't* like it. You've filtered out everything about you that's interesting so you can look good for people who don't matter. What happened to the Ava who named all the seagulls on the beach, even the manky old ones?"

"That Ava was a loser."

"That Ava had a mind of her own. The new one is a sellout who follows any cause that looks pretty in a picture."

"I'm not listening to this," Ava said.

She rose and stormed away through the carnival. Nets of dirty fairy lights rustled overhead. The waves crashed and hissed behind her. Time moved in snapshots of anger and hurt. One second, she was squelching up the steps toward the main square, wiping hot tears from her eyes before they fell. The next, she was back on dry ground, standing beneath the signpost with the broken arrows.

She barely remembered how she'd gotten there.

The square was empty. It was just her and the signpost with WHISPERS carved into the one remaining arrow. She raised her camera. Close up, with the moon shining on it through a rip in the clouds, the sign looked almost whimsical.

Do you believe in ghosts? a voice whispered.

She spun around, but there was no one there. "Jolie?" she called. No answer.

As she stood there, the air chilled, and the clouds seemed to judder across the moon. Ava felt like she was in a time-lapse video, losing second after second with nothing to show for it.

She blinked and took another photo. Then something made her scroll through the pictures of the signpost on her camera.

According to the time stamps, eighteen minutes had elapsed between the first and the last.

"Jolie?" she called again. Nothing.

The back of her neck tingled. She whipped around. Behind her was a puddle of water and a trail of wet footprints that she was sure hadn't been there before. The prints led all the way from the carnival steps to the puddle, then away again, around the side of the arcade. Someone had been standing there for long enough to make the puddle—standing so close that Ava should have noticed them approach or heard their breathing.

"No," she said. "I don't believe in ghosts."

She followed the footprints to what was left of a raised promenade that extended from the side of the island. There'd once been viewing platforms with coin-operated binoculars, a funfair, and dozens of small shops and food stalls. Whereas the carnival had been built on concrete right next to the beach, the decked area towered high above the waves. Or it had done.

The fire must have started in one of the kiosks. Nearly everything on this side of the arcade had been destroyed. Fairground rides had warped into forests of twisted metal and hardened lumps of melted plastic. Buildings were nothing but gutted black shells. The roller coaster was a burned-out skeleton, eerie against moonlit storm clouds. All that remained intact was a derelict carousel and an expanse of collapsing boards through which Ava could see the rocks and water below.

Ava automatically took a few pictures of the wasteland. But as she clicked the shutter, the clouds swelled and rolled in from the ocean, cutting off the light from the moon. A storm—perfect. She'd need to find shelter before it hit.

She'd taken only a few steps back toward the main square when she noticed heavy military boots swinging at the sides of one of the carousel's horses. Their owner's body was blocked from view by the other horses impaled on their poles, their mouths frozen in silent whinnies.

She took a step closer. The gears creaked into motion. Cheery music rose slowly in pitch as the carousel turned. Ava bent and grabbed a heavy piece of charred wood from the ground. Horses with melted faces and carriages of cracked fiberglass groaned past. The posts lifting the creatures moved jerkily with awful grinding noises. The horse on which the person was riding emerged slowly. Its monstrous face, then its neck, then—

"Where have they gone?" Ava gasped.

"Right behind you," a low voice replied.

Ava swung round, raising the plank and bringing it down again hard. The figure before her dropped to one knee with a cry of surprise. The carousel halted abruptly and fell silent. Ava blinked. She lowered the plank a little, but not too much.

"Noah?" she said. "Noah Park?"

In the year since she'd last seen Noah, the gangly boy she remembered had vanished. He'd been replaced by a grown man with long hair, Korean features from his dad, freckles from his mum. Except for the scar narrowly missing his right eye, he wouldn't have looked out of place as a model in a high-end fashion shoot.

The first spots of rain landed on his face. Quickly, it became a deluge.

"Don't bother acting surprised," he growled, straightening up. "We both knew who we'd find on this island."

Ava swept back her wet hair. She *wasn't* surprised. She hadn't known that Noah was back in town, but if she had, he'd have been at the top of her list of blackmailer suspects.

The boy who hated her more than anyone else.

But how had Noah had found out about the Oracle, and what did he want from her?

"No one's seen you in forever," she said, stalling for time. She wanted to run, but where to? Behind her, the burnt remains of the funfair were practically impassable. To her right was the carousel, and to her left, a flimsy barrier separating her from the storm-churned sea. The promenade was barely wider than the carousel itself, meaning Noah was blocking her path back to the main square. "I heard you'd moved away."

"You didn't give me much choice," Noah shouted over the sound of the rain.

"I only took the photos. You were the one fighting on industrial estates like some kind of—"

He stepped closer. "Like some kind of what?"

She swallowed heavily and glanced over her shoulder. The others were nowhere to be seen. All Ava saw was sheets of vertical rain.

"I have a police record because of you," he said.

"I didn't know they would see the pictures. I was trying to..." Her throat dried up and she couldn't finish.

"Go on, try to come up with an excuse. I'd love to hear it."

Ava shook her head. Her photographs of the beach sleepers trading punches after dark had felt like a metaphor for hopelessness and self-destruction. She'd posted the pictures online, trying to make a point about the marginalization of society's most vulnerable, although part of her had found the bleeding lips and bruised knuckles morbidly fascinating in the same way as derelict buildings and overlapping graffiti. The police had been waiting at the next fight, and Noah had been arrested after punching an officer in the face.

"Why were you even there?" she said.

"What do you care?" He stepped closer, snakes of wet hair clinging to his high cheekbones.

She stepped back. A thought hit her.

Charge at him now, and he'll go straight over the barrier.

The thought didn't feel like her own, but now that it had entered her brain, it fit.

Kill him before he kills you.

She gripped the plank tighter.

"Ava," Noah said.

She blinked, and the thought vanished into the storm.

"What's going on?" he said. "Why are we here?"

She wiped rainwater from her eyes. "I could ask the same of you. You're the one who brought me here."

He snorted. "Why would I want to spend a single second with the girl who ruined my life?"

"I'm not stupid, Noah," she snapped. "Only one person hates me enough to try to blackmail me." She pointed at his chest with the plank.

"Me blackmail you?" He reached into his jacket pocket and pulled out a piece of paper. "I thought you sent me this," he said.

Ava stared at the paper as raindrops spattered against it: a newspaper article about the parking lot fight where Noah had been arrested. Around the edge, someone had typed:

Eight o'clock. Portgrave Pier.

Can you keep a secret?

Ava's stomach dropped. "It wasn't me," she said.

"Then who was it? There's no one else here," he growled.

"There are others. Down at the carnival—wait, where are you going?"

He moved to push past her, and she raised the plank again.

"Get that away from me." He grabbed the end with one hand and twisted, unbalancing Ava with disturbing ease.

She let go with a yelp. He tossed the plank aside and splashed away toward the main square. His hands were balled into angry fists. Ava ran after him, calling for him to slow down. Her words were lost to the rain drumming on the boardwalk.

"Wait," she shouted. "Noah!"

She didn't expect him to stop, but abruptly, he did. She came within centimeters of face-planting into his back.

"What is that?" he said, craning his head toward the iron arch marking the edge of the island and the beginning of the pier.

"What?" Ava peered in the direction he was looking. The pier stretched off into the fog separating them from the seafront. Water ran from the roofs of snack shacks and trick-led between the planks of the boardwalk. Lightning flashed high in the clouds.

"The shadows. I think there's someone there." He pressed his lips together and continued on, quickening his pace.

"Hold up," Ava called after him.

He broke into a run, pounding through the puddles in his heavy boots. She couldn't keep up. She watched him dart beneath the arch and onto the pier.

He stopped. Backed away slowly with his hands raised

against something Ava couldn't see. She skidded to a halt at the arch. Noah glanced over his shoulder at her, his eyes wide and terrified.

"Stay back! It's a trap." His voice was shaking.

She frowned. There was nothing there. She placed one foot on to the pier, but a creaking sound made her stop. She looked more closely. The pier was swaying in the wind, boards popping out nails as they pulled away from each other.

"I think you should come back," she said.

And then the wind dropped, and there was silence. Noah took one step back toward the safety of the island.

The pier dropped away beneath him, and then he was gone, falling down, down, down.

No, not again.

Ava ran to the iron arch, which was now a gateway to the ocean. Below, wooden beams slammed against the rocks, turning and rolling, sinking beneath the waves. The churning water had swallowed twenty meters of the pier. It had swallowed Noah.

She lay flat on her stomach to look over the precipice. The water retreated. She could see him. He was lying facedown on top of broken decking that had fallen on the rocky edge of the island. The waves tugged at his legs and sloshed over his body.

It would be so easy to let the water claim him. That voice again—hers? She pushed it away.

She needed something to reach him with. A piece of rope, a long branch…

"What did you do?"

Ava bit back a shriek. Standing a few meters away was Livia. Her hair was plastered to her pale skin, and water streamed down her face, purple jacket slick with rain.

"Shit, Liv. You scared me half to death." She gestured frantically over the edge. "The pier collapsed, and Noah's fallen. Go find the others to help."

Livia didn't move. "I saw you chasing him," she said. Her voice was low and monotonous. "You hated him."

"Livia, no, I—there's no time!" Ava glanced down again at Noah's motionless body. "Just get the others," she called.

She hooked her camera on the archway, then lowered herself backward off the broken pier. She hung there while she mustered the courage to let go, then dropped onto the sharp rocks and debris from the pier. The impact wasn't as bad as she expected, but she lost her balance. She groped at the rocks as she slid down toward the water. Barnacles ripped the skin on her palms.

Waves colder than anything she'd ever felt lapped at her legs. She kicked herself higher up the rocks. From the surviving meter of pier beneath the iron arch, Livia watched, doing nothing, saying nothing. Ava screamed, a wordless noise of frustration. Her foot skidded on slimy algae and slid away beneath her, but she kept her grip on the rocks. Slowly, painfully, she climbed toward Noah. He wasn't moving. Glancing up again, Ava saw Livia still watching her. Only now she wasn't alone.

Another girl stood behind her. In the poor light, Ava couldn't pick out her features, only long, lank hair tangled over her face. Baggy clothes hung from her skeletal frame. Ava froze. The newcomer moved forward. With every step, her legs buckled beneath her, but she kept coming.

Her head lolled to the side on a broken neck, and then Ava saw her face.

Rachel.

"*He only needs one,*" Rachel gasped, and now her voice was close, her cold breath right against Ava's cheek.

The crashing waves swallowed Ava's scream and filled her mouth with water, freezing her from the inside out. There was a moment when she thought the ocean would drag her away. But somehow, she gripped the rocks with icy fingers until there was a lull between waves. With her last reserves of strength, she scrambled up to where Noah lay.

She looked up once more. Livia and Rachel had vanished. Had they ever been there at all?

She crawled over to Noah, who moaned and opened his eyes.

"Alfred?" he slurred.

"It's Ava," she said.

"Ava?"

"You know, the girl who ruined your life?"

He blinked woozily at her. "Why are you here?"

"I don't know."

"Surprised you didn't take my picture," he said, eyes closing again.

Ava shuddered.

"Hey, what happened?"

Ava looked up and saw Clem leaning over the edge, Olly and Scarlett behind him.

"The pier collapsed," she shouted back. "He's conscious, but I can't get him up by myself."

"Is that Noah Park?" Olly called down.

"What did you do to him this time?" Scarlett said.

"Can someone help?" Ava yelled. "The tide's coming in."

Olly jumped the two meters down to the rocks, making it look easier than it had felt to Ava. Together, they heaved Noah to his feet. He swayed unsteadily but remained upright. One on each side, they supported him over the rocks to an access ladder nailed to the pier's support posts. Olly went first, then Noah stumbled up the rungs. With Ava pushing and Olly and Clem pulling him, they got him to the top.

At the top of the ladder, Ava retrieved her camera. They all stood—Ava, Olly, Clem, Noah and Scarlett—soaked and shivering, staring across the divide.

Waves splashed over the sides of the pier, and dark rain obscured most of the fairy lights. Ava found it hard to believe Portgrave still existed. It didn't matter either way. The collapsing pier had opened up a gap of twenty meters, and there was no way across.

They were trapped on Allhallows Rock.

FOUR

The group huddled beside a roofless food shack, coats pulled up over their heads and clothes sodden. The shack was one of several encircling the main square and separating them from the jagged cliffs that surrounded the island. The buildings had once funneled visitors across to the arcade, where the path split into two, leading to the promenade and its funfair in one direction and the stairs down to the carnival in the other.

Ava didn't know which way to go, or what to do, or how to help Noah. He was leaning heavily against Olly, his lips moving faintly. He'd cut his head on the rocks, and the rain washed a steady pink dribble down his face.

"What the hell did you do to the pier, Park?" Scarlett said. "We're all stuck here, thanks to you."

"I don't think he planned for it to collapse underneath him," Ava said, her teeth chattering.

Scarlett glanced at her. "You don't think? Because it's all very *convenient*."

"For who, exactly?" Clem said, red glasses dotted with rain, eyes narrowed in irritation.

"What if he was the one who brought us here, huh? And now he's trapped us all here with who knows what. Ghosts or whatever the fuck."

"Ghosts?" Clem said incredulously. "*Ghosts?*"

Ava bit her tongue. No way was she mentioning how she'd seen a dead girl who looked like Rachel. Ava didn't believe in the supernatural. It had been her panicking brain, that was all, making shapes out of the shadows.

"We just need to figure this out," Clem said. "Everyone stay calm."

"Shut up," Scarlett said. "You're not the king of the pier."

"Guys!" Olly said. "Noah's badly hurt, and you're all arguing. We need to get inside before we die of hypothermia."

"Wait. What about Jolie and Livia?" Ava said.

"They're probably sheltering somewhere, like we should be," Clem said, sounding exasperated.

Ava shook her head. "But Livia was here just minutes ago. When the pier collapsed."

"It was only you and Noah when we got here," Olly said. He readjusted his hold on Noah, wincing. Olly was strong, but Noah was an awkward arrangement of uncoordinated long limbs, and it made him difficult to support.

"Maybe you're seeing things," Scarlett said, shivering in the rain. "Maybe we all are."

Ava shook her head. "No, Livia was right *there*, watching me try to help Noah. She must have run off before you appeared."

"Leaving Noah injured on the rocks?" Clem said. "They used to be friends, right?"

Clem was right. It didn't make sense. Livia was flaky and random and sometimes in a world of her own. But she was also funny and kind and selfless to a fault. Ava could remember Livia once running through traffic to reach a stranger who'd hurt themself on the opposite side. She simply wasn't the sort to abandon two people floundering in the freezing ocean and not try to find help.

Only now Ava wasn't so sure it had been the Livia she knew. There'd been a strange hollowness to her stare. Like someone else had been looking out through Livia's eyes.

"All right," Ava sighed. "Let's get Noah out of the rain."

"Finally," Olly said, grimacing. "Noah's bloody heavy."

"My bones are made of lead," Noah groaned. "Like Wolverine."

Ava took Noah's other arm to help. "Wolverine had adamantium bonded to his skeleton and superfast healing abilities. Get your science right," she said.

"Not sure that can be classified as science, what with it not being real," Clem said teasingly.

Ava met his eyes and then glanced away.

"I'll tell you what's real," Scarlett said. "Me catching the flu from being out here in the cold. I dressed for a party, not a tryout for the Navy Seals."

"You're so selfish," Olly said. "Noah might be about to die from internal injuries, and you're complaining about the cold."

"Hey," Noah said. "Noah's hearing is undamaged."

"Oh, please," said Scarlett. "He's not going to die."

"She's right," Ava said. "I don't think Noah's going to die. Not today, I mean."

"Reassuring," Noah said.

"Every year, close to half a million people die falling off things. But Noah fell less than four meters, and he's conscious and talking and making jokes about the X-Men. The statistics indicate he'll be fine."

Scarlett tilted her head back to the rain and made a noise best described as exasperated plughole.

"I'm glad to hear stats are on my side," Noah said. "Although I think I might have cracked a rib."

"And a splinter of bone could pierce his lung, and he'll drown in his own blood," said Olly. "Am I the only one taking this seriously?"

"You're a real comfort," Noah said.

"Adamantium bones don't splinter," Ava said. She squinted ahead. "Is that a light?"

"Over in the arcade?" Clem said. "I think it might be."

Scarlett wordlessly led the way through the shacks, across the main square. The arcade and club emerged through the driving rain and fog. The light Ava had seen shone from a window in the club. She tried the doors: open. Olly heaved Noah inside, and Clem shut the doors behind them. The sound of the storm dulled to a quiet patter. Ava breathed out slowly. Relaxed.

"What now, then, geniuses? I'm still freezing," Scarlett said.

"Lost property." Ava clambered through the cloakroom window to look for some dry clothes. She tossed a selection of old coats out to the others.

"The fur's mine," Scarlett said, snatching it up.

She dramatically swung the coat over her shoulders and struck a pose against the wall. She reminded Ava of a 1950s siren with her hair falling half over her face and her lips painted glossy red. Raising her camera, Ava took several photos, Scarlett switching her position in between each.

"It suits you," Clem said. "Hot AF."

"Duh," Scarlett said, prancing up the blue-lit stairs toward the club.

"It suits you," Olly mimicked, putting on a girlish voice.

Clem pulled a face at him but accepted a low five as they passed on the stairs. Ava sighed. Clem confused her. He was good-looking and talented and wrote clever things about art and activism. And then he opened his mouth, and Ava wished he hadn't.

Scarlett, Olly, Clem, and even Noah disappeared up the stairs to the club, laughing. Ava chewed her lip. What had happened to their fear and their panic? Thunder crashed outside. She quickly wrapped herself up in a men's floor-length military coat and followed the others upstairs.

The club was depressing. Perhaps it had been nicer back in the 1970s, but she doubted it. Every surface was painted matte black, and mirrors hung on most walls, except for one featuring a graffiti-style mural of swooping seagulls with Air Force insignias on their wings. Disco balls and spotlights were suspended from dodgy-looking scaffolds. The floor was filthy and covered with forty-year-old cigarette butts.

"What kind of club is called Flaps?" Scarlett said, placing her hands on her hips and staring up at a pink neon sign.

"Do you really want me to answer that?" Clem peered at her over the top of his red frames, crooked smile engaged.

They'd dated, Clem and Scarlett. The king and queen of Portgrave High. It hadn't lasted, of course. Scarlett had moved on to someone new, and Clem had accepted it without complaint, like that was the price you paid to be with a girl like Scarlett. Ava couldn't compete with her. She wasn't sure she wanted to.

"Get a room," Olly said. He plonked Noah down on top of a speaker.

"Been there, done that," Scarlett said.

"Seagulls," Ava blurted out.

Everyone looked at her.

She gestured to the art on the walls. "The name. Seagulls. Birds. Flap, flap, flap."

"Why would they name a club after shit birds?" Scarlett said.

"I once saw a seagull swallow a dead rat whole," Ava said. Scarlett and Clem stared at her openmouthed.

She was rescued by the sound of glass clinking in the next room.

Everyone but Ava took an automatic step back. Scarlett clung to Clem's arm. Ava looked at each of them in turn, but no one moved.

She tentatively approached the door. Inside, she could hear laughter. She pushed the door open just enough to peer into a large room with a long, mirrored bar on one side, lit by wall sconces.

Three more people: two girls sitting on stools, their backs to the door, and a boy she recognized standing behind the bar, a bottle in each hand. Teddy Stumpff-Montjoy Jr. In a tweed suit and flat cap over red cheeks, he looked like he was off to shoot some foxes. In fact, Teddy's pastimes probably did include various blood sports, along with burning money in front of poor people and drinking port.

He was two years older than Ava but had been expelled from his expensive private school for drunken behavior, and his parents were making him repeat year thirteen at Portgrave High as punishment. Mixing with the commoners was supposed to drum some humility into him. He'd wasted no time in befriending Clem and Olly, but only because they were popular. It was obvious he considered himself above everyone else.

"What's the holdup?" Scarlett said, no longer scared.

She pushed past Ava, followed by the others.

"Teddy, no way," Olly said, nudging Clem. "The dream team is reunited."

"Olly!" said Teddy, grinning. He glanced at the rest of them, and then froze, dropping his bottles with a clunk. He quickly grabbed them before they rolled off the bar. Someone's presence had spooked him. Ava glanced at her companions, trying to work out who.

No one was giving anything away. Noah still looked dazed; Scarlett was wringing the water out of her hair. Olly and Clem ambled over to the bar to greet their friend.

"Awesomesauce," Teddy said, recovering his cheesy grin. "Look what the storm blew in, ladies."

His companions had already spun around in their seats.

Ava recognized them too: Esme and Imogen, two more girls from school. Imogen was wearing a tight, shiny dress, and her over-straightened jet-black hair hung loose to her waist. She looked over Ava's vintage trousers and crop top with an unconcealed smirk on her washed-out face. Ava ignored it. She didn't put much stock in the judgment of someone who wore a cocktail dress to a derelict pier. And judgment seemed to be Imogen's default setting.

Next to Imogen was Esme. She briefly glanced up at them, then continued to rip a coaster into tiny pieces.

Esme. The ice queen. Bleached undercut with a messy quiff, tank top and ripped black jeans. Tattoos and makeup-less bronze skin. Turn Imogen inside out, and you'd get Esme. Ava trusted none of them. Not posh Teddy, not sneery Imogen, not mysterious Esme. Any one of the three could be the blackmailer.

"What happened to him?" Esme said, nodding at Noah.

"The pier collapsed," Ava said. "He fell. And we're trapped, by the way."

"The pier collapsed?" said Imogen. "We're trapped? Oh my god. Oh my god, oh my god."

"Relax. We just have to wait till the storm passes," said Clem. "Then we can signal to the mainland for help."

"And in the meantime…" Teddy said. He stretched out his arms to indicate the bar. "We were worried we'd have to drink all this booze by ourselves."

"You're joking, right?" Olly said, nervously eyeing the dusty bottles. For someone built like a superhero, Ava thought, he spent an awful lot of time fretting. "They must be forty years old."

"Live a little," Teddy laughed.

"Or, alternatively, die horribly," Olly said.

Noah flopped down into a velvet booth with a groan. "Talking of which," he muttered, "I feel terrible."

Ava looked him up and down. There was seaweed tangled in his long hair, and his ripped jeans were muddy and wet. His boots had a hole in one of the toes, through which she spotted a Star Wars sock. She returned her attention to his face and found him staring at her.

"Are you all right?" she said.

"Never been better," he said coldly.

She nodded. They didn't trust each other, and that was how it was going to be. She left him slumped in the booth and went to join the others at the bar.

"The open bottles will have gone off," Clem was saying. "But the sealed ones…"

"My man," Teddy said, sliding over a bottle of whiskey. As he moved, his jacket flapped open to reveal the wide sweat patches beneath his armpits.

"I don't know how you can drink neat whiskey," Imogen said. Her fingers darted to her lips, and she smoothed her hair with freshly licked fingertips.

Lick, stroke, lick, stroke. Ava couldn't decide who was winning the repulsive prize—licky Imogen or sweaty Teddy.

"I've got gin, Campari, rum..." Teddy rifled through the bottles behind the bar, looking for the ones that hadn't been opened. "Imogen, you look like you want something sweet."

"Just like me," she said, fluttering her eyelashes with no hint of irony.

Imogen was the kind of girl who treated boys like they were gods and other girls like they were means to an end. Ava remembered when she and Rachel had been best friends. Imogen had seemed far less desperate then. Happy, even. The two girls were always together, whispering and giggling behind cupped hands or trying to copy Scarlett's eyeliner in the bathroom.

Then they'd hit year eleven, and Rachel had started to waste away. One minute, she'd been Imogen's less irritating sidekick. The next, she'd been unreachable. Ava had still seen her around school, clinging to Imogen's hand with pale fingers, and she'd wondered what had gone wrong. She'd never tried to find out, though.

And then Rachel had died.

"Like you'd be sweet," Ava said quickly. Anything to avoid thinking about Rachel. "Gamey, more like. A cross between pork and veal, only tougher."

"You mean, like...to eat?" Imogen whispered.

Esme burst into gleeful laughter. She gave Ava an appraising look.

"You're funny, Ava," Teddy said. He took a swig from a bottle of red Campari. He coughed, spitting his drink all over himself and Imogen. He dabbed at the front of his shirt, made transparent by the liquid and all that sweat.

Scarlett swung herself onto a stool and took Teddy's bottle. She poured herself a large shot and swallowed it in one, then winked at Teddy. Glanced at Imogen briefly under her lashes. *I'm the hot one, not you*, her pout seemed to say.

Imogen laughed abruptly, with no joy. "You're so daring, Scarlett. Mother always says that drinking like a man isn't very ladylike, but what does she actually know?"

Scarlett curled her lip. "Is that her dress?"

"This would be far too small for her! No, I actually got this from a lovely little boutique on eBay."

"It shows." Scarlett poured another shot and swallowed it without breaking eye contact with Imogen.

"That's so kind of you to say," Imogen chirped.

There was an awkward silence. Esme rolled her eyes. Teddy gulped from the bottle again and gagged on the taste but went back for more.

"Are we really going to sit here and drink?" Olly said coldly, crossing his tree trunk arms.

"We're stuck here, aren't we? And in the meantime, a few drinks won't hurt," Scarlett purred. "It's not like anyone has to drive in the morning."

Teddy dropped his bottle on the carpet.

"Are you actually drunk already?" Imogen laughed.

Esme gave the faintest sigh. Then she spun around in her seat to address the rest of the group. "Does anyone know why we're here?"

Her gaze met Ava's like a challenge.

Of everyone on the island, Esme was the person Ava knew the least about. At school, she was top of the class for everything and the winner of every school award. But all the other parts of her were well hidden behind her knowing smirk and her complete disinterest in school corridor politics. Her only friend was Livia, although school gossip cast the two girls as more than just friends.

Ava remembered when they had first started hanging out. Livia had stopped cutting classes. She'd become more focused. But then, a few months ago, it seemed like something had changed between the two girls. The rumor mill said Esme had gotten cold feet, what with being made of ice and all that.

"No one has anything to say?" Esme said. "Anyone? Anyone?"

Ava climbed up on a stool to sit at the bar beside her. "Secrets," she said, eyeing Esme warily. "That's why we're here."

"Deep," Teddy said. "I thought we were here to drink and make terrible decisions."

Ava glanced at him. "Is that what your invite said?"

"Something along those lines."

"Let's see it, then," she said.

"It's a boring party invite to what is proving to be a boring party." He poured drinks for everyone.

"Except I don't think we're here for a party. Show me."

"Argh, you're so annoying. Fine, here." He passed her his piece of paper. It was a photo of Teddy, Photoshopped so he was wearing a comedy prisoner's outfit, complete with stripy jumpsuit and a ball and chain. And on the back, the familiar typed message.

Eight o'clock. Portgrave Pier.

Can you keep a secret?

"No one told me it was a costume party," Imogen said, peering over Ava's shoulder. "I love dressing up."

"It's more fun when you're not the only person in a costume," Teddy muttered, smoothing down his waistcoat.

"That's a costume?" Clem said, laughing. "I thought those were your normal clothes."

"Dude, this outfit is my father's."

"I think it suits you," Scarlett said. "And Jolie's wearing a ridiculous outfit like an idiot too, so you're not the only one."

"Jolie's here?" Imogen said. "Ew."

"Jolie and Livia," Ava said. "That makes ten of us. That we know of."

Ava, Jolie, Clem, Olly, and Scarlett. Livia, Noah, Teddy,

Esme, and Imogen. No obvious thread linking them all together. Some were in the same friend groups, and others barely spoke to each other. Some were popular, others outsiders. Some were nice people, others...weren't.

They each had a secret, though. Ava was sure of it. A secret that someone—quite possibly one of the ten—had discovered and used to bring them all to the pier.

She glanced around the room. Noah was still her prime suspect. One day, he'd been fighting in car parks, and the next, he'd vanished. No one had seen him for more than a year, yet here he was, back in town.

And then there was posh boy Teddy. Based on what Ava knew about him, he was more than arrogant enough to believe he was entitled to play people like puppets.

What about ice queen Esme? Another outsider, but with a clever coldness to her that set Ava's teeth on edge. That way she looked at people, like she knew something no one else did.

Noah, Teddy, and Esme. They were her top suspects.

But she couldn't discount the others.

Try-too-hard Imogen, with her clueless comments and desperation, didn't exactly shout "blackmailing mastermind." But she had reason to feel jealous of everyone on the pier, all of whom had someone to call a friend while she didn't.

And queen bee Scarlett wouldn't think twice about trampling her so-called friends to get what she wanted.

Maybe she saw blackmail as a way to get rich quick and escape Portgrave.

Then there was Livia and her stories about the pier and its ghosts. Maybe she was trying to freak them all out with her disappearing act.

Which brought Ava to fiery Jolie. Ever since her brother's accident, Jolie had been in a downward spiral of self-destruction and rage. Ava didn't want to suspect her best friend, but she couldn't deny that Jolie's absence right now was suspicious.

That left her with confusing Clem and sporty Olly. It was difficult to believe Olly was behind the blackmail. He was too nice, unless that was just an act. Olly's older brother had died tragically less than a year ago, and surely that was the sort of thing that changed a person.

Last of all, Clem—a cocky musician who was one person online and another in real life. What if neither of those personas was real? Something about Clem didn't ring true, and Ava couldn't put her finger on what it was.

She couldn't rule anyone out, and she couldn't pin down anyone for sure. Maybe the clue was in their secrets. She thought back over the invites. Her own picture of the car park, Jolie's freak show, Clem's club night, Scarlett's party boat, Noah's fight club, Teddy's prisoner outfit. That left Livia, Olly, Esme, and Imogen.

She nodded at Esme. "What does your invite say?"

Imogen jumped in before Esme could answer. "I'll show you mine, if you want."

She held out her invite, and Ava took it. It was a picture of her head badly Photoshopped onto a very thin bikini model's body with the words Just do it across the bottom. On the back:

Eight o'clock. Portgrave Pier.
Can you keep a secret?

"Why do you think someone sent you this?" Ava said.

"Well, at first I thought it came from a friend from Mommy Dearest, but then all of you turned up."

"Mommy...?" Ava said.

"Mommy Dearest. It's a forum for daughters of narcissistic mothers. My mother, well...she bullies me."

"To lose weight?" Ava offered, eyeing the bikini-clad figure.

"What? I don't need to lose weight!" Imogen shrieked. "Why would you say that?"

Ava held up her hands. "Sorry. I didn't mean you need to lose weight. I'm trying to understand the, um, invitation. It seems like it's encouraging you to look like that model."

"I already do look like that model, thank you very much," Imogen said. "Actually, I thought my friends online were inspiring me to finally stand up to Mother. I need to *just do it*."

"And the bikini?" Ava said.

"I guess they thought the color suited me." She snatched the invite back.

"I don't think it was your forum who invited you," Olly said gently. "Are you sure that picture doesn't..."

"What?"

"Mean something else?" Ava said, glancing over at Olly. It seemed that at least one other person got it. "Like, could it refer to a secret you have? Something someone might try to blackmail you over?"

"Don't be ridiculous," Imogen said with a tinkly laugh. But there was a dawning look of panic in her eyes. "It's a party invite, that's all."

"A party. And yet here we are, having no fun whatsoever," Scarlett said.

Esme cracked her knuckles one by one. As she did, she looked at everyone in the bar. Imogen, Scarlett, Teddy, Olly, Clem, Noah, then finally Ava. Weighing them all up. "Ava's right. This isn't a party," she finally said. "My invite was a shopping coupon. Hardly shouts party, does it?"

"Maybe they know that you're poor?" Imogen said, smiling sweetly.

"Seriously?" Esme leaned back against the bar with her hands behind her head. An amused smile played on her lips.

"I didn't mean it unkindly. But everyone knows you still get free school meals and..." She trailed off at the iciness of Esme's stare.

"You don't know me," Esme said softly. "Let's keep it that way."

"Please," Scarlett cried dramatically. "Can we give it a rest for *one minute* and have a drink?"

"Good idea," Teddy said, "since we're here all night."

"Not a fan of sleepovers," Esme muttered. "Especially ones involving blackmail."

"No one's blackmailing anyone," Teddy said.

"I'm not so sure," Olly said.

Teddy pushed one of his lined-up shots across to Olly. "Have a vodka and chill."

"Stop it already! You know I don't drink. I haven't since Jack died, so quit offering." Olly stormed away to join Noah in the booth. He rested his head in his hands.

The rest of the group shuffled uncomfortably. It had been eight months since Olly's older brother was killed in a hit-and-run. Suspected drunk driver, never caught. For a few weeks, it had been in the paper every day, and then the news had inevitably moved on. Ava figured she'd struggle to last a week before she was forgotten.

She picked up one of the shots and knocked it back. The liquid burned as it hit her throat. She closed her eyes and saw Rachel's corpse staggering toward her, closer and closer. Rachel, whom she had spent six months trying to forget.

Ava wrenched her eyes open. "We can't wait till morning,"

she said, not realizing she'd spoken out loud until everyone turned to look at her. "We need to get off the island now."

"In this weather?" Clem said, raising an eyebrow. "Be my guest. Maybe you can stand on the pier and perform an interpretive dance, because it's not like we have phone signals. I'm sure someone will see you. In the dark. Through the fog."

"I have a bad feeling about..." She gestured around. "About this."

Teddy leaned over and poured her another drink. "We'll find a way off this island in the morning. Until then, let's try to not be boring old fogeys, all right?"

She nodded slowly and picked up the shot. They were right. One night on the island, and then they'd find a way home.

She gulped down the drink, this time barely feeling the burn. And as the alcohol hit her stomach and sent its warm flush up through her cheeks, she started to forget why she'd wanted to leave in the first place. A wave of contentment washed over her, and she wasn't sure it was just the vodka at work.

Teddy poured more shots and toasted everyone in the bar. "Here's to forgetting all our troubles," he said, swallowing his drink in one.

Ava raised her glass. "To forgetting."

FIVE

A fire burned on the dance floor. Olly had ripped the wood from the DJ booth, and the black paint fizzed and crackled. There was melted plastic in there too—Ava could smell it, like someone had tossed in their phone or wallet. The fumes felt almost soporific. Ava's movements and thoughts slowed, like a honeybee made woozy by smoke. Time was thick and flowed in heavy globules, all or nothing.

Something about this reminded Ava of a film or a book; she couldn't remember which. An island of lotus flowers that lulled sailors into a blissful state of forgetfulness, trapping them there forever. She frowned and shook away the thought.

Jolie had reappeared, her panda fur matted with mud and soot, with no explanation for where she'd been. Her hair was a candy floss halo, so Ava knew she'd been caught in the rain. But when Ava had told her about the collapsing pier, Jolie had feigned surprise and changed the subject.

"Let's get a drink already," she had said, and that was the end of the conversation.

No Livia, though. Ava thought she should be more concerned, but she couldn't muster up the feeling. Blissful forgetfulness again.

The group passed bottles of spirits around the fire. Laughing, chatting. Ava lifted her camera and began to take photographs. Her earlier unease crept back as she looked through the lens. It distorted whatever spell had fallen over the group, revealing flashes of uncertainty and suspicion so fleeting only the shutter could see them.

They should have been running. No one was running.

Scarlett got up to dance, the tinny sound of music from her phone quieting the chatter. Her fur coat lay discarded like roadkill. Ava took photographs, but the camera captured exactly what Scarlett wanted it to and nothing deeper. Ava refocused her attention on the others. Teddy, watching Scarlett with an almost predatory expression. Clem, rolling his harmonica over his fingers, slipping it up his sleeve then out again. Olly, lying on his back and staring up at the shadows on the ceiling. Jolie sneering. Imogen preening. Noah, snoring in the booth, his muddy hair dried in crusty snakes.

Esme was more interesting. She was beautiful in the same way as the derelict buildings that caught Ava's imagination. Heavy lines and abrupt slashes of light. Striking and fascinating, but only if you could see them from the right angles. And like derelict buildings, Esme was surrounded by an aura of mystery.

Esme caught Ava watching her and smiled slowly. Ava didn't look away.

"Hey," Scarlett cried. "Stop it!"

Ava looked up abruptly. "What?" she said.

"The flash, it's blinding me."

Ava stared. "I'm not using the flash," she said.

"What's that?" Scarlett spun around, hand clasped to her chest.

The mirrors above the bar flickered with reflected flames. Scarlett's eyes were locked on them. The music playing from her phone finished, and a new track didn't start. Raindrops pelted the roof. Scarlett jumped again, her eyes wide like a startled animal.

"I don't see anything," Ava finally said.

"There was a bright light. In the mirror," Scarlett said. "Are you all screwing with me?"

"Maybe it's the ghosts," Olly said sleepily. He was still lying on his back on the floor, sober and serious. "Wooo-ooo."

"Ghosts?" Imogen said, shuffling closer in her now-grubby dress. "Is this island actually haunted?"

"Don't be ridiculous," Clem said. He'd taken off his woolly hat to reveal a messy man bun. Him calling anything ridiculous was rich, given his hairstyle. "Ghosts aren't—"

The double doors burst open. A figure stood silhouetted in the frame, dripping a pool of water onto the floor, dark hair plastered across her face. Rachel.

Ava screamed and scrambled back. She fell over, coating herself in old cigarette butts and thick grime. All of this happened in the space of two seconds...the same amount of time it took her brain to process that the new arrival was not Rachel's ghost but Livia.

"Whoa," Livia said, brushing her hair off her face. Her purple leather jacket squeaked with the movement. She noticed Esme and frowned, but hid it with a quick smile.

"Am I missing something?"

"I suspect we all are," Esme said, patting the floor next to her. "Good timing, though. Where've you been?"

Livia shrugged in reply. She sat down by the fire and poured rainwater out of her boots. Ava was hit by a waft of her ratty old coat. It stank like concentrated urine, and the rain seemed to have made it even more pungent. Ava knew it had belonged to Livia's granddad, who'd died over a year ago, which made it impossible for anyone to mention the smell. Livia must have gotten used to it.

"I didn't expect to see you here," Livia said, not looking up from her boots.

"You know me," Esme said gruffly, as if that explained everything.

"Which is exactly why I'm surprised. The Esme I know would have ripped the invitation in half and refused to come."

Esme chuckled quietly, then took a piece of paper out of her pocket: her invite. It was taped together across the middle. Ava caught sight of the familiar typed words.

"You aren't wrong," Esme said. "But I wanted to know who sent me this. Wasn't you, was it?"

Livia looked up with a start. "Me? How could you even think that?"

Esme shrugged. "You've been off with me lately."

"And whose fault is that?" Livia went back to her boots with a shake of her head. "I don't want to talk about this here."

"Don't mind us," Scarlett said acidly. "We're all dying to hear more about your boring little tiff. Seriously. Keep talking."

Esme stared at Scarlett, her expression unreadable. Even when Scarlett nervously opened a compact mirror and reapplied her blood-red lipstick, Esme continued to stare.

Ava cleared her throat. "Livia, about earlier. Did you see anything on the pier? After Noah fell?"

Rachel, standing beside Livia on broken legs, her gaping mouth a hideous black pit. *He only needs one*. What did that even mean?

Livia chewed her lip like she was thinking about speaking, but she didn't. Instead, she rummaged through her bag until she found a lipstick case containing a bag of white pills. Ava looked away as she popped one in her mouth.

"Anyone want one?" Livia said, overly brightly.

The group murmured, "No thanks."

"I'd rather keep my wits about me," Esme said.

"And I'd rather not," Livia said. "Keep my wits about me, I mean. This place is…too much."

"You did see something, didn't you?" Ava said.

"Bad memories, that's all." She put her pills away and stilled her shaking hands in her lap. "It reminds me of my granddad. He worked here for years, and he didn't exactly talk about this place fondly."

"Did you see his ghost?" Ava asked.

Clem clapped his hands together and laughed. Livia stared steadily at Ava.

"Are we really talking about ghosts?" Noah said. His voice was hoarse with sleep. He staggered over to join them around the fire. He nodded at Livia.

"Hey, man, good to see you." Livia reached up to bump fists with Noah as he passed. "What's with your face?"

He touched the cut on his head and winced. It had stopped bleeding, at least.

"What's with *your* face?" he replied, grinning at her. "How've you been, Liv?"

"Same as ever. I still see your mum about town," Livia said. "You going to pay her a visit?"

Noah's smile broke. "I think I've put her through enough already. Besides, we have ghosts or whatever to contend with first."

"Come on, there's no such thing as ghosts," Clem said.

"I believe in ghosts," Esme said unexpectedly. She tossed an old peanut from behind the bar into the fire. The flames fizzed hungrily.

Clem played a few notes of something creepy on his harmonica. "See, I've watched *Ghost Hunters* or whatever it's called, and they never find any proof that ghosts are real."

"I didn't say they were real," Esme clarified. She threw a peanut at Clem, laughing when he ducked. "Just that I believe."

"What's the difference?" Jolie sneered.

"Lots of things aren't real, but people still believe in them. Love, for example. Love is nothing but a chemical trick, yet it's still the root of all evil in this world." Esme glanced at Livia when she said this, then quickly looked away.

"Wow, that's a pessimistic view of love," Noah said. "And of the entire human race."

"Is it?" Esme accepted the bottle of vodka from a half-asleep Olly, who'd passed it on without drinking. "Guess it depends whether you feel like you need someone else to be enough. Me? I'm self-sufficient. I've got everything I need right here." She tapped her own chest.

Livia snorted coldly. "Esme's problem is that she likes to

think of herself as a lone wolf, and love doesn't fit with her image."

Esme stared back at Livia over the rim of the bottle, touching her lips to the glass but not drinking. "I'm too busy living my life to worry about my image."

"That's what you're doing? Huh."

"We're sixteen," Esme sighed. "We have our whole lives to settle."

"*Settle?* Wow." Livia grabbed the bottle from Esme, swigging deeply. "Good to know. Thanks."

Ava raised her camera, drawn to the static bristling between the two girls. Livia hid her face inside her purple coat, but Esme turned to look defiantly into the lens.

"How do I look?" She jutted her chin up at Ava, angling her head to reveal words tattooed on the side of her neck. ENOUGH IS ENOUGH, it read in curling script.

"Sorry, I should have asked first," Ava said, lowering the camera.

Esme's lips curled into a grin. "Take as many photos as you want. I'm not shy."

Jolie clapped her hands. "I'm bored. Let's play truth or shot."

"At last, something fun." Teddy went to grab glasses and extra alcohol from the bar. He stumbled when he returned. Cheeks red, huge sweat patches darkening his shirt. Drunk. Drunker.

"I'm going to ask the first question," Jolie said. "And this one's for...Ava."

This wasn't going to be good. Jolie had that vicious look in her eye.

"Can I just have the drink?" Ava said.

"No, don't be a turnip," Drunk Teddy said. "You have to answer the question, and if we think your answer is a washout, then you drink."

"Fine. Whatever," she said.

Jolie smiled slowly. "Kill or kiss. Out of everyone in this room."

Ava puffed up her cheeks and stared at the ceiling, trying to work out how to play this. Normally, she'd have picked Jolie to kiss and then tried to lick her on the face, making her squeal with laughter. This time, she was half tempted to pick Jolie to kill just for asking the stupid question. Jolie to kill, then. Livia to kiss.

"I would have to kill..." She hesitated, struck by a sudden, strange need to be honest. "I would have to kill..."

Scarlett, Scarlett, Scarlett. She's a terrible person and you hate her. Scarlett, Scarlett—

"Scarlett," Ava found herself saying.

Scarlett flinched. "That's mean," she said softly.

"Ouch." Clem bit his fist, wincing. "Shit got real."

Esme laughed, a low, throaty chuckle. "I'm so glad I came tonight. You're all awesome in a really terrible way."

Ava forced herself to grin at Scarlett. Like it was all a joke. "It's nothing personal. I've seen you fight, and now I know you're an easy target."

"Easy target in a fair fight, maybe," Jolie growled, "but she'd stab you in the back, given half a chance."

"I have a strong sense of self-preservation," Scarlett said, glaring at Ava and Jolie in turn. Her eyes flicked up to the mirror, and her gaze faltered.

"And what about, um, you know?" Imogen said.

"Kissing?" Jolie said, staring down Imogen. "You can't bring yourself to say *kissing*?"

"I don't want to kiss anyone," Ava said, tired of the game.

"That's not what you told me earlier," Jolie said.

"Jolie, don't," Ava said.

"Are you embarrassed? Because you shouldn't be. You're in good company. Scarlett, you had a thing with Clem, didn't you?"

Scarlett shrugged. "Whatever."

"And..." Jolie followed the curve of the circle with a pointed finger. "Livia too?"

"We were eleven," Livia said. "And then I discovered I like girls."

"What's the point you're trying to make?" Clem asked.

"There you go, Ava," Jolie continued, ignoring Clem. "The boy all the cool girls want. He's perfect for your new image."

Ava closed her eyes. The thing was, Jolie had a good point. Clem was perfect for the Ava she wanted to be. The real-life Ava, however, was struggling to go along with the plan. The real-life Ava was a bitch and didn't know what was good for her. Everyone else wanted Clem, so why couldn't she be happy he'd picked her?

When she looked up again, Clem was watching her across the circle—a question, an accusation. Before they'd kissed, Ava had daydreamed about him nonstop. The softness of his lips, the touch of his hands. She had been sure he would be the one to see who she truly was. Ava wanted that feeling to come back—she *wanted* to want him like she had before—but something was missing.

She downed her shot and looked anywhere but at Clem. "Is it my question now? Because this is for Esme. Could you kill someone?"

Esme leaned back on her elbows and watched Ava with interest. Her white hair flopped across her face. "Yeah, I think so. Sure."

"That's it?" Teddy said. "You don't even want to consider it?"

"No, not really," Esme replied, sweeping her hair back, her eyes on Ava.

"You need to have a shot of vodka," Clem said. "I don't want to be stuck on this island with a sober psychopath."

"I'm not a psychopath," Esme laughed. "But if I had to

kill someone to save my own life, I don't think I'd feel all that guilty about it. Every girl for herself."

"What made you ask her that?" Jolie interrupted. She narrowed her eyes at Ava.

"I don't know," Ava said, when what she really meant was that she didn't know her own answer to the question. Could *she* kill someone? She wouldn't have thought so before tonight. But out there with Noah on the viewing deck…

"Could you?" she asked Jolie, moving the conversation on.

"Sure," Jolie said. "If I didn't have to look at them. Like, I could kill them from a distance by pushing a button or something."

"Or run them over with your car," Scarlett said. "If it was dark, you wouldn't see their face or anything. Bump, drive on."

"That's horrible," Imogen whispered.

"Yeah," Teddy said quietly. He reached for the bottle.

"Slow down, mate," Olly said, opening one eye. "You'll be wasted by midnight."

"Maybe that's a good thing," Teddy muttered.

"Is it my question now?" Scarlett purred. "Teddy, then. What's the worst thing you've ever done?"

He stared at her, and something passed between them that Ava didn't understand. He stood up. "I'm not playing this game anymore."

She watched him push open the double doors and

disappear outside. After a moment, Scarlett followed. Since when did girls like Scarlett run after boys?

Olly sat up with a sigh. "What's going on with them?"

"Teddy's dad has a boat. Therefore, Scarlett likes Teddy," Clem said.

"She'll eat him alive. I thought he was smarter than that," Olly said.

"Not after a few drinks," Clem said. "And have you *looked* at Scarlett?"

"My type tends to be taller and hairier."

A few people laughed, but Ava couldn't. A part of her wanted to run and keep on running. Only there was nowhere to go. And even if the pier hadn't collapsed, she still wasn't sure she could leave. She couldn't walk away when someone knew her secret. She needed to know who it was. And then she needed to stop them from bringing her whole carefully constructed life crashing down around her.

"Ava, can we talk?"

Clem was standing over her. The rest of the group had moved away from the fire, forming little pockets in the booths. Imogen, Livia, and Esme. Olly and Noah. Teddy and Scarlett, back in the room now, still together, talking intensely. Jolie alone. She stared across the room at Ava, flicking her lighter on and off.

"Is something wrong?" Clem said, sitting down to face her. "You're acting weird around me."

"Everything's fine," Ava said. Her eyes were on Jolie's lighter flame. Off. On.

"It's just...after the other night, you never replied to my texts. And now it's like you can barely look at me."

Ava tore her eyes away from Jolie's flame and focused on Clem.

He sighed deeply. "I thought maybe we'd give it a shot. You and me, I mean." He shrugged hopefully.

"You and..." Her heart skipped a panicked beat. "I have a lot on my mind right now. It's not good timing," she said.

"Yeah. We all do. But stuff like being stranded on an abandoned island is meant to bring people closer, right?"

Or break them apart. Ava supposed it depended on the strength of their foundations.

Clem was good-looking and popular, and it followed that she should like him. But Ava had never liked the good-looking and popular version of Clem. She'd liked a version that might not even exist in the real world.

Jolie would have called her a hypocrite. After all, Ava only ever felt like her true self when she was safe behind a screen and a series of carefully edited photos. Maybe Clem was the same. Or maybe Jolie was right, and the person Ava was trying so hard to be was as fake as Clem's online persona. Maybe the things they *did* mattered far more than the people they hoped they were. And Ava didn't like what that meant for her.

"That's it, then?" Clem said. "You're not going to even talk to me?"

Ava glanced up at him. She knew she was meant to say something, but the words had vanished. Clem shook his head and walked away to sit with Olly and Noah.

Across the room, Jolie extinguished her lighter with a laugh. Her laughter hurt more than Ava wanted to admit. There'd been a time when they were always on each other's side, no matter what. Through Ava's dodgy crushes and Jolie's adventures. Through fights and mistakes and bad haircuts. There had been a time when Jolie never would have laughed at her.

Then again, there had also been a time when Ava would never have kept secrets from her best friend.

Ava automatically reached for her camera, wanting to feel its reassuring weight in her hands. Except she realized the casing was vibrating.

Everything was vibrating.

The chatter in the club stopped, replaced by the low hum of electricity. Ava could feel it in the same way that standing next to a concert speaker made the pit of her stomach vibrate, hear it like the sound of waves drawing back from the shore. Her hair prickled with static.

Something was coming.

SIX

The hum brought everyone outside with their hands clapped over their ears. Pulsing sound bounced droplets of water out of puddles. The pier burst into life in an eruption of blinding light. Neon signs thrummed and crackled. Flashing words promised FUN and GAMES and PRIZES. Power surged around the island, awakening ancient fairground rides and attractions. In the arcade, video games played their repetitive opening sequences in a clash of electronic noise. Slot machines whirred with spinning wheels and the fake sound of coins clattering into trays.

"Who's doing this?" Clem shouted.

"Show yourself," Olly cried, raising his fists. "Come out, you bastard."

Ava swept her bangs out of her face, scanning frantically for a clue as to what was happening. But she couldn't think. The wind whipped through her hair and carried whirlwinds of seaweed and litter across the square. The all-encompassing noise made her want to curl up somewhere dark, but the brightness of the lights had burned the night into artificial day. There was no escape.

"You're asking the wrong question," Noah said, holding his hands over his ears. "Not who, but how. *How* are they doing that? How does everything still work?"

Scarlett clawed at handfuls of her hair, screaming silently. "Make it stop," she gasped. "I can't breathe, I can't think."

"But this is a good thing!" Imogen said. "The people on the mainland will see the lights and hear the music. Someone will come to help us."

"No one's coming to help us," Esme said. She sounded almost bored. "The fog's too thick, and the wind is blowing the music out to sea."

"Fuck," muttered Teddy. He ran a hand through his curly hair, damp with sweat. "We're all fucked." He dropped suddenly onto his hands and knees and projectile vomited half a liter of red alcohol.

Imogen shrieked and jumped back from the spreading puddle. "I need to get out of here! I need to go home."

"Freaking out isn't going to help," Jolie spat.

"Neither is yelling!" Clem yelled.

Ava took a step back. And as she did so, it felt like someone had flicked a switch in her head, making the argument and the noise of the pier fade into the background. She watched from the outside as the others paced and cried and accused. She raised her camera and snapped a photo of the group. When she viewed it on the screen, most of their eyes gleamed red and angry. Esme, though, looked emotionlessly into the lens, her eyes an eerie pale gray.

"Did you invite us here?" Ava asked.

"Me?" Esme said. She looked amused more than anything.

"You still think one of us is doing this?" Livia said. "You honestly think one of us could have set all this up? The noise, the lights? It's the ghosts."

"There's no such thing as ghosts," Clem said.

"Tell me you're not seeing things," Livia cried. "Tell me you're not hearing voices whispering in your ear. Seeing dead people."

"No, because unlike you, we're not on drugs," Jolie said.

"I've seen something," Olly admitted. They all looked at him. "A ghost, or what looks like one. My brother."

"Oh, come on," Teddy said. He had wiped his face and looked calmer now. "We're all blotto and getting a tad overexcited. There aren't any ghosts here."

"I agree something Jar Jar Binks–level weird is going on," Noah said. "I don't know what, but turning on each other isn't going to help."

"You're not even meant to be here," Imogen said. "You left town, remember? Are you doing this?"

Scarlett laughed dementedly. "You're all such idiots," she half sobbed, turning to stare up at the lights flashing overhead. She even managed to make desperation look graceful. "What do you want?"

"Who are you talking to?" Imogen said.

Scarlett's voice climbed in a way that made them all look at her. "Leave me alone, just leave me alone!"

"Steady on," Teddy said. "Someone's hysterical."

"Scarlett?" Clem said. He snapped his fingers in front of her face.

"He only needs one," Scarlett sobbed, a distant look in her eyes. "Confess and you'll be free."

The noise of the island stilled. The music quieted, and the beeps of the arcade faded. No one spoke. Everyone stared at Scarlett.

"I use people." Scarlett swayed, still staring off into the distance. Her voice was monotone and not quite her own. "I destroy relationships to get what I want, and I hurt people who get in my way."

"None of this is news to us," Jolie said.

"I let men think that I like them. I make them trust me so that they tell me *everything*, and then I use it against them. I force them to buy me things, and then I tell their wives anyway."

"Did you use me to get close to my dad?" Teddy asked.

"You only wanted to come to that boat party because my family's rich, not because you liked me, right?"

Scarlett wasn't listening. She turned her face up to the rain. "You hear me? I confess. Now let me go! Choose one of them, not me."

"Choose one of us for what?" Ava said.

Scarlett's eyes drifted to Ava. Her gaze was blurred, unfocused. "The guilt will eat you up inside," she said. "How long can you keep a secret?"

"What are you talking about?"

Scarlett blinked once, then again. The faraway look vanished from her face. She curled her lip like she'd smelled something awful. "Uh, why are you freaks all staring at me?"

"Um, your weird confession just now?" Jolie said. When Scarlett continued to look blank, Jolie raised her eyebrows. "Adultery? Extortion? Greed? You were admitting to basically being the worst person in the world."

"Me? No, not me. I know for a fact that other people here have done far worse things than me." She glanced over at Teddy. "For a *fact*."

"Don't you dare," he spat. "You keep your mouth shut, or I'll—"

"What?" Scarlett interrupted. "Daddy's not here to buy your way out of trouble, so back off."

"I'm warning you, Scarlett." He pointed a wavering finger at her.

"Go have another drink—you know you want one. And maybe if you have enough, you'll forget to be scared." She rapped a finger against her temple. "He's already in your heads, and he's coming for your confessions."

"Who's coming?" Olly said.

"He's in the mirrors. He sees everything." Scarlett jabbed one pointed nail at them. "He only needs one. The rest of you are dead."

She laughed, then turned and ran off into the darkness, toward the carnival staircase. Her heels made an uneven clacking noise with every step.

"Scarlett?" Imogen whispered, covering her mouth with a hand. "Oh my god, what's wrong with her?"

"She's had a lot to drink, that's all," Clem said. His face was ashen. "Or she's inhaled hallucinogenic mold or something."

"Should someone go after her?" Olly said. "She seems pretty out of it."

No one moved. Scarlett's footsteps faded away, and still no one followed. Ava shuffled uncomfortably.

"I guess no one likes Scarlett much," Esme mused.

"This is messed up," Noah muttered, although Ava wasn't sure if he meant Scarlett's strange confession or the fact that no one had followed her into the darkness.

"All right, this is all too much," Olly said. "What's happening to us?"

Livia was pacing nervously, gnawing at her fingernails. "Whispers is behind all of this, I know it."

"The man in the portraits?" Ava said.

"He's not a man," Livia said. "My granddad called him a monster."

"Like, a literal monster?" Imogen said.

Livia stared at her, wide-eyed. "He needs our guilt to walk among us."

Clem held up a hand. "So we're all here because some supernatural thing called Whispers wants us to confess our secrets. That's what we're going with?"

"You got a better explanation?" Livia said.

"Maybe you're trying to scare us," Ava said, rounding on Livia. "You're the one who keeps going on about ghosts. About Whispers. Maybe this is part of your plan."

"Oh, you suspect me now?" Livia said. "A minute ago, you were accusing Esme."

"If it's not one of us, then there's someone else on this island," Clem cried. "Monsters in mirrors aren't real!"

"Just because something isn't real doesn't mean it can't hurt us," Esme said. "As long as someone believes."

"I don't even know what's real anymore," Olly said. "There's a voice in my head bringing every bad thought I've ever had to the surface. Trying to make me do all these terrible things."

"It's called too much alcohol," Clem snapped.

"I haven't been drinking! Remember?"

The two best friends stared at each other, chests heaving. It was Clem who looked away first. "Look," he said, "someone is trying to mess with our heads, and Scarlett cracked under the pressure. There's nothing supernatural going on here."

"But why?" Imogen sobbed. "Why is someone doing this to me?"

"They know our biggest secrets, and they're using them against us," Ava said.

"But I don't have any secrets," Imogen stammered.

Ava rounded on her. "You sure about that? Because Scarlett's invite was to a boat party, just like the ones where she likes to pick up rich men to extort."

"Like my dad," Teddy muttered.

"So what?" Imogen said.

"So, her invite hinted at her darkest secret, just like mine and like all of yours too." Judging by the nervous shuffling, most of the group knew she was right. She suspected that half of them had known this wasn't a party before they'd arrived and, like her, they had only turned up to head off any attempt at blackmail.

"I was invited to a party," Imogen said weakly.

"What kind of party invite has a picture of your head on a bikini model's body? *Just do it*? What does that mean to you, really?" When Imogen didn't answer, Ava rounded on

Clem. "And that flyer from Black Box. What happened at the club, Clem?"

"Don't!" Clem shouted. "You don't get to... Just back off." He turned and jogged toward the funfair.

"Chill out, Ava," Jolie said. "You're giving me a headache."

Ava bit back a surge of fury. "So that freak show poster means nothing to you? No dark secrets involving what happened to your brother?"

"Shut up," Jolie snarled. "Enough with the detective act."

"I'm trying to work out what's happening, and our secrets are the key!"

"Forget it, I'm not playing anymore." Jolie stormed off in the same direction as Clem and disappeared into the shadows.

Ava watched her leave, then returned her attention to the others. "Are you all going to deny what's happening? Pretend that someone hasn't discovered our secrets and brought us here?"

"This is all beastly," Teddy said. "I'm going to get another drink."

"Of course you are," Ava said, watching him stumble off toward the club. "Anyone else want to bury their head in the sand? Or a bottle of vodka?"

"Getting mad isn't helping," Livia said.

"I'm not mad, I'm—" Ava was interrupted by the sound of a child's ride jerking to life, playing a cheery tune with whooshing sound effects and flashing lights. Ava squinted at the cartoon features. It was meant to be a boat with a big smiley face, only the elements had scoured the pupils from its eyes and scarred its peeling paint with rusty wounds. It stopped abruptly, tilted to the right, with those awful empty eyes staring at Ava.

"That's creepy," Ava said, but when she turned back to the others, they were gone.

She hadn't heard them leave, and she could only have looked away for a few seconds, but now the main square was dark and deserted apart from its creeping shadows. The music had fallen silent. She checked her watch.

Her stomach dropped. Somehow, two hours had vanished.

Ava pulled her coat tighter and began walking quickly back toward the club. A light around the side of the building made her stop. She hadn't noticed before, but there was a photo booth there. One of the old-fashioned ones that took four pictures.

As she approached, Ava caught sight of her reflection in a small vanity mirror bolted to the side of the booth. She looked scared and grubby. She slowly drew back the flimsy curtain. White light pulsed blindingly in her face, and she recoiled.

She rubbed her eyes with her palms, blinking away the brightness of the flashes. The reds and whites cleared from her vision, but there was still an image bleached onto her retinas.

A young man's face with black-painted lips and smudgy eye makeup. The man in the mirrors. Whispers.

Ava scrubbed at her eyes. But when she closed them, she still saw his face staring back at her. His mouth spread into a wicked smile.

Can you keep a secret? he whispered inside her head. *Will you be the One?*

SEVEN

Ava woke with a start. She sat up and bashed her head against something hard.

Disoriented, she blinked at her surroundings. She was in a photo booth, and the bright morning light was streaming in through holes in the moth-eaten curtain. The memories rushed back with a flood of panic. The man from the mirrors inside her head. Whispers.

She scrambled out of the booth and tumbled to the muddy ground.

Silence. Outside, the pier was a derelict wasteland. She hadn't noticed in the dark, but there were piles of debris littering the main square. Broken pieces of wood, crumbling bricks, litter blown in on the wind. The neon lights were cracked and full of filthy water; the signs were all broken bulbs and loose wires. Her breathing slowed. The pier hadn't come to life last night. Forty-year-old alcohol had given her nightmares, that was all.

She pulled herself upright, holding onto the photo booth. Her fingers brushed against something inside the tray. Straightening, she picked up a strip of four pictures. They were of her and Scarlett. In the top one, they were laughing and hugging like best friends. In the second, pulling silly faces. In the third, their foreheads touched, and Scarlett was pursing her lips into a pout. In the fourth—

"What the..." Ava lifted the strip closer to her face and squinted. In the fourth picture, their bottom lips grazed. Ava's tongue was brushing Scarlett's.

In what universe would Ava *kiss* Scarlett? She'd thought about it once, maybe twice. But it was only ever a thought. Real-life Scarlett was as horrible as she was beautiful. Ava touched her lips, trying to imagine the ghost of Scarlett's mouth against her own, but any memories were gone.

"Hey, hey, what's going on here?" Teddy appeared behind her and made a grab for the pictures. He stank of alcohol and old sweat.

Ava jerked the photos away and pocketed them quickly.

"Drunk pictures?" he said, blearily. "Please say they're nudes."

She ignored him. "Where is everyone?"

He grimaced, then burped unpleasantly. "I don't know. I drank way too much whiskey last night." He lifted a bottle of vodka and took a swig, then noticed Ava's horrified expression. "It's a clear spirit, if you're going to be a bore. Anyway, it's well past lunch."

"What?" she gasped, checking her watch. He was right; it was two o'clock.

"What did you get up to last night?" he said. "Your hair looks like crap."

Ava was about to tell him that the red vomit stains on his suit were hardly attractive when she caught sight of herself in the little rectangular mirror on the booth. There were scraps of blue-painted wood in her knotted hair. Her skin was pale and chalky, her lips swollen and pink.

"Wild party, right?" Teddy said. "I can't believe someone rigged the whole pier to light up."

Ava's stomach plummeted. So it had been real. In which case, what else had happened? And why couldn't she remember anything? She tried to get her memories in order. The last thing she recalled was Scarlett vanishing into the darkness. However, the photos suggested there'd been more to the night.

"Um, have you seen Scarlett this morning?" she asked.

"No," he said, freezing with the bottle halfway to his lips. "Why would I have seen her?"

"Didn't she..." Ava trailed off, trying to remember. "Did she confess to being the world's least ethical gold digger?"

"Oh. That. Yes, that happened." He grinned at her. "You're very interested in Scarlett. There's a fine line between love and hate, dear girl."

Ava felt her cheeks reddening. "You and she seemed close last night."

"Close," he muttered. "Not so much, it would seem."

He plonked himself down on a bench and swigged some of his vodka. Ava sat at the other end and tried to not breathe in his fumes.

"We went out a couple of times, but it turns out she was using me," he said. "I thought she liked me. I mean, we had a jolly good time at that boat party. We took a few bottles of Armand de Brignac up to the top deck and played spot the hair transplant from above."

"Give it a few years," Ava said, peering at his mop of greasy hair.

"I know, I know," he said, patting his own head. "Might be the only thing I inherit from my father."

"Isn't he a multimillionaire?"

"In my experience, the richer someone is, the more possessive they are of their money. And he doesn't approve of my career aspirations." He put on a low, croaky voice that sounded like a bad impression of Winston Churchill. "What do you mean you don't want to be an industrial chemist? The Stumpff-Montjoys have always been chemists."

"What do you want to be?"

"Who cares? It's not like I even need to work. The companies all look after themselves. But Daddy thinks I need a degree to run them." He put on the voice again. "My son will not be a playboy. I will not tolerate it."

He went back to sipping from the bottle, back hunched, eyes closed. Ava took his picture. His expensive suit made a nice contrast to the rubbish-strewn pier. The picture would say something about the excesses of wealth in the face of global ruin.

"It's all a test," he muttered, almost too quietly for Ava to hear.

"What's a test?" she said, lowering the camera.

He didn't open his eyes. "How far will you go?"

"That's a bit cryptic for the morning after the night we had."

"What?" He looked up at her, his hair falling across bleary eyes.

"You were saying something about..." She trailed off at the blank look on his face. "Never mind. We should find the others."

"What for? They're acquaintances, not friends," he said, suddenly angry. "If I wasn't rich, I daresay no one would give me the time of day. Scarlett certainly wouldn't have lowered herself to speak to me if I was poor."

"I don't think it's personal," Ava said, thinking about how Scarlett was unfailingly horrible to everyone.

"She made it personal. I told her things. I opened up. I thought she was different, but all she cared about was herself." He bashed the bottle down on the bench. The bottom smashed, and vodka trickled through the gaps in the wood.

"Watch it!" Ava said, standing up so it wouldn't soak her trousers. "All right, well, I'm going now."

"You do that. Run along and have fun with your fake friendships with fake people."

Ava hurried toward the club. Glancing back, she saw Teddy slumped on the bench, holding his broken bottle. She was so busy eyeing him that she didn't see Jolie emerging from the old funfair.

"Look where you're going, will you?" Jolie's panda costume was black with soot, and her hair a frizzy mess. She glared at Ava, then walked on.

"Hey," Ava said.

Jolie sped up with her head held high.

"Look," said Ava, running alongside her, "I know I shouldn't have mentioned your brother last night, but you're blowing this out of proportion. We have more important things to worry about."

"It's not just Max. It's the way you're always hiding things from me. I don't even know you anymore, and I definitely don't trust you."

"You have secrets of your own too."

"Don't turn this around on me." Jolie stopped and turned to face Ava. "You're the one who has been slowly retreating for the last six months. What is it? You too good for me these days?"

"What are you talking—"

"I get it! In five years' time, you want to be having adventures in big cities with your stupid camera, but I'll still be here, rotting away like the rest of this shitty town. Better toss this old wood aside before I drag you down too."

Ava crossed her arms. "Feel better for that?"

"A little," Jolie muttered. She walked on, but at a slower pace so that Ava could keep up.

They found the others congregated in front of the arcade, chatting tiredly. Jolie nodded in their direction but stopped short of joining them. Ava watched the puffs of steam winding up from everyone's mouths, clouds in the cold air. It had to be close to freezing, yet Ava had slept outdoors, and she hadn't lost any limbs to frostbite. At the very least, she should have developed hypothermia.

"Where did you sleep last night?" she asked Jolie.

"The roller coaster ticket booth."

"Sounds comfy. I slept in a photo booth."

"Always with the pictures," Jolie said, but the anger was beginning to drain from her voice.

That reminded Ava of the pictures of her and Scarlett. Maybe her own photos would jog her memory when it came to the previous evening. She unlooped the camera from around her neck, turned it on, and began to scroll through the pictures.

Some of them she remembered. The argument in the square. Red eyes glowing. And hungover Teddy, sitting on his bench minutes ago. But everything in between felt like a big, bright space, like film exposed to light.

One of the unrecognizable photos was time stamped four a.m. It was impossible to make out; a patch of gray concrete, maybe. Some blurred shapes. Ava turned the camera to look at it from a different angle. It seemed that the camera had been lying on the ground when the picture was taken. And now she looked closer, the camera's casing was scratched where it must have been dropped. Perhaps it had slipped out of her hands after one too many drinks and the jolt had triggered the shutter mechanism.

"Bit of a long shot," she muttered.

"What's that?" Jolie said. "Let me see. Wow, your talent is unsurpassed. What is it?"

"I was trying to work that out."

Jolie turned the camera again. "Is it me, or does that bit look like a face?"

Ava snatched the camera back. Jolie was right. Among the blurred shapes, there was what looked like a gaping mouth and shadowy eye sockets. Ava shuddered and turned the picture over so the concrete was at the bottom again.

She could still see the face, albeit upside down. She shut the camera off.

"I'm getting creeped out by all this."

"And yet no one seems in any hurry to escape," Jolie said.

Ava nodded. She'd had the same thought. What was it Scarlett had said? *He's already in your heads.* She was reminded of an article she'd read about some parasite found in cat poo. Apparently, it could deliberately change its victims' behavior, making them more prone to taking risks. Mind games. Puppets on a string.

"Are you listening?" Jolie said, nudging Ava to get her attention.

"Sorry. What did you say?"

Jolie sighed dramatically. "I said, have you seen Scarlett this morning? Everyone's here except for her."

Ava glanced up. Teddy had joined the group. Nine of them were present. Scarlett was the only one missing.

She shook her head. The photos of her and Scarlett kissing felt heavy in her pocket.

Jolie clapped her hands to get the attention of the others. "All right, weirdo nerds, we're going to look for Scarlett. She's probably hiding so we don't see her without makeup. But because we all love her so much, we're going to check that she's all right."

"Oh, please," Imogen said, arms folded over her ruined dress. "You all hate poor Scarlett."

"Your understanding of sarcasm is unsurpassed," Esme said coldly. She was leaning up against a wall with her legs crossed at the ankles. The only colorful thing about her was an abstract bird tattoo on her forearm; everything else was shades of black and white. Black jeans, white hair, gray eyes.

"Um, thanks?" Imogen said.

"You're *so* welcome."

"Brilliant," Clem sighed. He was rolling his harmonica over his knuckles and studiously watching its progress. "Shall we get going, then? Where do we start?"

"We last saw her right here, so I guess the buildings around the main square, then fan out?" Ava said.

"I'll try the carnival," Clem said. The opposite side of the island. He continued to stare at the harmonica as if his life depended on it.

"Oh, you two. Awk-ward," Jolie said, then cracked up. "Come on, then, what's everyone waiting for?"

As if in reply, music started up from behind one of the food stalls close to the iron archway and Baldo's billboard. They all tentatively followed the sound. It was a familiar tune, but the notes were garbled, and Ava couldn't make it out. As they got closer, the music was punctuated by a grinding sound: metal on metal.

"What is that song?" she asked, trying to keep her voice steady.

"It's 'Row, Row, Row Your Boat,'" Clem said.

"Gently down the stream..." Livia sang nervously, pulling the purple jacket tighter around her body.

"If you see Scarlett, don't forget to scream," Jolie finished. Ava hesitated. Then she made herself turn the corner, even though something told her she wouldn't like what she found.

Like with the photo on her camera, it took her a moment to process what she saw. An upside-down face with a gaping mouth and staring eyes.

Scarlett lay half in the children's boat ride with her head dangling back. Her hair hung in matted tangles that swept the concrete as the ride jerked to and fro.

Someone screamed, but Ava barely heard. With shaking hands, she switched on her camera. The four a.m. picture. Now the colorful smudges fitted together like a bloody puzzle. The camera fell limply from her hand, and as it hit the ground, the flash went off.

"I think I..." Ava said, gagging on her own words. "I think I might have killed Scarlett."

EIGHT

Everything was circles, round and round, no beginning and no end. Ava could feel the Earth rotating a thousand miles per hour, so fast it might fling her off into space or suck her down deep into its molten core. She reached out for a wall to steady herself. Her legs still gave way, and she slumped to the wet ground. *Stop*, she told her thoughts, but they didn't listen.

"It wasn't you," Noah whispered. "It was me. I think I killed her." His expression was stricken. "I remember I wanted to, and now she's dead."

Crack. The planet recentered its endless spin around Noah. Ava could see him with painful clarity. Every strand of his hair, no longer caked in mud. A maintenance worker's jumpsuit, arms tied around his waist. White T-shirt, clean, heaving with his short breaths. Ava placed a hand on her own chest. She was breathing too fast, and each breath burned like a lungful of seawater. *Stop*, she told herself. *Slow down.*

Clem stepped toward them. His eyes were wild. "No, it was me. She ditched me for another guy and expected me to just roll over and take it. She didn't even say she was sorry."

"Yeah? Well, she ditched me too," Noah spat. "We were together for four months, but the second things got complicated? She was gone."

Clem stumbled back. His harmonica clattered to the ground. He laughed joylessly, disbelievingly. "You and Scarlett? Like she'd go with you."

"I was on the football team. Ask Olly."

Olly was pacing, muscles tensed, muttering under his breath. He stopped. Looked over when he heard his name. Frowned. "Noah was on the team. Two years ago. Up until..." He trailed off, frowning.

"Until that accident in training tore my cruciate ligament? Yeah," Noah said.

Ava tried to force herself to remember, but the memories weren't there. Noah had appeared on her radar less than eighteen months ago, a long-haired, snarling loner who paced the corridors with fists for hands and threw punches with the beach sleepers at dusk. Who had he been before that? A football star cliché, complete with beautiful girlfriend?

"No one is who they say they are," Ava said, only realizing she'd spoken out loud when the others looked down at her.

"What are you doing sitting in a puddle?" Jolie said, sounding almost hysterical. Jolie didn't do hysterical. "Get up."

"You don't look good," Livia said. "Did you take something?"

Ava shook her head. People looking at her made everything worse. She tried to wipe the sweat off her face. Tried to will her hands to stop shaking. *Pull yourself together*, she told herself.

"Stop it already." Jolie tried to drag Ava to her feet.

"I can't breathe," Ava gasped. "My chest hurts. My heart."

Even as she spoke, she knew it wasn't real. It was never real: the twisting pain that seared her muscles and tugged her ribs inward, tighter and tighter; the pounding heart that tripped over itself with every trembling beat. Shame found its way through the cracks. She knew that when the panic attack stopped, sometimes as quickly as it had started, the shame would be all that remained.

"You didn't kill Scarlett," Jolie cried. "You don't have it in you."

"I was there! There's a photo of her dead on my camera. Why would it be there if I didn't do it?"

Clem snatched up her camera and flicked through the pictures. Paused. Turned the camera toward her. "This picture? Yeah, that's Scarlett. But the time stamp is from five minutes ago, right before you dropped the camera. I saw the flash." He tossed the camera into Ava's lap.

Ava shook her head. "It was on my camera before we found her. Jolie saw it too."

"Stop!" Jolie kicked at the puddle. Dirty water splashed the bare skin between Ava's trousers and her shoes. "You didn't kill Scarlett. I did. I was angry because we'd fought earlier and she'd pushed me over. I hated her."

"Not as much as I hated her," Clem muttered. "She treated me like I was nothing."

"She treated all of us like we were nothing," Livia cried. "She used to call me names. Take the piss out of my granddad for his drinking. Everyone hated her."

"I didn't," Imogen sobbed. "We were friends. We really were."

"She was horrible to you, Imogen," Livia said. "She was a bully who pranced around the school like she owned it, and I'm glad I killed her. Oh god, did I kill her? Why can't I remember?"

Clap. Esme stepped into the middle of the group. She clapped her hands a second time. "Stop. All of you."

Voices faded until all that remained was Ava's heaving breaths. She hadn't known how loud they were. Shame reared its head again. *Stop*, she told herself. *Stop being so fucking stupid*.

"Is there anyone here who *doesn't* think they killed Scarlett?" Esme asked. Her white hair blew in the wind, making her look almost elvish.

No one said anything. Livia fumbled in her leather coat and pulled out a packet of pills. The foil cracked as she pushed two out onto a shaking palm.

"Oxycodone hydrochloride. I took that for my knee injury," Noah said softly.

"Takes the edge off," Livia said, her teeth chattering. "Makes it all less…just less."

"Raise your hand," Esme said. "Who here feels like they might have killed Scarlett?"

One by one, the group raised their hands. Noah, then Clem, then Jolie with a half-hearted shrug. Esme, Livia, Olly, and finally—reluctantly, woozily—Teddy. Everyone except for Imogen.

"Well, I know I didn't," she said, her voice slightly too high-pitched. "Why would I want to kill Scarlett? We got on so well. You all know that, right? We were friends."

"Sure you were," Jolie muttered. She smoothed her filthy panda costume, only succeeding in smearing soot deeper into the fur.

Noah ran his fingers over the cut on his forehead. "This is crazy. Why do we all think we killed Scarlett?"

No one answered. The group shuffled uncomfortably, eyes darting over to where Scarlett lay, then quickly away again.

Ava dared a look. Nausea rose thickly in her throat. All that blood. She couldn't have done that to Scarlett, even if she felt like she had. She focused on holding each breath until the pain in her chest began to subside. The panic ebbed away, leaving behind exhaustion and shame but also a sense of clarity.

She coughed to clear the tightness from her throat. "It's like someone's trying to trick me into thinking I killed Scarlett. But the thoughts don't quite fit."

"So we're talking about mind control?" Clem said incredulously. "Hypnosis?"

"I *feel* like it was me," Olly said. "How is that possible?"

"I don't know," Ava said. "Maybe we've been drugged. Someone's playing mind games with us and making us doubt our own memories."

Noah shuffled his worn boots on the ground. "It's like this island is bringing all my worst thoughts to the surface. Trying to convince me that I'm a bad guy who'd do something like this."

"Yeah," Olly agreed. "There's a voice in my head that wants me to turn on everyone else."

"Whispers," Livia slurred. "I told you. It's him."

"Or maybe you're making up this Whispers story so we won't suspect you," Imogen said.

"Or maybe you should take me seriously before we all end up dead!"

"Listen to yourself," Clem said. "A magical mirror

monster didn't do *that* to Scarlett. Monsters don't exist!" He picked up his harmonica and wiped it clean on his trousers. Made it disappear up his sleeve.

"Depends on how you define *monster*." Olly glanced at Scarlett's body. "Someone killed her, and we're the only ones here."

The group exchanged looks. They all had motive.

Clem, Noah, and Teddy had all been casually dumped by Scarlett. Everyone else had been a victim of her bullying at some point. Jolie still had the bruises to prove it. The truth was, Ava couldn't rule anyone out, not even herself.

"But *why* are we here?" Noah said quietly.

"Because of our secrets," Ava said.

"If it's blackmail, then why haven't we gotten any demands?" Esme said.

"Maybe the blackmailer wants to punish us instead," Ava said.

"But how did they find out our secrets? I never told anyone mine," Olly said.

"Well, I did," Clem said coldly, staring at his friend.

Olly's jaw tightened. "Me? I'm not a snitch, or whatever it is you're accusing me of."

"I don't know." Clem looked away, shamefaced.

"We know enough," Ava said, rising on shaking legs. "We have to get back to the mainland before anyone else gets hurt. We never should have come here."

Olly nodded. "You're right."

Jolie flipped the panda hood over her head. "Let's get the hell off this mind-screw of an island."

"There used to be a lifeguard station here, right?" Olly said slowly. "What if there's a boat? Or a radio?"

"It must be round the back of the island, or we'd have seen it," Noah said. "We could radio the coast guard for help."

The group moved toward the club, but Ava remained rooted to the spot. "What about Scarlett? The coast guard will find her body. Are we really going to tell the police what happened?"

Everyone stopped. Clem stared down at the ground. Olly closed his eyes.

"Shit," Jolie muttered. "We can't tell them we all have amnesia. It's too suspicious."

Ava's panic had been replaced by numbness. The shock she had felt over Scarlett's death was slipping away. She wasn't even upset anymore. She knew she should be, but she wasn't.

"We can push her into the sea," she said. "Tell the police we came here for a party and she must have fallen."

Esme and Noah exchanged looks.

"Is this another of those uninvited thoughts?" Noah said.

Ava shook her head. "No. That one is all me."

"Cold," Jolie said, but she didn't argue.

"I don't know if I can," Olly said.

"Ava's right," Teddy said, pacing to and fro. "If the police find her body, then we're all screwed. No way am I going to prison over someone like her."

"But we can't just push Scarlett into the sea," Imogen said. "Fish will nibble on her, and Scarlett wouldn't like that at all."

"Scarlett's dead. She doesn't care," Clem said. "How else are we going to explain this without incriminating ourselves?"

"We could tell the truth," Imogen said in a tiny voice. "Mother always says that honesty is the most important thing."

"What *truth* is that?" said Clem. "That we think a monster in a mirror did it? Or that one of us is a killer, but we don't remember who?"

Imogen closed her eyes. A tear ran down her face, taking a trail of makeup with it.

"I already have a police record," Noah said. "I can't take the risk."

"And I have a future I've worked too hard for to toss it away," Esme said. "I'm not taking the fall for anyone."

"It sounds like you've all made up your minds, then," Olly said.

"Everyone needs to promise to stay quiet," Esme said, glaring between Olly and Imogen. "If anyone talks, all our secrets will come out, and we'll have to explain what really happened to Scarlett."

"Yeah, whatever," Jolie said.

"I mean it," Esme said, her voice taking on a dangerous edge. "I'm not going to let one of you assholes wreck my life."

"Don't threaten me," Jolie said.

"Don't test me," Esme retorted.

"We all have our reasons to stick to the pact," Clem said. "There's no need for threats."

Esme looked away from Jolie with an irritated hiss. "Promise. All of you."

One by one, the others nodded their agreement. Livia, Teddy, Noah, Jolie, Ava. That left Imogen and Olly.

"Yeah," Olly finally agreed, closing his eyes. "I promise."

"Imogen?" Livia said. "Do you really want to risk going to prison for Scarlett? Is that what she would have wanted?"

Imogen didn't answer. Esme took a step toward her and lowered her voice to a quiet growl. "We're all sticking to the same story. It's going to be your word against all of ours."

"What will your mother say if you're locked up for murder?" Ava added.

"All right! I'll do it. Happy now?"

"Not really," Esme said. She raised an eyebrow at Ava. "We're doing this, then?"

Ava nodded mutely, and the pact was sealed. It felt like a line, one Ava was surprised she had crossed so easily. Maybe she was simply capable of worse things than she wanted to believe. But the panic attack had left her too exhausted to care.

Even when they lifted Scarlett's body out of the boat, Ava still felt nothing. Scarlett was heavier than she'd expected, and she fell into the water with a gracelessness that would have disgusted her, had she been alive. Ava stared down at the churning water. It was too late for second thoughts.

"What now?" Ava said.

"I'm going to check out the boat situation." Esme smoothed her hair back, but it sprang up again. She jutted her chin at Ava. "You've got blood on your coat."

Ava glanced down. A dark smear ran the length of her sleeve. She quickly ripped the coat off and hurled it over the barrier into the ocean. The waves swallowed it up.

"Shit," she said, wiping her hands on her trousers again and again. "Shit, shit, shit." It was too late for second thoughts, but that didn't stop Ava from having them.

She turned away from the ocean and froze. Standing on the arcade roof was Rachel.

The ghost stared at her, her lank hair still even in the wind. Ava stood in terrified silence and watched as Rachel stepped off the roof. The ghost dropped faster than anything human would ever fall: a blur of black, and then nothing.

Ava felt something then. A presence standing right behind her. She couldn't move; she couldn't speak. Cold breath against her ear. Scarlett's voice, as bored and mocking as it had been in life. *Can you keep a secret?*

NINE

Ava ran toward the arcade and the narrow path that led around the back. Find a boat, go home. It was all that mattered. Her boots pounded against the concrete, sending wobbly vibrations up her legs.

"Ava, slow down," Noah called, jogging to catch up. He was favoring his left leg and wincing with every other step.

She slowed to a breathless walk, unable to maintain her pace.

"You ran off like there's a turbo laser trained on your ass. Did something spook you?" he said.

She laughed bitterly. "What, other than Scarlett's murder? Other than everything?"

He frowned. "Yeah. I know. I know."

"Why am I the only one who seems freaked out?" She gestured at the rest of the group as they ambled over. She could hear them arguing about boats and radios. Jolie was laughing. Like she hadn't just thrown someone's body into the sea.

Noah chewed on his lip and blinked his chestnut-brown eyes. "It already feels like a long time ago."

"Not to me." But even as she spoke, she could feel the memories fraying at the edges. The threads unraveled and stole away the desperation that had made her run. The fear was still there, but it was diluted, almost as if it belonged to someone else.

"What's happening to us?" Ava said.

"When you said your thoughts don't feel like your own... do you really think someone's putting thoughts in our heads?"

"I don't know," Ava said. "But the sooner we get out of here, the better."

They waited for the group to catch up. Ava led the way behind the arcade and stepped out into a dingy area where several large dumpsters sat, full of stagnant water and cardboard porridge. Hidden behind them, a utilitarian barrier overlooked a narrow staircase down to the shore. At the bottom, there was an old boathouse and jetty at the edge of a concrete quay where cargo had once been unloaded. A makeshift boxing ring stood in the middle of the quay. Ten by ten, surrounded by moldy ropes.

"Oh yes," Jolie said, cracking her knuckles. "Who wants to fight me?"

"Um, no one?" Livia said.

"Thumb war, then." She eyed Clem. "It's all in the wrist, apparently, and I bet your wrists get a lot of exercise."

"Very funny," he said dryly.

"I don't get it," Imogen said.

"Of course you don't." Jolie marched down toward the boxing ring. The others followed behind her, except for Ava and Noah. They hung back, watching from above as Jolie and Clem clambered through the ropes and pretended to limber up.

"I don't get how they can play games right now," Ava said quietly.

"We all have our ways of dealing with bad things," Noah said.

There was an edge to his voice. Was he making fun of her panic attack? Ava glanced at him.

"I, of course, favor a more self-destructive option involving letting people punch me in the face," he continued, smiling sheepishly.

Ava laughed despite herself. "*That* was a coping strategy?"

"Football was my thing, and after I screwed up my knee, there wasn't much left for me. Or that's how it felt at the time."

"Oh. Sorry." Her smile vanished.

He watched her with interest: an intense, suspicious stare tinged with curiosity. "I should probably thank you, if I'm entirely honest. You did me a favor with those photos of yours."

"The ones that ruined your life?" She raised an eyebrow.

"It was already on a steep downward trajectory when you came along." He mimed an aircraft crashing into the ocean. "For a while, I figured I was coping okay. I was taking a lot of those pills that Livia likes so much. I told myself I needed them for the pain. Then my parents got wise to it and cut me off."

"They were trying to help, but they made you worse," she said. Jolie always responded to Ava's panic attacks with a tough love approach. It only made her feel ashamed.

"Yeah. So I started hanging around on the beach to get away from everyone's worry and disapproval. That's where it all went even more wrong."

She wasn't sure she'd get away with the question, but she had wondered about it for so long that she had to ask. "How did you end up fighting?"

He shrugged. "One of the beach sleepers said I could make easy money if I wasn't afraid of taking a few punches. But I never really did it for the money. It was like…like the only way I could get outside my own head."

"Yeah, I get that," Ava said. Photography let her take one step away from real life. The world wasn't so scary when you weren't part of it.

"And you obviously know what happened next. After I was arrested, I kept overhearing my parents whispering about how I'd ruined my future, and my mum would start crying. It hit me that it wasn't just my life I'd screwed over but theirs too. They were better off without me, so I vanished. Got a job in the city. Tried to forget all about this town."

"Everyone thought you were dead."

"I checked in with Livia after a few months, and she said they were all doing better without me. So I left them alone."

She narrowed her eyes. "And that's it? That's the truth behind Noah Park's mysterious disappearance?"

"Yeah, pretty much."

Ava didn't believe him. There was something he wasn't saying. Ava suspected it had to do with the secret that had brought him back home. The secret that had brought him here.

Below, Jolie appeared to be trying to twist Clem's thumb off his hand. He was laughing, although there was a pained edge to it.

"We should get down there," Noah said, "before they start trading punches for real."

By the time they made it down the stairs, Clem was shaking out a thumb injury and Jolie was celebrating by trying to swat the hat off his head. In five years at the same school, Jolie had never paid any attention to Clem except to laugh at him from a distance. It was weird seeing them together.

Ava looked away. The rest of the group was chatting at the ropes, except for Teddy. He'd found a spot on the rocks and was sitting with his head on his knees, back shuddering with sobs. He still clutched his broken bottle of vodka.

Was he mourning Scarlett or the person he'd briefly hoped she was? If it were Ava who died, how would she be mourned? Not as the person she wanted to be, that was for sure. And if her secret came out, it would be all anyone would remember her for. That would be it. Escaping the island wasn't the end of it. Life wouldn't be life as she knew it if the blackmailer revealed what they knew.

Teddy looked up, and Ava realized he wasn't crying but laughing hysterically. Tears ran down his face; his mouth was twisted into a demented grin.

We all have our ways of dealing with bad things, Noah had said. But this didn't seem right. Teddy didn't look like himself.

"He only needs one," he gasped, and then his head whipped forward and back again, like he'd come to a sudden halt.

"What did you say?" Ava stammered.

Teddy blinked up at her, bleary-eyed and puffy. He'd bitten his tongue, and there was blood in the corner of his mouth. "What?"

"You said, '*He only needs one.*'" The exact words Scarlett had said right before she died.

"No, I didn't." He stood up unsteadily and ambled down

from the rocks. "You're hearing things. Are we going to find this boat or not?"

They joined the rest of the group outside the boathouse. A small stone building at the top of a launch ramp, its double doors were all peeling strips of black paint and rusty hinges. The roof looked primed to fall in. If the fresh splinters on the ground were anything to go by, the padlock and chain had only recently been torn off.

Someone had been there already.

Jolie and Clem entered first, jostling to be the first through the door. Inside, there was a huge wooden lifeboat, like something out of a history book. It lay at an awkward angle, half supported by a four-wheeled trolley that had collapsed on one side. One of the wheels—taller than Ava—had lost most of its tread, leaving behind a sunburst of spokes and not much else.

"Boat looks seaworthy," Noah said, knocking a fist on the wood as if that meant anything.

"It must weigh four tons," Olly said. "No way we can get it down to the water."

Noah kicked the broken trolley, and the boat creaked ominously. Ava ducked under the lopsided boat to explore the rear of the building. The walls were hung with old tools and life jackets that seemed to be made from pieces of cork sewn into musty fabric. She pushed aside a loop of rope to approach what looked from a distance like an unlit bonfire.

She blinked through the dusky light. The pile of wood was actually a small rowboat—or what was left of one. It looked like someone had taken one of the lifeboat's heavy oars to the rowboat, tossing the oar aside once it broke and starting again with a second. The boat's main beams were still intact, curved like a whale's rib cage, but the planks on the outside were either hanging loose or lying on the floor in a mess of blue-painted splinters.

Ava's hand automatically reached up to touch her hair.

Blue splinters.

Livia came to stand beside her. "Someone hulked out on it," she said.

"Who did this?" Jolie said, bending down to pick up a handful of shattered wood.

"Look, the edges of the broken wood are clean," Clem said. "This must have happened in the last few days."

"Someone doesn't want us to get off the island," Olly said.

"It was one of you!" Imogen cried. She dropped to her knees in front of the ruined boat. "No, no, no."

Ava swallowed. *Had* it been her? Creeping into the boat hut in the night to destroy their best chance at escaping? But that didn't make sense. Ava wanted to go home, she wanted to escape. Didn't she?

"You've got something…" Teddy reached over to remove a piece of wood from Ava's hair. He brushed it off his hands and grinned at her. The blood from his bitten tongue had outlined his teeth in red, making him look unnervingly monstrous. "I can keep a secret," he said softly.

Ava took a step back, knocking against a reel of heavy rope. Teddy moved closer, still grinning. "He's already in your head, you know. He's in all of our heads, testing us to see who is the strongest. Are you strong, Ava? Will you be his *One*?"

"What are you two doing?" Jolie said.

"Jesus." Teddy cricked his neck, and he was back to himself again. "Who the heck knows? Any sign of a radio?"

"Nothing in here," a muffled voice called.

They circled the lopsided lifeboat. Olly had clambered up on to the deck and disappeared into the cabin. He reemerged to the ominous sound of creaking wood. "Can't have been used for close to a hundred years. You seen those life jackets? Everything is Victorian. I'm not sure radio waves even existed back then."

"Physics isn't your subject, is it?" Esme said dryly. "There are tin drums of petrol lined up against the wall. This place has been used more recently than that."

Ava counted four huge oil drums, rusty and seeping out the heady stench of boat fuel. She glanced across at Livia, lighting a roll-up. *Click, click* went her lighter, but nothing exploded.

"So there still could be a radio," Olly said, jumping down from the huge lifeboat. "Let's look closer."

Ava half-heartedly tugged ropes aside and opened cobwebby cupboards. There was nothing there except for flaky old hooks and crusty tins of varnish. She was about to say as much to the others when she opened a small wooden door and something moved. A furry creature erupted from the dark space with long yellow teeth bared.

Ava screamed and jumped aside. The thing—a rat, now she'd had time to process the matted brown fur and scaly tail—landed on the floor with a loud thud. It scuttled toward Imogen, making her squeal and throw herself at Clem. The rat ran between Noah's legs, over Jolie's foot, and down through a hole in the floorboards.

Ava clutched her chest and tried to get her breathing back under control. Rats had always terrified her. Her heart thumped with adrenaline, like it had when they'd found Scarlett. Scarlett…

She tried to stop the thought, but it was too late. Scarlett's ghost flickered in a dark corner, then vanished with a laugh.

"Uh-oh, Ava's about to freak out again," Imogen said.

Ava forced herself to look away from the place where Scarlett's ghost had stood. She slammed the cupboard closed and breathed out slowly. "It made me jump, that's all."

"So you're not going to start crying? Because you look like you're going to cry," Imogen said.

"Leave her alone," Jolie said. "I'm the only one who gets to mock Ava for being such a pussy."

Ava ignored them both. She bent down to examine the hole through which the rat had vanished. Her legs shook, but she wasn't going to let anyone see how spooked she was. She concentrated on the hole. The floorboard had been eaten away, probably by the rat's many, many brethren. Underneath, Ava could see only darkness. She stood back up and stomped on the floor. It echoed hollowly.

"I think there's a room underneath us," she said.

"There's no way down," Olly said. "We've searched this whole place."

Not the *whole* place. She crouched down and swept aside the sawdust and broken pieces of wood from the rowboat. It left behind a square outline cut into the floorboards: a trapdoor.

Esme pulled down a metal hook from the wall and used it to pry up one side of the hatch. Olly heaved it open. A dark ladder stretched into an unlit pit.

"Don't suppose anyone has a flashlight?" Esme said.

"Who needs a flashlight when we have fire?" Noah said, waggling his eyebrows. He grabbed a rag from a shelf and wrapped it around a broken piece of wood. There was a jar of something thick and white by the boat—wood wax, Ava presumed. He smeared it over the rag, then snapped his fingers at Jolie for her lighter.

Jolie hesitated, then shook her head.

He grinned slowly at her. "What's the worst that can happen?"

She didn't smile back. "Don't go there."

"I've got one," Livia said, passing Noah a lighter.

"Thanks." He flicked it on. "Stand back. This might explode."

It didn't, which was a relief, given the drums of petrol. Instead, the rag burned hungrily, filling the room with thick smoke. Noah descended the ladder with the torch bobbing dangerously in one hand. He jumped the bottom rungs and landed with a squelch.

"It's stinky down here," he called up. "And any time now, it's probably going to be full of toxic smoke. Anyone tempted to join me?"

"I'm not going down there," Jolie said. "I'm not stupid."

"I don't want to wreck my shoes," Imogen said. "Mother would be so cross."

"Anyone?" Noah repeated, coughing on the smoke.

The rat had gone down there, probably to join hundreds of its friends and family. A whole inbred rat army: one of Ava's biggest fears. But if Ava were to die that minute, she would be remembered as the girl who panicked at everything. Maybe it was time to actually *be* the person she wanted others to see when they looked at her.

"All right," she said, stepping into darkness. "I'm coming down."

TEN

The tunnel stank like death, more like a sewer than somewhere humans were supposed to venture. Noah swept the torch in an arc. The flames were enough to reveal all the dark nooks and twisting shadows. Not enough to reassure Ava when it came to rats and other horrors.

She tried to pretend she was Jolie. Fearless, confident Jolie.

Thin fingers gripped Ava's arm, and she yelped, but it was only Livia stepping off the ladder.

"Oh, exciting. No one's ever found anything bad in a secret tunnel," she said cheerfully.

"Challenge accepted," Ava said, finding that she sounded more at ease than she felt.

Esme followed, jumping the last few rungs of the ladder. "Mmm, what is that lovely aroma?"

"I like to call it Eau d'Cay," Ava said, putting on a thick French accent.

Livia frowned. "I don't smell anything."

Probably because she was constantly surrounded by the acrid reek of her coat. Ava cleared her throat awkwardly and peered up the ladder. "No one else is coming down?"

"They're going to carry on looking around upstairs. We don't need them." Esme marched off ahead. In her tank top and boots laced over jeans, she was perfectly dressed for exploring an abandoned tunnel. Ava's vintage flared trousers dragged across the muddy ground.

"All the more treasure for us to find," Livia said, hurrying behind Esme and Noah.

"And a radio," Ava added, but no one was listening. She jogged after the others, her trousers slapping damply against her ankles.

A little ways down the tunnel, they paused to examine what looked like a jacket hanging from a peg on the wall, rotten and falling apart. The black fabric had formed itself into a twisted mass. "Do you think this was the Magnificent Baldo's?" Ava said.

A handsome man in a black suit with chains wrapped around his waist. A fleeting vision crossed Ava's mind like a memory, only more faded and not her own. Baldo standing on the rocks with the ocean behind him. A flamboyant bow to the crowd. Applause.

"He was the dude who owned the pier, right?" Noah said.

"Yeah. Granddad said no one knew his real name, so after the fire, they didn't know who would inherit what was left," Livia said.

"So he died in the fire?" Ava said.

"He vanished. They presumed he was dead, but no body was found."

"That explains why they left the pier to rot," Esme said, "but not why Baldo would want a secret tunnel under the island."

"He was an escape artist," Livia said. "A seventies version of Houdini. Maybe this tunnel was part of his act."

"A puff of smoke, and he's gone," Esme said. "But where did he come from in the first place?"

"He was a nobody. Granddad said he'd been to prison for burglary a couple of times, and then suddenly he turned it all around."

"And bought an entire carnival?" Noah said. "Not to mention an island. Where did he get the money?"

"I'd love my own island," Livia sighed.

"Not this one," Ava said. "No one would want this one."

"Surely there's a lifetime of photo ops here," Esme said.

"I'm not that dedicated to my art," Ava muttered.

Esme looked up. "The people who make it in this life are

the ones who take risks. Nothing's going to hold me back from getting where I'm going."

"Where *are* you going?" Livia said, frowning.

Esme paused to think about it. "Away," she said. "Move it or lose it, ladies."

As they walked, the tunnel started to feel less like a man-made structure and more like something scraped out of the earth by an animal. Where Noah's torch lit up the walls, there were strange black roots snaking through the mud like wet, tangled hair. In places, the roots were wound into funnel shapes that reminded Ava of spiders' nests. The ends of the funnels led down into pitch-dark holes in the mud. Ava tried not to imagine what might live in the holes. Tried, and failed.

"Did your granddad ever mention anything like, I don't know, mutant spider-rats?" she whispered. "Just so I can prepare myself."

"He only talked about the pier when he'd been drinking. And then nothing he said made much sense. Mutant spider-rats feels kind of tame compared to the reality."

"He worked here for ten years, right up until the fire?" Noah said.

"He was a handyman with the funfair." She forced a grim smile. "How did you know that?"

"A guess," Noah said quickly. "How come he stayed in Portgrave after the fire? None of the other pier workers stuck around."

"I don't know. Sometimes, I'd hear him arguing with himself after he'd been drinking. 'I should run far, far away. Why can't I run?'" She paused, chewing her lip, then put on a man's slurred voice. "'Are you guilty, Olivia? Guilt has roots; don't let it pull you down.'"

"What does that mean?" Ava said, glancing at the slimy roots all over the walls and ceiling.

"I don't know. He'd tell me that this whole island was made of guilt, but the fire had destroyed it. Like he was trying to convince himself it was true. And then he'd pick up the bottle of whiskey all over again."

"Was the drinking how he ended up sleeping on the beach?" Noah said.

Livia didn't answer. They walked on until the ground turned to stone and the walls to rock. The slimy black roots still swarmed over every surface. Noah's torch filled the passageway with coiling smoke, making Ava feel like they'd stepped out of this world and into another.

"It wasn't the alcohol," Livia finally said, her voice taking on a faraway tone. "Some money went missing at home, and my mum kicked him out. Six months later, he was dead on the beach."

"I'm sorry," Ava said.

"Me too," Livia replied.

"It was his choice to pick up the bottle," Esme said. "His life, his decision."

"That doesn't stop me from feeling—" Livia broke off and stopped walking. "Um, people?"

"What is it?" Noah swung his torch in her direction.

He jumped. "Holy goats!"

Ava leapt back with a gasp, but she felt no rush of panic. If it hadn't been for Scarlett's murder, she probably would have freaked out. But as it was, a human skeleton only dented her composure rather than shattering it. It helped that the skeleton looked more like a Halloween prop than a real person.

It was sitting up against the wall, held together by strips of fabric. It had rusty chains over its shoulders and a padlock around its waist.

"Baldo," Ava whispered.

He must have died at the time of the fire. But the screwdriver protruding from between his ribs strongly suggested it hadn't been the flames or smoke that had gotten him. Without thinking, Ava stooped down to wrench the screwdriver free. As she tugged it out, Baldo's lower jaw shook loose and clattered at their feet, making Livia clap a hand over her mouth. Ava spun the screwdriver on her palm. There were initials engraved on the handle: AQH.

"Let me see," Livia said, taking it from her. She frowned.

"Number five Phillips," Noah said. "Good choice."

Ava shot him a look. "Next time I stab someone with a screwdriver, I'll bear that in mind."

"The Magnificent Baldo," Esme said. "The heck happened to you?"

"We're meant to be finding a way off the island, not solving a forty-year-old murder mystery," Livia said, pocketing the screwdriver. There was something oddly evasive about her tone. "This is all too weird."

"If you think that's weird..." Noah was holding the torch up to some graffiti scrawled on the stone wall.

"Hold your tongue," Esme read.

"There's more." Noah rotated, casting smoky light over each wall and the ceiling. The same phrase was written perhaps a dozen times, along with others.

KEEP YOUR SECRETS. NEVER SPEAK.
WHISPERS. WHISPERS. ONE. ONE. ONE.

"I'm usually against armchair diagnoses," Ava said slowly, "but I'm beginning to think Baldo had some serious psychological issues."

"'*He only needs one*,'" Esme said. "That's what Scarlett said."

"Do you think Baldo was the *One*, whatever that means?" Noah said.

"You're talking like it's all real," Ava said.

The others exchanged looks. "What else did Scarlett say?" Esme asked. "'*Confess and you'll be free.*' Only Baldo's graffiti says the opposite. '*Hold your tongue*,' see?"

"Confessing hardly did Scarlett any good. She confessed, and hours later, she was dead," Noah said.

Ava shivered. For a few minutes, she'd forgotten why they were there. The memories rushed back, soaked in blood and regret. "There's no radio here. Let's get back to the others."

Esme shook her head. "I want to see where this tunnel comes out. We must be nearly at the far end of the island by now."

"We're not here to explore," Ava started to say, but Esme interrupted her.

"Go back if you want, but I'm going this way."

When the other three continued on, Ava followed.

They weaved around more strange, funnel-shaped holes leading down into blackness. Burrows. Dark places where dark things lived. Ava shuddered and quickened her pace. A chilly sense of space announced that they'd stepped into a large cavern. There were lanterns on the walls, so Noah lit them with his torch. They filled the space with a flickering orange glow.

The cavern was full of stuff. Old stuff, like a museum that had been picked up and shaken. Objects were scattered across the floor and stacked up into immense piles. Some were games and attractions from a nineteenth-century carnival. There was what looked like a pinball machine and a miniature recreation of a gallows. One farthing, and the trapdoors opened, hanging a threadbare doll from a noose.

"How long has this carnival been here?" Noah said.

"Hundreds of years, from the look of things," Ava said. "Baldo wasn't the first person to own a carnival here."

"It's not just carnival stuff." Livia held up heavy cast-iron handcuffs. There were piles and piles of them. "You don't think this island was involved in the slave trade or something?"

"And this looks like a Roman centurion's helmet," Esme said, putting on a crumbly metal headpiece. She jumped into a battle pose, but the helmet fell off and rolled across the floor.

Noah turned slowly, taking in the vast room.

"There's been something here on Allhallows Rock for thousands of years?"

"Maybe longer," Ava said, squinting at faint images drawn on the walls. "Noah, bring that torch over?"

Noah held the flames up, showing a mural daubed on the walls of the cavern. It appeared to show a group of men killing each other with spears. Nearby, there was a black smudge with ten swirling arms, like some kind of demonic jellyfish. Each of its limbs reached out to encircle the necks of the fighting men.

"Looks like the Sarlacc on Tatooine," Noah said, his voice half laughing, half trembling.

"That's a strangely specific thing to say," Ava said.

"I resort to Star Wars trivia in times of great stress."

Ava hugged her arms over her stomach. She glanced

around the cavern, noticing more of the strange black holes with the funnels of roots at the top. They were everywhere. Some were tiny, while others were bigger than a person. It felt a bit like being inside a giant piece of coral or a moldy sponge. The roots twisting over the walls all seemed to grow from the funnels, slithering out of the darkness on black slime.

"I have a bad feeling about this place," Ava said.

"All right, scaredy-cats, come on, then." Esme pointed to a tunnel leading out of the cavern. "It looks like it gets lighter up ahead. That way must lead outside."

Esme went first. Ava paused to cast one more glance at the cave painting and the strange black jellyfish creature.

The drawings had to be tens of thousands of years old. Had there been something on the island for all that time?

A sudden scream. She ran after the other three and skidded to a halt in front of one of the funnels. Esme had slipped into a hole hidden in the shadows. She'd fallen just a meter before snagging on the sticky roots. They were wrapped all around her, seeping black liquid onto her clothes and skin. She reminded Ava of a puppet with tangled strings.

"I'm all right," Esme said, staying very still. "But if I try to move, the roots are going to break."

Livia dropped onto her stomach and tried to grab Esme, but she was too far away. Noah dangled his long arms into the hole. He got closer, just a fingertip away from reaching her. Esme stretched toward him. One of the roots broke, and she jerked down another few centimeters. Gasping, she swung slowly above pitch darkness.

"Esme!" Livia cried. "Just…just hold on."

"That's awesome advice," Esme said. "Thanks so much."

"Okay, okay." Noah stood up, a hand over his mouth. "Think. Think."

"The cavern," Livia said, setting off at a run. "There will be something there we can use."

Noah followed her. Ava stared after them. "Ava, stay?" Esme said. "Keep me company."

Ava nodded slowly. She forced herself to kneel down as close to the edge of the hole as she could manage. She looked down, past Esme. The darkness had weight, like it was a something and not a nothing.

"If there's a mutant spider-rat climbing up to eat me, I don't want to know," Esme said.

"No spider-rats," Ava said. "Or Sarlaccs."

"Reassuring. You think you could maybe talk to me? Keep my mind off the whole falling to certain death thing?"

Ava swallowed heavily. Falling. Falling. She closed her eyes.

"Ava, stay with me, all right?"

Ava pulled herself back to the here and now. She forced a smile. "I'm here. Just…hold on."

"Tell me something. Something that matters. Where are you going to be in ten years?"

"Anywhere but Portgrave," Ava said, her voice shaky.

The words spilled out without any editing. She didn't usually share her dreams out loud. "I want to travel the world with my camera and nothing else."

Esme laughed quietly. "Nothing, or no one?"

"Both," she admitted. "What about you?"

"University, as far away as I can get. Job in a big city. Lawyer, architect, banker. Something like that." She shifted slightly, and the roots creaked beneath her.

"You want to be rich?"

"I want to be free. I don't want to depend on anyone else, only myself." She took a deep breath in and out again, wincing. The roots were tightening around her arms and legs. It must have hurt, but she couldn't move without them snapping. "That's why I came to this island. Because some bastard is trying to control me, and I'm not going to let that happen."

"You're a lone wolf," Ava said, repeating Livia's words.

Esme smiled at a memory. "We were watching some lesbian werewolf film, Liv and me. But it ended with us arguing over whether we'd let the other bite us if they were a werewolf. That's where the whole lone wolf thing came from."

"Sounds like Jolie and me. We always manage to argue over the silliest things."

"But you guys always make up."

Ava chewed her lip and didn't say anything.

The roots holding Esme creaked again. Ava glanced over her shoulder. No sign of Noah or Livia. She turned back to Esme. For all her bravado, Esme was beginning to look scared. The roots creaked and strained under her weight.

"I have something I want to ask you," Esme said. "Why did you ask me that question back at the club? About whether I could kill someone?"

"Curiosity, I suppose."

"The real reason. Now feels like a good time for truths."

"All right." Ava's knees were burning, so she shuffled onto her bum. "I was thinking about how far I'd go to stop whoever it is who brought us here. I used to believe I could never be a killer. But what if I could be?"

"That's your point of no return. We all have them."

"What's yours? The one thing you will never do?"

"I don't want to be anyone's puppet. The moment I let someone make my choices for me, that's when I'll know I've lost."

One of the larger roots snapped. Esme jerked and slipped. Her legs scrabbled against the side of the hole. Her arms were looped through the remaining tangles, but the roots were stretching and fraying, one strand at a time. Clods of earth and broken roots fell away.

"That's the real reason why I'm so anti-love," Esme continued, talking louder, as if she could blot out the reality of her situation. "As soon as another person comes along, your life kind of stops being your own. Before you know it, you're pretending to be someone you're not to keep them happy."

A crack. A drop. Ava held her breath and waited for Esme to fall.

ELEVEN

Roots snapped. Esme grabbed at the remaining tangles, but they slid through her fingers. It was too late. Ava staggered back from the hole. She couldn't watch her fall, not again.

But then Noah and Livia were there, lying on the ground to dangle two long chains into the hole. Esme's fingers reached for Noah's chain just as the last of the roots failed. She dropped. Noah cried out as he took her full weight. Her feet kicked over nothing.

Noah groaned with the effort of holding her. But then Esme managed to grab Livia's chain with her other hand, and the pair of them heaved Esme out of the hole. She flopped onto her back with her hands over her face. There were black stains all over her, like someone had splashed her with ink.

"Holy moly," Noah said, trying to catch his breath. "What were we thinking coming down here?"

"I have no idea," Livia said. "Also—*holy moly*? Are you eighty?" She grinned at him and laughed.

After a second, Esme joined in with their laughter. She sat up and swept her hair out of her face. Her hand came away sticky with black slime. "That was an experience," she said.

"Are...are you okay?" Ava stammered, still standing back from the hole.

"My heart's going at about three hundred beats per minute, and I look like a demon has puked on me, but otherwise I'm just perfect." She frowned at Ava. "You don't look too good, though."

"I'm not the one who nearly died." Ava tried to force a smile. She sat down against the wall and clasped her hands together so no one would see they were shaking. She closed her eyes and focused on breathing slowly. After a few seconds, a wisp of smoke drifted into her face, sweet and skunky. She waved it away.

"Sorry," Livia said, flapping her arms about as if that was going to clear the smoke from her joint. "Anyone want some?" She offered it to Noah.

"Nah, I don't do that anymore," he said. "Bad memories and all that."

"And that's the exact reason I still do," Livia said, an edge to her voice.

"Your granddad?"

She watched him with clenched teeth. "Yeah. I was the one who found him, you know? Sitting on the beach with a tin of beer in one hand. Like he'd just *stopped.* All the life floating out of him like..." She gestured to the smoke.

"I'm sorry, man. He was a good guy," Noah said.

"How did you know him?" Livia said, frowning.

"I saw him around. We didn't talk much, though." He swept a hand through his hair and looked anywhere but at Livia.

Livia sighed. "Well, according to him, he was the opposite of a good guy. 'Guilt has roots, Olivia. Don't let it pull you down like it has me.' Back then, I didn't know what he felt guilty about." She trailed off and took a deep drag from her joint.

"Maybe he never got over his time here," Esme said. "I can vouch for it being a mentally scarring experience."

"Yeah. You're right. It always seemed like he'd left part of him behind," Livia said. "Those roots again."

Ava glanced over at the black roots covering the walls, growing out of those funnel-shaped holes. They reminded her of a monster's tentacles that would bleed if cut. She shuddered at the thought. But where did guilt come into the story?

"What do you think they are?" she said, pointing at the roots.

"Nothing good," Esme said. "They felt *wrong*. Like the exact opposite of alive. I am not a fan."

Ava shivered. "Their source has to be at the bottom of the holes, right at the heart of the island."

"It's Whispers down there," Livia said, her voice slowing. Ava shot her a quick glance. Something wasn't right. "I can feel him."

"Whispers is a gigantic black fungus with a million arms?" Noah said. "I can't wait to meet him!"

"He's the voice inside your head, the knife in your hand, and the secret in the shadows," Livia said.

"That something your granddad used to say?" Esme said.

"Huh?" Livia said, blinking. "What?"

"I saw him," Ava blurted out. "Last night. The photo booth flash blinded me, and for a second, I could see a face."

"What did he look like?" Esme said.

"Just like the man in the portraits. Young, with black paint across his eyes. Like a hot clown, basically. Only evil."

"I flipping hate clowns," Noah said.

"More than you'd hate a gigantic fungus with millions of arms?" Esme said.

"It's a close call." He shuffled over to the hole that had nearly eaten Esme. "Hello? Whatever you are, please leave us all alone, thanks, bye."

"You don't really think there's something down there, do you?" Ava said. "This isn't real, right?"

No one answered. Esme used her foot to give one of the chains a shove over the edge of the hole. It dropped soundlessly. They waited for the clank as it hit the bottom, but nothing came.

"Really glad I didn't fall down there," she said.

Ava shook her head. "Sorry I wasn't much help. I kept panicking and—"

Esme cut her off with a wave of her hand. "What happens in the hole stays in the hole," she said. "And that goes for both of us."

The version of Esme who'd opened up about her feelings was gone again, hidden away under a thick sheet of ice.

"We're all alive, and that's what matters," Noah said. "Except for Baldo. Baldo is still dead."

"It stinks down here," Livia said abruptly. "Let's get out of here before I vom."

She staggered ahead without waiting for the rest of the group to join her. Shrugging at Noah, Ava followed. The tunnel turned from stone to mud, and the funnels became fewer and farther between. Light seeped in from a natural doorway ahead. The tunnel brought them outside into a hidden passage between rocks. Shingle crunched beneath Ava's feet. She weaved through the rocks and stepped out onto the beach, breathing in the fresh air.

"Where are we?" Noah said.

"At the far end of the carnival," Esme said. "Those are the

backs of the tents over there. The tunnel brought us through the cliff." She pointed at a rocky outcrop curving out to sea, marking the edge of the cove.

Ava tried to get her bearings. If Esme was right, then the portrait hut would be nearby, hiding behind the tents at the edge of the water. She walked down to the swash. She couldn't see the hut anywhere.

Frowning, she looked out to sea. There was something half submerged—a wooden jetty lined with benches. People sitting on those benches would have had a perfect view of the rocky outcrop that separated the carnival from the boathouse cove.

Noah pointed toward the outcrop. "There's a cage up there. Like a medieval gallows."

He was right. Up on top of the rocks, there was a metal scaffold. Chain, ratchet, person-sized cage. From the length of the chain's reel, Ava suspected it could plunge the cage all the way down into the water. The audience would be able to see its full descent and the splash when it hit.

"You said Baldo was an escape artist," Ava said. "That had to be part of his act."

Esme nodded. "He must have been chained up in the cage as it dropped into the ocean. Then he freed himself and swam clear while the audience watched for him to reappear."

"Only he didn't really," Noah continued. "He followed the currents around the outcrop to the cove on the opposite side, then clambered out via the lifeboat ramp."

"And then he used his secret tunnel to change into dry clothes before reemerging behind the audience as if by magic," Esme finished. "To rapturous applause."

"What's that?" Livia said, pointing across the beach. "Where did that come from?"

They turned to look. Ava's skin prickled. Close to the line of rotting tents was the ramshackle hut with the portraits. Ava was sure it hadn't been there a second ago.

Her first thought was to run, but she stopped herself. Pretending she was as brave as Jolie, she marched over to the hut.

"Wait a second," Noah said. "You're going in there?"

"It has something to do with why we're here," she said. "There might be answers."

The door blew open as she approached. She peeked inside. It looked the same as it had the day before. On the walls, there were portraits of all ages and sizes and that gold-framed mirror.

She tentatively stepped inside and approached the jar on the table. Slugs, tongues, jelly sweets? "It's just a prop," she said, mostly to herself. "Designed to scare us."

A round of applause made her jump back from the table. It seemed to be coming from the mirror. Ava walked closer. Instead of her own reflection, Ava saw what looked like a jerky old film of the Magnificent Baldo. He was standing in front of the benches on the beach, basking in the adoration of his audience. They clapped and cheered and threw money into his black hat, so much money that it overflowed. The wind whipped bills into the air, and they swirled in a tornado around Baldo.

As quickly as it had appeared, the vision was gone. Ava found herself staring at her own reflection. As she watched, the other three stepped into the hut behind her.

No, not three. Four.

A fourth figure was hidden behind Noah. The stranger craned his head to the side to get a better view of Ava. A beautiful young man with black face paint and a hungry grin.

Ava screamed and spun around. The spot where he had stood was empty. "He was here...did you see him?"

Noah looked around the hut with a frown. "It's just us. And lots of old white dudes."

"There was someone else here! I saw him in the mirror." More blank looks.

Confess, and you'll be free, warm breath whispered in her ear.

A wave of claustrophobia made Ava need to get out, and get out now. She shoved her way past the other three and rushed outside. She breathed slowly until her heart resumed its normal rhythm.

"You saw something in that mirror?" Esme said, following her.

"I feel like I'm losing it, just like Scarlett did. And Scarlett's dead!"

"You've got this," Esme said quietly.

"I really don't," Ava sobbed, clapping a hand to her mouth. "I'm scared of everything."

"You're scared, but you're not running away. You're the one who volunteered to follow Noah into a rat-infested tunnel. You kept me distracted after I fell down a massive hole of doom. You're the first person through the door every time. That makes you the bravest person here, if you ask me."

Ava managed a weak smile. "I don't feel very brave."

"It's OK to be scared. But you're going to get through this."

"Thanks," Ava said. She wiped her eyes. "You're good at pep talks, you know? When you're not being an ass."

Esme fired double finger guns at her. "Tell anyone, and I'll push you off a cliff." She clapped her hands together, summoning Livia and Noah. "All right, it looks like it's going to get dark soon, so let's find the rest of our merry band before anything else weird happens."

They made their way up through the flooded carnival. Dusk thickened around them, and gradually Ava's fear started to fall away. She didn't know if it was the island's magic or being with Noah, Esme, and Livia. Feeling like she was part of something real was nice. Part of something that, she was ashamed to admit, didn't involve Jolie. That was the thing about being Jolie's friend—it didn't leave much room for anyone else.

The calm feeling was interrupted by splashing footsteps. "There you are! Where've you all been?" Imogen tottered over on her impractical kitten heels. She was wearing a familiar-looking fur coat. "You've been gone for hours."

"Is that Scarlett's coat?" Ava said.

"It's sexy on me, right?" Imogen struck a pose against a candy floss hut. Bent one bare leg at an awkward angle. Pulled a face like she was holding back a sneeze. Ava didn't take her picture, even though it was obvious that Imogen wanted her to.

"Seriously?" Esme said, shooting Imogen an icy look.

"Oh, fine, then." Imogen stopped posing, and her face fell into its default expression—peevish, disgusted.

Ava quickly raised the camera and took Imogen's picture. Downturned mouth, furrowed brow, chin tucked back into her neck. Ava wasn't usually so cruel, but it felt good.

"Let me see." Imogen reached for the camera. "Oh my god, that looks nothing like me, take another one."

Ava took the camera back and switched it off. "Why are you wandering around by yourself, Imogen?"

Imogen looked confused. "Teddy was here. I don't know where he went, though. Teddy? Teddy!" she called.

"Where's everyone else?" Noah asked. "Did you find a radio? Because we didn't have much luck."

"Radio? What radio?" Imogen pulled a face. "Come on, you're going to be late for the party."

Exchanging looks, they followed Imogen through the tents. A party was the last thing on Ava's mind. But as night swallowed up the day, she felt herself forgetting why, and all thoughts of escaping the island faded into the background. One by one, the lights switched on, and the pier shimmered into life. Ava's worries floated away on a cotton-candy-scented breeze. Despite everything, she found herself smiling. Music, magic, sparkling lights. The carnival called to her.

TWELVE

A bonfire burned at the foot of the freak show stage. Shadowy figures danced around the flames like spirits risen from the dead. Ava raised her camera. She focused on Jolie, who was dancing with Clem. Her arms were raised above her head, her eyes closed. Clem bit his lip and moved his hips so close to her that their bodies were almost touching.

"That's something no one wants to see," Esme muttered, slouching into one of the back benches.

Ava laughed nervously. Jolie and Clem together was a ridiculous thought. Jolie hated Clem. Yet as she watched, Jolie lowered her arms and placed them on Clem's shoulders, smiling as he looped his arms around her waist.

Ava padded up the aisle between the benches. "Hey," she said. "What's going on?"

No one noticed her. Not Jolie and Clem, dancing closer and closer. Not Olly and Teddy, tapping their feet in time to music Ava couldn't hear. Ava felt like she shouldn't be there. Like she was watching something private. Then a shrill wolf whistle brought the dancers out of their trance.

"You're welcome," Esme said, taking two fingers out of her mouth and winking at Ava.

Jolie stepped away from Clem and looked Ava up and down with a frown. "You're back, then?"

"How long were we gone?" Noah said.

"Hours, days, who knows?" The fire leapt and crackled, and she took a step away. "But now you're all here, so let's get this party started."

Ava accepted a drink from Drunk Teddy, but she couldn't relax. There was something she was forgetting. She could feel the empty space where the memory should have been. So while the others laughed and danced, she watched on the camera's screen. She snapped images of swirling fire and wild laughter and the gaps where something was missing.

She looked through the photos as soon as she'd taken them, as if trying to convince herself they were real. The whole scene felt strangely dreamlike, as if someone had pulled a veil in front of her eyes, blocking out the real world and dulling her senses. There was something she needed to remember, but it remained infuriatingly out of reach.

"Roll up, roll up," Clem cried.

Ava looked up from her camera. Clem stood on the stage. He lifted a musty top hat and bowed deeply. He waited patiently for nonexistent applause to die down. Then he addressed the benches. "Good ladies and gentlemen, please welcome to the stage the Fantastic Mr. Oliver Okeke, strongman extraordinaire and owner of the best abs in all of Portgrave."

Olly bounded through threadbare curtains to whoops and shouts. He'd changed into a tiny red-and-white leotard that had belonged to a carnival strongman. There were moth holes dotting the fabric. Jolie wolf whistled, and Olly gave an embarrassed smile.

Olly held up one finger to quiet the catcalls, then dragged a strange-looking contraption to the center of the stage. It appeared to be a pair of seats welded at the opposite ends of a long metal bar. "I need two volunteers," he called. "Ladies?"

"Come on," Jolie laughed, grabbing Ava's hand. "Let's do it."

"No, Jolie..." Ava objected, but Jolie was already dragging her off the bench and up onto the collapsing wooden boards of the stage.

Olly took Ava's hand and twirled her around to applause too loud for six onlookers. Ava squeezed her eyes shut, trying to shake off the fog that had descended over her. Maybe she was drunk, although she didn't remember drinking anything. She didn't remember much at all.

"Thank you to my beautiful volunteers," Olly cried, helping them step into the seats.

He crouched down to grip the bar. His leotard made a worrying ripping sound. Ava held on to the bar as it jerked off the ground. Jolie screamed in delight. Another thrust, and Olly locked his arms above his head. Ava clung on as the contraption rocked perilously. Then they tilted the other way, and every muscle in Ava's body turned to stone.

"The thing I didn't consider," Olly stammered, staggering around the stage, "is that normally I, like, throw my weights down."

"What's that mean?" Jolie said.

"I don't know how to put this thing down without dropping you."

Jolie laughed fearlessly, throwing her head back so the wind caught her hair.

"Don't you dare drop me!" Ava said. Her heart doubled its tempo. Her vision narrowed.

She caught sight of a figure watching them from the back of the audience. The light from the fire shifted and revealed that the figure was Scarlett. Blood streamed down the side of her head, soaking her dress and pouring down her bare legs.

Ava remembered. The blackmail. Scarlett's murder.

Dumping her body in the sea. Baldo's skeleton and that strange underground cavern with all its slimy black roots.

And that man watching her from the mirror. Whispers.

A high-pitched, strangled cry crept out of her mouth, and she jerked away from the vision. The seats unbalanced, and she fell. She screamed and kept screaming, visions of twisted metal and protruding bones jumping into her head.

Somewhere in the distance, Jolie was still laughing.

And then she stopped falling.

Esme and Noah were there, each catching an end of the contraption. They helped Olly gently lower it to the ground. Esme hauled Ava out of her seat and slapped her on the back.

"Heights aren't your thing, huh?"

Ava scrambled away from her. "What are we doing?" she cried. "Scarlett's dead, and we're playing stupid games? What's wrong with you?"

The rest of the group stared at her uneasily.

"It's a wake," Imogen said quietly. "For Scarlett. To remember her."

Except it felt like everyone had forgotten. Everyone except for Ava. She blinked away the memory of the blood-soaked ghost. "We're meant to be escaping. Why aren't we trying to get away?"

"We have a plan," Jolie said. "We're going to try and fix the boat trolley so we can get off the island. But that has to wait till morning."

"What?" Noah said. "That boat is the size of a bus. No way can we lift it."

"You got a better idea?"

"Stop!" Ava said. "This is what happened last night. We sat around drinking and arguing instead of running away, and Scarlett died."

"Relax already," Jolie said. "Have a drink and stop being so dramatic."

"I don't want a drink." Ava climbed down from the stage and sat with her head in her hands. No one was listening to her. The island had cast its forgetfulness spell on them and washed away their memories.

The bench creaked as someone sat down next to her. She glanced up. It was Jolie. "That was an adventure, huh?"

"No, not really." She pushed away the bottle Jolie was trying to force into her hand. "Leave me alone." But even as she protested, her rage ebbed away like the tide.

Jolie rolled her eyes and shuffled a small distance away along the bench. "Drama queen."

On the stage, Clem readjusted his top hat. "Our next performer is..."

"Songbird," Imogen pronounced, jumping up from her seat.

"Song what?" Jolie heckled.

"It's my stage name," Imogen said sniffily. "You'd know if you'd came to any of the school concerts. I headlined the last one."

"Headlined?" Jolie said. "Is the school recital now Portgrave's answer to Coachella?"

Imogen looked confused. "It could be. I'm singing at a professional level now."

"All right, all right." Clem swept his arm in a grand gesture toward Imogen. "Everyone, Songbird!"

The group fell silent as Imogen began to sing. It was a gentle melody unlike all the blaring tunes of the fair. An opera aria that Ava thought she had heard before, but not in the way Imogen sang it. Her entire body relaxed, and once again, she forgot all about her panic.

"What a loser," Jolie snorted.

"Stop being so horrible," Ava hissed. "It's getting boring."

"Not as boring as you. I knew you before you reinvented yourself as a hipster artiste, remember? I could tell everyone just how boring you really are."

"You don't want me to change because you're scared I won't need you anymore," Ava said, the realization hitting her hard. "This is all about your own insecurities."

"Says the girl who's scared of her own shadow."

Ava stood up to leave, but Jolie pulled her back down again.

"Don't go," Jolie sighed. "It's this place. The freak show. I keep thinking about my invite, and it's making me cranky."

Ava's irritation faded to shame at not having spotted the truth behind Jolie's bad temper. Her brother. The freak show stage. Ava opened her mouth to speak, but no words came. Jolie had never talked about the fire, and Ava didn't know what to say.

"The fire department said he must have fallen asleep smoking a cigarette," Jolie said quietly. "And our house was full of all this flammable shit, so it all went up in seconds. It's like our parents went out of their way to buy only things that would burn. The curtains, the sofa, even the wallpaper."

"I'm sorry," Ava said.

"He didn't look alive," Jolie continued, almost viciously. "When they brought him out, I thought he was dead. Did I tell you that? What he looked like?"

Ava stared down at her hands. Jolie breathed heavily, short, sharp breaths.

"*Ora pro nobis peccatoribus*," Imogen sang.

"I would do anything to forget," Jolie said more softly. Ava knew how she felt. There were some things that stuck with you, and after you'd seen them, you were a different person. It felt like they left marks on your soul and nothing would ever wash them out. All Ava's grand ideas of becoming a new person? That was painting over the stains beneath.

"*In hora mortis nostrae. Ave Maria.*"

Silence. Even the electronic music of the attractions seemed to fade away.

No one applauded. They watched Imogen smugly saunter down the steps and return to her seat. The group sat there, dazed, until Clem finally returned to the stage, minus the swagger.

"Um, does someone want to follow that?" he asked. Silence. "Anyone?"

"Yeah, I will," Noah said, standing up. He ambled behind the curtains to half-hearted clapping.

Jolie eyed Imogen on a nearby bench. "Seems unfair that someone like Imogen gets to be so talented. Everyone here except for me has a talent. One day, you'll all be famous one way or another, and I'll still be where I am now." It was an uncharacteristic display of vulnerability from Jolie.

"I don't want to be famous," Ava said. "I just want to matter."

"Isn't that the same thing?"

Ava smiled tightly but didn't answer. "Anyway, you're the fearless Jolie. You can be anything you want to be."

"Anything that doesn't involve using my brain," she muttered.

"Become a stuntwoman. Lycra, scars, death metal theme song."

Jolie seemed to consider this, then snorted in amusement. "Maybe someone will sponsor me to do stupid shit that everyone else is too scared to try. Professional daredevil."

"There you go," Ava said. "I've never heard such a realistic and achievable ambition."

Jolie grinned at her, and briefly, she was the friend Ava

remembered. Then Noah bounded back onstage and Jolie's smile faded again.

Noah was holding a bottle of vodka in one hand and what looked like a giant match in the other. No, not a match—a fire juggler's torch. Ava winced as he poured alcohol on the torch and lit it. Then he took a swig from the bottle. Jolie's knuckles turned white as she gripped the edge of the bench.

"Is that safe?" Clem said, stepping back.

Noah swallowed, then shrugged. "Probably not."

"That's beyond stupid," Jolie muttered. "He could kill himself if he inhales."

Noah took another swig. He paused, then spat it out in an arc, lighting the liquid with the torch. The burst of flames seemed to come from nowhere, bright blue with purple and orange wisps. It looked almost otherworldly, and Ava felt like if she reached out to touch it, the flame would feel cool. It was beautiful. And then the wind changed direction.

The ball of fire exploded into long fingers that twisted outward like monstrous tentacles. The fire seemed to move in slow motion, reaching toward Ava with curling claws. Screaming faces were trapped within each flame. A fine spray of the alcohol dusted Ava's face, followed by a brief sting of heat.

Livia, Esme, and Olly cheered as Noah smiled sheepishly, the burning torch dangling from his hand. He tossed it into the bonfire and bowed.

"Ta-da," he said nervously.

"What the hell is wrong with you?" Jolie yelled.

She climbed onto the stage in a few strides and shoved Noah in the chest.

"I'm sorry," he said, raising his hands. "Are you all right?"

"No, I'm not all right," she spat. "Nearly killing us all doesn't make you cool."

"OK, I didn't *nearly kill* anyone—"

"You think this is funny? Have you ever seen someone with fourth-degree burns on their face? With so much damage you can see their fucking bones?"

Ava scrambled to Jolie's side and tried to take her arm. "He didn't know about your brother."

"And here comes Ava, rushing over to protect a stranger over her *best* friend," Jolie cried.

"That's not what I—"

"You're like a dog in heat," Jolie screamed. "Throwing yourself at every man who even glances your way."

"Whoa, time out," Noah interjected.

"Back off!" Jolie shoved him again, and again, and again, and he didn't try to defend himself. With each push, he stumbled back, but he let her keep on hitting him. If anything, this seemed to make Jolie more angry. She slapped him hard across the face, once and then twice. "Come on, then. Take a swing at me."

"I'm not going to fight you," he said.

"Too good to hit a girl, are you?" She struck him again.

"I'm not going to hit *anyone*. Not anymore."

She swung at him again, but this time he blocked her.

Jolie laughed, although there was no joy in the sound. "Such a good boy," she sobbed. Ava couldn't tell if she was still talking to Noah or someone else. "Rescuing me from myself."

"I'm sorry?" Noah offered.

Ava put her arm around Jolie, trying to lead her away from Noah, but Jolie was crying too hard to notice. She'd pulled the cigarette lighter from her pocket and was clicking it on and off, on and off.

"I'm sorry," Noah repeated.

"Stop saying you're sorry!" Jolie screamed.

She shoved him again. The way the flames of the bonfire were blowing cast Noah's and Jolie's shadows on the back of the stage, only the shadows weren't right. They moved independently and twisted into a violent scene of horror. Scarlett, slumped on her knees with her arms raised to shield herself. A second figure holding a rock aloft. Bringing it down again and again.

Ava cried out and stumbled back. She teetered at the edge of the stage, barely keeping her balance. The smallest gust of wind, and she'd fall into the fire. Noah made a grab for her and pulled her away from the edge.

"It's always about you, isn't it?" Jolie said softly. Her anger gone, she marched down the steps.

"Jolie, wait. I thought I saw something." But Jolie had already vanished into the darkness.

A memory resurfaced: Scarlett storming away from the group and into the night. The next morning, she was dead.

"We have to go after Jolie," Ava said. Her heart pounded against her rib cage, panic rising, a sense of foreboding and impending doom. "Before something terrible happens."

You'll be too late, Scarlett's voice mocked. *Just like before.*

THIRTEEN

Jolie had left behind footprints that slowly faded as water seeped into the indentations. Ava knew they were hers thanks to the long scuffs made by the flapping feet of her panda costume. But Jolie herself was nowhere to be seen. The beach, with its huge black rocks like alien obelisks, was silent.

Ava followed the footprints to the ocean. The backwash sucked hungrily at the shore, pulling small stones and pebbles down toward dark water. Ava's boots sank into the shingle with every wave. Maybe if she stood still for long enough, the beach would swallow her whole. It was as if it had swallowed Jolie. The footprints ended where the water began.

"Maybe she's making a swim for it." Livia shivered and huddled tighter inside her leather jacket with its bulging pockets and cigarette burns on the sleeves.

"The water's about ten degrees." Olly knitted his hands behind his head and paced in the swash, searching the moonlit waves. "And the riptides would have swept her straight out to sea."

"No," Esme said. "This island isn't that easy to escape. If she went in the water, there's a good chance the current carried her around to the cove."

"Like the Magnificent Baldo's act," Livia said. "If Jolie has any sense, she won't fight it."

"If she had any sense, she wouldn't have gone into the water!" Olly said.

Esme shrugged. "I'm not so sure she did."

"What about the footprints?" Ava said.

"What footprints?" Esme gestured to the ground with a sly smile.

There was nothing there.

"Um, I have a question?" Clem raised his hand.

Esme wearily gestured to him. "Yes?"

He put his hand down and spread his arms in an exaggerated shrug. "Why are you talking about Baldo?"

"He owned the carnival," Livia started to explain.

"Yeah, I know who he was." Clem produced the harmonica from his sleeve as if by magic and rolled it nervously across his knuckles. "I just don't see how a dead magician has anything to do with Jolie."

"An escape artist, not a magician." Ava nodded to the cage dangling high on the outcrop. The moon lit it up like a goth metal album cover. All it needed was a squawking crow and a bolt of lightning.

"Who cares?" Clem exclaimed.

Ava glanced over at Esme, then at Livia and Noah. None of them had mentioned Baldo lying dead in his cavern. It felt like something important they shouldn't have forgotten about until this moment. But the nighttime magic of the island had swept them up, and his death had drifted into insignificance. Even as Ava actively thought about him, she struggled to hold on to the memories.

Wetness against her calves brought her attention back to the beach. She blinked down at her feet, or the place where her feet had been. She'd sunk into the shingle all the way past her boots, and she hadn't even noticed it happening.

"Damn it!" She struggled to free herself.

Olly single-handedly heaved her out. "You zoned out there, huh?" he laughed, his eyes crinkling with a grin.

"Did I?" Ava said. It didn't feel like she had, not for longer than a few seconds.

"Time doesn't work right on this island," Livia said. "Don't you feel it passing us by?"

"Do we feel *time*?" Clem said, shooting Livia the sort of look that accused her of swallowing her stash in one go.

Livia nodded slowly. "I keep feeling it shift beneath me. Slow, then fast. Sometimes it jumps and I have memories of things I don't think I ever lived through."

Ava was about to agree, but before she could, she felt the rushing sensation Livia had described. Time spun away. The hands of her watch rotated with the sound of whirring gears. The tide slipped out to reveal an expanse of sticky mud where there'd once been water. Stars changed position overhead.

None of the others appeared to have noticed. They were still talking in small groups, their conversations alien to Ava. She was at the center of a time-lapse video, standing still while the world surged past her. Storm clouds swarmed across the sky, stealing the stars. The first specks of rain dotted Ava's cheeks and—*crack*—time slowed.

"We need to get back to the club," Clem said, "before the storm hits."

"Wait, what about Jolie?" Ava said.

Clem turned to her with a start, as if he'd forgotten she was standing beside him. "What about her?"

Ava weakly gestured to the ocean, but the others looked at her like she was mad. "She disappeared?"

Livia frowned. "I don't remember seeing her. Did she go back to the club with Teddy?"

Ava glanced over to where Teddy had been standing. He was gone too. She was sure he'd been there moments ago.

Thunder rumbled ominously. "Let's go already," Clem said.

The others followed, except for Ava and Olly. Olly paused to frown up at Baldo's cage, then jogged after Clem. Ava glanced at the cage too, wondering what he'd seen. Another crack like a whip, and lightning seared away the night. Arteries grew down from the clouds, flashing as they branched into a dozen zigzags. Where one touched the water, it became a thick column of fizzing light with flames at its tip.

For less than half a second, the lightning lit up a figure standing beside Baldo's cage.

"Up there!" Ava cried. "There's someone up there."

Jolie.

Ava set off for the outcrop at a run, ignoring the others calling for her to stop. The rocks made a natural staircase to the peak, but they were sharp and slippery and scraped at her knees and elbows as she climbed. She skidded into seawater pools and crunched on snails. Seaweed was slimy beneath her fingers.

"Wait," Olly called from the beach. "I don't think that's Jolie."

Ava kept climbing. Halfway up, she had to pause to catch her breath. She risked a look over her shoulder. She could see the whole carnival, from Baldo's flooded stage to the creepy portrait hut to the steps leading up to the main square. Everything appeared to center around a circular building she hadn't seen before. It was hidden away at the center of the clustered tents and carnival games: the secret midpoint of a maze. All of the strings of fairy lights from the entire carnival started there, stretching out from the point of its roof like forks of lightning.

"Careful," a voice shouted up.

She looked down. Olly and Clem were climbing up toward her. Olly leapt nimbly from boulder to boulder, sometimes swinging from just one arm as he searched for a foothold. Then he reached down to take Clem's hand and pull him up. They worked well together, Ava realized with a pang of resentment. Why was their friendship still strong while hers with Jolie had crumbled the moment they set foot on Allhallows Rock?

"Don't move," Clem said to her. "Just don't move."

"I'm fine," Ava started to say, but Clem was looking past her at something she couldn't see.

The two boys continued to help each other climb with clasped hands and shouts of encouragement. Ava scrambled up behind them. She finally heaved herself over the top behind them. She shakily stood up. The wind whipped at her face and made her feel exposed and unsteady. Clem and Olly were slowly advancing on the tip of the outcrop, where a figure wobbled precariously. Not Jolie. Teddy.

"Come away from the edge, mate," Olly said.

Teddy was hanging on to the cage's metal skeleton with one hand. In his other hand, he held a nearly empty bottle. How much had he drunk? Ava tried to think back to the freak show, but it felt like so long ago. She could picture him in the audience, rarely speaking, always drinking. In fact, she couldn't think of a moment in the past twenty-four hours when he hadn't had a bottle in hand.

All that alcohol had taken its toll. His skin was pale and clammy, his movements uncoordinated. He kept shaking his head, either telling himself off or trying to clear his mind. The wind caught him, and he briefly swung out over the edge of the rocks, barely managing to keep his feet rooted on the ground.

"Hold on." Clem's voice was shaking. "Just don't let go."

"Hold on?" Teddy said. "It's too late for that now."

"It's okay." Clem walked toward Teddy with his hands out, but Teddy backed closer to the precipice, skidding on pebbles. Clem stopped.

"Can't you hear him?" Teddy said, his eyes unfocused and bloodshot.

"Who?" Olly said.

"Whispers, whispers, right in my ear. They never stop."

"What are they saying?" Ava asked, tentatively edging toward the three boys.

They all glanced back at her, and for a second she was

back in the corridors of Portgrave High. Clem and Olly, shiny and smiling, always together. Teddy, slouching on the periphery of their bromance in his expensive leather deck shoes and sunglasses. The popular boys Ava would never have dared to approach. Then they were back on the rock, the wind threatening to carry Teddy out to sea.

"Confess and you'll be free," Teddy slurred, then laughed croakily. He swung off the scaffold again, this time rotating all the way around the metal pole and back onto solid ground. He hung there with his eyes closed, half-conscious but somehow still clinging on.

Clem and Olly went back to ignoring Ava. "We're going to have to grab him," Olly whispered. "On three?"

Clem closed his eyes and breathed out slowly, then nodded.

"Okay, then." Olly slowly stepped closer to Teddy, an arm's reach away. "One—"

Teddy's eyes flicked open. "Which one of you will be the *One*? Who can hold on the longest?"

Olly and Clem froze. Exchanged worried looks. "What does that mean?" Ava said, moving closer.

She remembered the graffiti surrounding Baldo's body. *Whispers, Whispers. One, One, One. Hold your tongue*. Olly held out an arm to bar her way. She stepped around him. "Do you know what the *One* is, Teddy?"

"He only needs one," Teddy said, surprisingly clearly. "*One* to tie him to this world with their guilt."

"And that's the alcohol speaking," Clem said, his voice wobbly with fear.

"I don't think it is," Ava said. "Where did you hear that, Teddy?"

He knocked on the side of his head with a fist. "The voices in my head won't stop. They want me to confess."

"Scarlett heard voices right before she died."

"I killed Scarlett," Teddy cried. He stumbled and fell against the cage. The chain creaked and slipped on the winch.

"That's just this place messing with our heads," Olly said. "When we get home—"

"She was going to tell," Teddy interrupted. "She knew my secret, and she was going to tell."

There was a firmness to his voice now. A finality. Ava believed him.

"What happened?" she said quietly.

"I told her everything," Teddy said. "Everything! I thought I could trust her. But then last night, she kept dropping these hints. Like she was going to tell just because she could."

"You killed her?" Clem said disbelievingly.

Teddy laughed manically, but then the smile faded, and he looked confused. "I'd have gone to prison. I couldn't go to prison. You have to understand."

His invite: the picture of him in the prison uniform,

locked up behind bars. His biggest secret—the worst thing he'd ever done.

"I found her last night near some photo booth," Teddy whispered. "She kissed me, but then she started laughing, calling me pathetic and weak. Said the whole world would know what I'd done. And then there was a voice in my head telling me to pick up a brick and hit her with it. So I did. I hit her and hit her until she was dead, and then I put her in that boat like the voice told me to."

"The blood," Clem whispered. "Where's all the blood?"

Teddy pulled his suit jacket aside. The pink stains on his shirt: *blood* mixed with sweat, not Campari. "None of you noticed," he laughed. "You were all too busy arguing about which one of you did it."

"Shit, Teddy," Olly said. "But listen. It wasn't you, it was these voices. It's not your fault—"

"I wanted to do it," Teddy cried. "Who was she to reject me? I'm a thousand times better than someone like her."

He stumbled backward and caught hold of the cage's open door for support. He rocked there, feet on the ground, shoulders leaning back into the cage. The chain creaked.

"You're a good guy," Clem said, sounding like he didn't believe it. He stepped closer to Teddy. "We can work this out. Come away from the edge, all right?"

Teddy glanced at the inside of the rusty cage. "We're *all*

good guys, aren't we, Clem? That's what you tell yourself, isn't it?"

Clem's expression darkened. "Come away, and we'll go get a drink together."

"A drink, a drink," Teddy laughed. "I only had a few, you know? Five, maybe. Six? Who cares. That was your excuse too, wasn't it, Clem?"

"That's enough, mate," Clem said coldly.

"One little mistake," Teddy continued. "And before you know it, everything has changed. That night at Black Box—"

"I said, enough!" Clem cried, but Teddy wasn't listening. "I got kicked out. Too drunk, the bouncers said. Screw them. And you were *too busy* to share a taxi, so I drove myself home."

"Drunk?" Olly said, taking a step back. "What kind of person drives after six drinks?"

Teddy rounded on him, spittle flying out of the corners of his mouth in his fury. "What kind of stupid idiot goes wandering around the streets in the fucking dark? How was I supposed to see him, huh?"

Thunder rumbled, then silence. "Jack?" Olly stammered.

"Oh my god," Ava murmured. Teddy in his striped jumpsuit with the ball and chain. Teddy had killed Olly's brother. This was his secret.

"You just...you drove off," Olly stammered. "You didn't even call for an ambulance."

Teddy blinked like he was waking from a dream. "It would have wrecked my life." His tone changed from anger to syrupy pleading. "Do you know what would have happened to me if I'd gone to prison? Someone like me doesn't go to prison."

"Murderer." Olly gritted his teeth, balled his hands into fists.

Murderer, murderer, murderer, a voice whispered in Ava's ear. *He deserves to die.*

Lightning split the sky. Ava turned away from the blinding light. The crack resounded inside her head, making it impossible to hear or think or remember.

How far will you go? the voice taunted. *How long can you hold on?*

The air was heavy around her, and she could feel every hair floating up from her skin. The camera hanging round her neck vibrated loudly. Another flash of lightning, this time exploding shards of rock from the tip of the outcrop. Baldo's cage buzzed as the electricity wrapped itself around the metal. Teddy went rigid, his back arching. Smoke poured from his hands.

He fell backward into the cage, slamming against the bars. The chain creaked, and the winch slipped. The cage dropped an inch and swung perilously. Teddy lay there, moaning softly, fingers twitching.

This is where he's meant to be, the voice said.

Ava clamped her hands over her ears, but the voice still whispered inside her head. *He deserves it. Pull the lever, pull the lever.*

Ava let her hands drop from her ears. She reached toward the winch lever. She could make sure Teddy would never hurt anyone again.

FOURTEEN

Lightning struck again farther off, out to sea. It lit up the cage where Teddy lay and Ava's fingers inches from the lever. She snatched back her hand.

"Why are you trying to make me into a murderer?" she screamed.

Another spear of lightning exploded rocks from the outcrop. Ava closed her eyes, but the brightness scoured through her eyelids. The rumble of thunder followed. No, that wasn't right. This sound was a groan, not a rumble. The sound of a chain unraveling, creaking metal and grinding gears.

Ava opened her eyes with a gasp. Teddy's cage was gone, plummeting down toward the dark sea. She rushed to the edge of the cliff—nothing but darkness below. A single scream. A splash. Silence.

Time lurched forward with no memories to show for it. One second, Ava was standing with Clem and Olly, staring down into the pitch-black water. The next, she was waking on the freak show stage with algae under her nails and jumbled memories.

Bright sunlight marked the passage of time, night to morning. But how she'd come to be asleep on the stage, Ava didn't know. The only thing she was sure of was that Teddy was dead and one of the three other people who'd been on the rock had killed him: Clem, Olly, or her. Rather than being horrified by this knowledge, she felt oddly numb. Like it was all a dream.

She sat up stiffly and took in her surroundings. Most of the others were gathered on the stage too, either still asleep or slowly stirring. But Jolie wasn't there, and neither were Olly and Clem. Ava's stomach flipped at the memory of Jolie storming away into the night. The footprints on the beach. The crashing waves.

"The heck happened up on the rocks?" Esme said croakily, sitting up. "Did I just dream that Teddy was hit by lightning and fell into the sea? Nights on this island are wild. I hate not knowing what's real."

Ava pulled herself out of her thoughts. "It was real. Teddy's dead," she said. "He confessed to killing Scarlett. She was threatening to expose his secret: that he hit Olly's brother with his car."

Esme sat up straighter. "That was him? Explains Scarlett's taunts about drunk driving."

"You noticed that too."

"I see everything," Esme said in a mocking whisper before grinning widely.

Livia ambled over to join them. She sat heavily beside Esme, making the boards creak, and rested her head on Esme's shoulder. Esme stiffened, but Livia didn't appear to notice. "Is it just me who's lost half a night?" Livia said.

"No. Not just you." Ava flicked through the pictures on her camera—nothing after the performances on the stage. "I don't remember anything after Teddy died. I barely remember that part," she said.

"Did you kill him?" Esme said, not sounding all that bothered what the answer was.

Ava thought back to the moments before Teddy fell. The flashes of lightning that had disorientated her. And then there had been the whispers, compelling her to murder Teddy. But she hadn't. She had stopped.

"No," she finally said. "But Clem and Olly both had motive to do it."

"Olly I get, but Clem?" Esme said.

"Teddy was hinting at something. I think he knew what Clem's secret is."

"They've both been acting strange this morning," Livia said. "Creeping around like rats."

"You've seen them?"

"Bad dreams woke me up. It was around dawn, I think. Olly jumped up like he'd been bitten and ran off toward the beach. And I heard Clem about twenty minutes ago, arguing with Jolie."

Ava sat up straighter. "You've seen Jolie? Is she all right?"

"Um, yeah? Why wouldn't she be?"

"Last night, she disappeared into the sea, and we..." Ava trailed off. Livia was staring at her. "You don't remember, do you?"

"Neither do I," Esme said. "Are you sure it wasn't a dream?"

Ava thought about it. "I'm sure. You were both there. We all talked about the currents that carried Baldo around to the cove."

Livia cocked her head to one side. "I do remember Jolie storming off after Noah's fire breathing, but I'm sure she was with us later on."

Ava pressed her hands against her eyes. Her head was woolly, as if someone had held her upside down and shaken her until all her thoughts were scrambled. She felt numb, like Teddy's death didn't matter all that much. Another of the island's tricks? Two people were dead now. Scarlett, Teddy...

Stop, she told herself. She tried to focus on the things she could still fix. "Do you know where Jolie is now?"

"I heard her tell Clem she was going to the boathouse," Livia said, "to find a way off 'this squirrel fart of an island.' Her exact words."

Ava jumped up. She needed to find Jolie. She wouldn't be able to accept that Jolie was okay unless she saw her with her own eyes.

She stepped out of the freak show enclosure and past the ring of huts that surrounded the stage. The rest of the carnival stank even worse in the cold light of day. Stank like it had once been alive and now wasn't. With a hand over her mouth and nose, Ava hurried toward the beach.

She didn't get far. Clem appeared out of the shadows like he'd been waiting for her. He looked a mess. His hair had mostly escaped its elastic band and stuck up like he was the one who'd been struck by lightning, not Teddy.

Ava leapt back, splashing filthy water up her legs. "You made me jump."

"No rats here, only me," he said, trying—and failing—to force a crooked smile. "Where are you heading in such a rush?"

"To find Jolie. Apparently she didn't drown last night."

Clem's expression changed, eyes widening almost imperceptibly, muscles tightening.

Ava frowned. "Livia said you'd seen her this morning."

His jaw twitched. "Yeah. Briefly. But I don't know where she went."

That wasn't what Livia had said. Ava's stomach pitched. Something was wrong. "I should get going," she said.

He quickly reached out to touch her arm. "Ava, wait. Can we talk first?"

"Talk?" Panic rose up in her. "You want to talk?"

"Before you go looking for Jolie," Clem continued.

"Why?" she said. "What have you done to Jolie?"

"Nothing! Nothing at all. I keep trying to talk to you, and then something happens, and I need to get this off my chest, all right? It's *nothing* to do with Jolie."

That was a lot of *nothings*. Ava continued to stare at him until he looked away nervously and produced the ubiquitous harmonica from his sleeve.

"Yes?" she said, somewhat impatiently.

"I like you," he blurted out.

Now it was Ava's turn to widen her eyes, tighten her muscles. This was an awful conversation.

"And I thought you liked me too, although now I'm not so sure."

Ava managed a shrug but nothing else.

"It's driving me crazy," Clem continued, "watching you come on to Noah Park when you've barely said ten words to me in days."

"What? Are you jealous?"

"Are you trying to make me jealous?"

"No! I'm trying to *not die*." This was all too much. "I need to look for Jolie. I can't do this right now."

"Ava, please!" He caught her hand again, and this time when she tried to pull away, he tightened his grip. Like a boa constrictor, squeezing, squeezing. "What's going on with us? You and me."

"Nothing," she said, trying to pull free. Maybe it was her anxiety making her feel so squicky at being touched against her will. Clem was a nice guy. Everyone loved him.

"I don't get it, Ava. What did I do wrong?" he pleaded.

Other than expecting her to pine over a single kiss rather than worry about the two people who'd *died*? But she wasn't Jolie, so she didn't say this out loud. Instead, she mumbled, "I'm sorry, it's just that my best friend is missing."

"Best friend," he muttered, rolling his eyes. "Yeah, right."

He loosened his grip enough for Ava to snatch her hand back. She cradled it to her stomach, rubbing the red mark he'd left with his thumb. "What does that mean?" she asked.

"I don't think you should trust her, that's all. She makes things up. Lies about people."

"Jolie doesn't lie," Ava said. "It's her biggest strength and weakness all in one. She always tells it like it is. Her interpretation of reality, at least."

"Yeah, well, her *interpretation* isn't always right. That's all I'm saying." He folded his arms.

"Why don't you want me talking to Jolie?" she said, watching him closely. He was acting about as shifty as it was possible to be. Like Ava finding Jolie was the last thing in the entire world that he wanted to happen.

"I think you can do better than someone like her," he said, not meeting her eye. "It feels like she's the reason you've stopped talking to me."

"Jolie has nothing to do with you and me," she said slowly. He glared at her with wet eyes.

"I have to go." She moved to leave again, but he blocked her way. One hand up against the wall. His body angled so she'd have to push past him to escape. Not touching her, but close. Too close.

"I keep having these dreams about you," he said. "You and Noah. You and Olly. You and Teddy."

"Oh my god, that's just..." Ava shuddered.

"And then I see you flirting with everyone, even Esme."

"I'm not flirting with anyone! Look, I get that this island is messing with everyone's heads, and I've had my share of weird dreams, but—"

"Dreams about who? *Noah?*" There was an unpleasant whine to his voice.

"Not that sort of dream!"

"Then what?" he said, leaning closer. Close enough that she could feel his breath on her face. Too hot, too stale.

She swallowed heavily, the indignation draining from her.

Something else rose up to replace it. It was the same feeling that came after a panic attack: shame and anger in one, mainly at her own messed-up feelings. Clem was a nice guy; everyone knew that. So why was she so uncomfortable?

"Can you let me past, please? I feel a bit anxious when people get too close to me," she said quietly. Apologetically. She even managed a self-deprecating smile.

Clem didn't step back. "I want to talk, that's all. Is this a game to you? Because if you're playing hard to get, then stop it already."

"You're making me uncomfortable," she forced herself to say. "I need to go."

"Why are you being like this?"

He moved to take her hand again, closing her in with his body, his leg pressing against hers. No. Too much. Ava needed to get away right now. It was the same feeling as getting her head trapped in a hot, itchy jumper. Prickly wool, suffocating, suffocating, she couldn't breathe—

Clem cried out and dropped to his knees, his mouth a perfect O. Ava stared down at him. He was clutching his groin. She'd lashed out without even thinking.

Noah picked that moment to run around the corner. He skidded to a halt. "Um, am I interrupting something?" he said disbelievingly.

Clem looked up with red-ringed eyes. "Piss off, this has nothing to do with you."

"Everything okay?" Noah said to Ava.

"She's fine, so you can get lost," Clem said. "We don't need you."

"Well, clearly *she's* fine," Noah laughed. "You, though..."

Clem staggered to his feet. "Stay away from her, Park. She's not interested."

Noah snorted. He pointed a thumb over his shoulder. "Shall I go back for my dueling sword?"

Clem shuffled nervously, jiggling up and down like he wanted to take a swing at Noah but knew what a bad idea that would be. Everyone knew Noah's reputation and how quick he was to raise his fists.

Except Ava was only seeing aggression on Clem's side. Maybe Noah wasn't that person anymore. Or, more likely, Ava wasn't something he cared to fight over.

"I'm on to you, Park," Clem spat. "I know exactly what kind of man you are."

"Then maybe you can enlighten me, because I don't have a clue," Noah laughed.

Clem spat on the ground. With one last look at Ava—longing or fury, she wasn't sure—he stormed off.

Ava breathed out heavily. "That was weird."

Noah's smirk was gone. "Are you all right?"

Ava flushed. "Yeah, I'm fine. I think I overreacted, and now I feel like an idiot, but other than that..."

Noah frowned. "I heard you tell him he was making you feel uncomfortable. He had you up against the wall."

"He just wanted to talk, and I..." She stopped, unsure why she was making excuses for Clem. She was so used to blaming herself for all her anxious thoughts that she struggled to know which ones were justified these days. Sighing, she hopped up onto the counter of a ring toss game. "I don't want to sound overly dramatic, but I think I might be losing my mind."

"This island seems to be pushing our sanity to the limit."

Ava nodded, not meeting his eye. "Maybe this place is getting to him. Clem, I mean."

"It's getting to all of us." Noah leaned his head back against the wood of the booth and stared at the ceiling. "Last night I dreamed I was fighting again. And I snapped and kept on hitting until there was nothing but blood and bone left. Screwed up, huh?" He looked at her.

"It feels like a test," she admitted. "Like whoever's behind all of this knows our biggest weaknesses and is trying to turn us into the last people we want to be. They're pushing and pushing to see if we break."

"Break and kill each other?"

"Something like that." But not quite. There was something they were missing. She frowned as a memory surfaced. "Last night, Teddy said something weird. '*Which one of you will be the One? Who can hold on the longest?*' Maybe the last person standing gets to be the *One*."

He laughed. "Brilliant. We're all part of a deadly game show with a prize I suspect no one actually wants."

Ava laughed too, despite herself. Then she remembered that two people had already died. "So the person who holds on the longest wins. But holds on to what?"

"'*Can you keep a secret?*'" Noah said, frowning. "Scarlett couldn't. She confessed that first night, and then she was murdered."

Ava nodded slowly. "And then Teddy confessed right before he died. Teddy killed Scarlett, then someone killed Teddy."

Confess, and you lose the game.

Lose the game, and you die.

"Do you think Teddy's killer will be the next to confess?" Noah said. "Do you think it was Clem?"

Ava shook her head. "We need to find Olly," she said. "And I think I know where he is."

FIFTEEN

Olly was standing high on the rocks with Teddy's cage swinging behind him. It was empty except for a single piece of paper on the rust-eaten floor: the remains of Teddy's invite, water-sodden and plastered to the metal. Olly was staring down at the carnival, toward the circular tent right at its center. He was cradling one of his hands in the other, a dirty cut across his palm just beginning to clot.

"We should clean that, mate," Noah said, stepping closer. "It looks nasty."

"The wheel slipped while I was winding it up," he said, not looking up. "Teddy wasn't inside. Maybe he escaped and..." He trailed off. They all knew there was no chance he was still alive.

"Did you throw the lever last night?" Ava said quietly.

Olly didn't reply. He just stood there, staring. Like his thoughts were spinning so fast he didn't have the energy to move. Ava knew what that felt like, to be trapped in your own head and frozen on the outside.

"It'll be okay," Noah said.

"No, it won't!" he cried. "I let the voices in. They were telling me to kill Teddy, and I did."

"I've heard them too. Telling me to hit Jolie back when she pushed me. Telling me to lose my temper with Clem and break every bone in his face," Noah said. "The voices are assholes. It's not your fault."

"But I listened to them," Olly said. "And now they just won't stop."

"What are they saying?" Ava said.

"'*Confess and you'll be free*,'" he said, choking on the words.

He staggered and stepped closer to the precipice.

"Just come away from the edge, okay?" Ava said.

Olly frowned and glanced down, like he was only just realizing how close he was to falling from the cliff. He stared at the water, mouthing silent words.

"Olly," Noah said. Olly didn't appear to hear him. "Olly!"

Olly turned with a start. Stared at Noah and Ava like he'd forgotten they were there. His eyes were strangely hollow and his voice slurry. "I cheated. My trainer gave me some pills. Steroids. To help me build up my muscles. I knew they were illegal, but I didn't have enough time to train for the bodybuilding competition." He pulled a piece of paper from his pocket and handed it to Noah.

Olly's invitation was made up to look like a prescription for something called trenbolone acetate. On the back:

Eight o'clock. Portgrave Pier.

Can you keep a secret?

This was Olly's secret. His confession.

"Olly, stop!" Ava said. "Don't tell us any more."

Olly looked at her with unfocused eyes and continued. "The worst thing, though? My brother found out the week before he died. He was so mad at me. He called me a coward and a cheat. We never made up."

"It was a mistake," Noah said.

"That doesn't stop me from feeling guilty. Shit, bro, I'm so sorry." He clasped a hand over his mouth and sobbed loudly, staring at something neither Ava nor Noah could see.

Ava and Noah exchanged looks. This was what had happened to Scarlett and Teddy. Soon after their confessions, both had died—Scarlett murdered by Teddy within hours, and Teddy killed by Olly within minutes.

"Olly, man," Noah said. "Let's get back to the others."

"There can only be *One*," Olly whispered. "*One* to tether him to this world. Guilt has roots."

He tensed like he was going to launch himself off the cliff. Noah and Ava reacted at the same time. They both grabbed him, sending them all slamming down on the rocky ground. Noah pinned Olly's arms above his head. Ava sat on his legs.

"Let me go," Olly pleaded. "I killed Teddy. That's not something I can come back from."

"You weren't in your right mind," Noah said.

"I *wanted* to do it," Olly said. "I wanted him to die."

"But you never would have pulled that lever if you weren't here on this island."

"Maybe the island is making us into the people we really are. Back on the mainland, we were all pretending to be good people, only we're not. We all covered up Scarlett's murder. We all have our secrets."

"But we don't deserve to die," Noah said. "Do we?"

Olly lay still for just long enough that Ava and Noah relaxed their hold on him. Then he kicked out with both legs and flipped over onto his stomach. He scrambled on his hands and knees toward the edge of the cliff. Noah grabbed Olly around the ankles and yanked him onto his belly, but Olly continued to wriggle for the edge, too strong for Noah to hold.

"Your brother was right," Ava called out. "You are a coward."

Olly stopped struggling.

"What about all the other people on this island? Are you really going to leave us here to die?"

"I..."

"This will be all we remember about you," she continued. "Olly, the coward who killed Teddy and abandoned his friends."

"Ava," Noah said, a warning tone to his voice.

"Is that what you want?" she said more gently. "Is that who you really are?"

"Maybe I am," Olly said, voice thick with tears.

"Because that's not how I see you. Remember that sports day when you were going to win the eight hundred meters, but you hung back so that Alfie Morris didn't come last?"

He shrugged. "He has asthma," he said. "He shouldn't have been running."

"What about the time Livia got her head trapped in the school railings and you bent the bars to get her out?"

Noah tried to suppress an amused snort. "Seriously? You did that?"

"I was showing off," Olly said.

"What about when you used your year eleven Sportsman of the Year acceptance speech to come out to the whole school, all because you'd heard one of the younger students was being picked on for being gay?"

Olly rolled onto his back and sat up with a weary sigh.

"Montage me sounds like a loser. Can't you throw in some of the times I was awesome? Like all those goals I scored, or the time I wrestled a bear?"

"You never wrestled a bear," she laughed.

"Not yet." He smiled weakly. "But there's still time for me to do better. I'm going to do better."

"So you'll help us escape?" Ava said hopefully.

He nodded. "I reckon there's something in the boathouse that might just do it." He stumbled to his feet and began the climb down from the outcrop. He paused, and his eyes met Ava's. "But as soon as we're back home, all these lies stop. No more secrets."

Ava froze. She watched him making his way down the rocks. That had sounded a lot like he intended to back out of the agreement they'd all made after Scarlett's death. If Olly went to the police and told the truth about Scarlett's and Teddy's murders, what did that mean for the rest of them?

"No more secrets?" Noah whispered. "I'm not sure I'm ready for that."

Ava nodded. She'd been so intent on distracting Olly from what he'd done that she hadn't stopped to think what might happen when he got home, full of repentance. She'd saved him from himself, and now that choice could end up destroying her future.

"I guess we'll cross that bridge when we get there," she said. "Our secrets aren't worth anyone else dying."

She was almost sure she meant it.

They found Jolie in the boathouse. She was sitting on the lopsided deck of the ancient lifeboat, kicking a hole into the rotting hull. Her panda hood was pulled low over her eyes, so all Ava could see of her face was her tightly set mouth. She noticed Ava, Olly, and Noah's arrival, paused for a second, then went back to kicking the wood.

Ava felt a rush of relief that she was safe, followed quickly by irritation at how worried she'd been. "Where did you go last night?" she said, more snippily than she'd intended.

Jolie stopped. Looked up. Her hair stuck out of the hood in disheveled clumps. "What's it to you?"

"I was worried! We followed your footprints to the sea. I thought you'd gone in."

Jolie shrugged. "I went for a paddle. It was colder than a penguin's nutsack, so I was hardly going to swim in it."

"But your footprints just stopped."

"I guess the tide came in, Sherlock."

"Forget it, then," Ava said. "Sorry for caring."

Jolie returned to her kicking. Ava knew something was eating away at her, an abscess opened up by the pier that had been festering under the surface for much longer. She knew the right thing to do was to take a deep breath and be the bigger person. Make a joke. Offer an olive branch. But Ava still couldn't do it.

"Bitch," she muttered, almost too quietly for anyone to

hear, like she was testing the word out on her tongue to see how it tasted. Bitter.

Jolie stopped kicking. Silence. Ava's heart felt like it was full of dust. She walked away.

Her hands were shaky, so she lifted the camera and watched the world through the screen. *Focus on the balance of light, focus on the shadows*, she told herself. With the right lighting, you could change your perception of the whole world. She photographed an old anchor, flaking with vivid rust. It was a hundred different shades, from red to black to a bruised purple, like the bark of an ancient metal tree coated in lichen.

"Don't you ever want to photograph something happy?" Noah asked.

She glanced up at him. He was watching her with curiosity. "I don't want my pictures to make people happy, just to make them feel. Same way people read sad books or watch sad films to experience the whole spectrum of human emotion, and afterward they feel more aware of their own small share of good fortune."

"Deep," he said, smirking.

She felt her cheeks grow hot. "And the colors are beautiful too."

Jolie made a puking noise and jumped down from the lifeboat. "Get over yourself. You're one armpit away from photographing car crashes and saying the blood splatter is modern art."

Something inside Ava's chest twisted at that. "There's art in the ugliest things," she said, turning her camera on Jolie and taking a picture. "Jealousy and bitterness, for example."

Jolie, for once, didn't have a comeback. She just stared at Ava with an unreadable expression. Ava stared back. It was Jolie who looked away first.

"Guys," Noah said, "we need to stick together. This island is—"

"Don't," Ava interrupted. She hurried over to join Olly before Noah could continue with his lecture.

Olly was looking up at the ropes hanging on the walls. "You know, I've done a bit of climbing. Maybe we can set up a Tyrolean traverse across the broken part of the pier."

"A what-what?" Ava said.

"Like a rope bridge you dangle from," Olly said. "There are rescue lines, hooks, and harnesses in here. Everything we need."

Noah came to stand on Olly's other side. "One of us would have to set it up. And there's no way to swim or jump over the broken section."

"I can make a grappling hook from some of the lifeboat gear. I'll toss it over and climb across first to secure it."

Jolie laughed cruelly. "You'll go straight in the water."

Olly shrugged, then grabbed one of the old life jackets and held it aloft. "There, perfectly safe now."

Jolie bit her lip. "You really think it would work?" she asked, no longer rough and abrasive but desperately hopeful.

"Yeah," Olly said. "We'll make it work."

"About time one of you losers came up with a plan." Back to her usual self. She slapped Olly on the back. "The sooner we're out of here, the sooner I can pretend none of this ever happened." She walked outside without offering to help.

Olly watched her go, then went back to the ropes. "Let's get these ropes over to the pier, and then we can go home."

Everyone else was hanging around in the main square. As Clem's gaze landed on Jolie, Ava saw him still. He dropped his harmonica, then rushed to pick it up. Ava looked at Jolie. She was staring at him like her eyes might set him alight.

"What's going on?" Ava said. "Did you and Clem argue?"

"What did he say?" Jolie said.

"Nothing, really. He seemed keen I not talk to you. Did you say something to him about me?"

"Everything's not about you." She pushed past Ava and marched up to Clem. Shoved him hard, and kept shoving until he was under the pier's iron archway. She faced him with her hands on her hips. Ava could see her lips moving, a torrent of words spilling out, but couldn't hear what she was saying.

"What's that all about?" Noah said.

"I have no idea," Ava replied.

She walked closer, Olly and Noah following. The rest of the group gathered around as well.

"I don't remember," Clem was saying. "I don't know what happened."

"That's convenient!" Jolie retorted.

"Are they talking about Teddy?" Olly whispered, dropping the ropes in a pile.

"I don't think that's it," Ava said.

"Do *you* remember?" Clem said. And then, when Jolie was silent, "No, I didn't think so."

Jolie shook her head in exasperation. "I don't know what I remember! This place keeps putting all these memories into my head, and I don't know what's real."

"Well, that makes two of us, so you can quit acting like you're the injured party in all of this."

Jolie's face twisted cruelly. "Who do you think the police would believe, huh?"

Clem went still. "If you go to the police, then I—"

"You'll what? Yeah, I didn't think so."

He made a grab for her. She slapped his hand aside. "Don't you dare touch me!"

"Guys, stop," Olly said, stepping forward to intervene. "And Jolie's right. When we get back, we're going to the police."

"Oh, that is not what I said," Jolie snapped.

"Well, maybe someone *should* say it. Two people are dead, and we're going to pretend nothing happened?"

"We made a pact," Esme said, stepping forward to join the argument and bringing her eerie calm with her. The eye of the storm, or still waters hiding danger beneath the surface.

"*You* made a pact," Olly said, rounding on her. "Some of us got…swept along with things."

"There's no backing out now," Clem said. "Deal with your own shit, and don't drag us all down with you."

"Don't worry, Clem," Olly said quietly. "Pretty sure you're more than capable of dragging yourself down. You didn't learn anything from Black Box, did you?" He briefly glanced over at Jolie.

Clem's reaction was instantaneous. He shoved Olly in the chest. Olly stumbled. Skidded. Teetered at the edge of the broken pier and only just kept his balance. Ava gasped. She lost her grip on her camera, and it fell from her hands. She batted it back into the air and managed to catch it.

Jolie turned to face her, as if only just then realizing she had an audience. "Have you been taking pictures?" she snarled.

"No, I wasn't."

"Give me that." Jolie snatched the camera and switched to playback mode. Angrily bashed at the buttons to scroll through the images.

"Give it back," Ava said.

Jolie lifted it out of her reach, taking advantage of her height. Then she slowed. Stilled. Stared. "What is this?" she said quietly.

"What?"

"You were *watching*?" Jolie said. Her expression hardened. She began to press the delete button, the camera beeping each time. Six times. Then Jolie shoved the camera back at Ava. "You disgusting freak."

"I don't understand," Ava said. "Watching what?"

"Don't give me that crap," Jolie said. "I know you followed us last night. I just saw the photos."

"What photos?"

"Whoa, whoa, let's calm down," Clem interrupted. He looked twitchy, like a cornered rat.

"Shut up," Ava and Jolie yelled in unison.

"I have no idea what happened last night," Ava said, gritting her teeth. "I wasn't there."

"Liar!" Jolie took a step forward. "Stay away from me, you pervert." She lifted a fist as if about to throw a punch. She laughed at Ava's flinch, then strode away toward the funfair.

"Jolie?" Ava said weakly, but her friend was already gone, head held high, no backward look.

"Have I missed something?" Livia said, bleary-eyed in a cloud of smoke.

"If you have, then I have too," Ava said, looking at Clem for an explanation. He walked away too without another word.

"Olly?" Esme said. "You know what that was all about?"

Olly watched Clem go. "It's not my secret to tell." Then

he turned to the group with a grim smile. "Let's get out of this place before anyone else loses their shit."

He made his way over to the pile of ropes. On the way past, he rested a hand on Ava's shoulder. "It's the voices. Remember that. We'll get back home, and everything will go back to normal."

Ava nodded. If only she could believe him.

SIXTEEN

The grappling hook arced gracefully through the air and clattered against the rusty girders. Olly tugged on the rope, and with a clank of metal on metal, it pulled taut. He tightened the rope through a carabiner and clipped it in place. Yanked on it again for good measure. The grappling hook rattled but didn't budge. It wasn't supporting the weight of a person, though. Not yet.

Olly laughed almost disbelievingly, then high-fived himself. "Yay," he said quietly.

"Can we climb across now?" Jolie said, reaching for a harness. "Let's go already."

"No, no," Olly said. "I'm going first to make sure the other end is safe. Those girders got pretty twisted up when the pier collapsed. I'm going to retie the line securely, and I need to attach the safety rope."

"Safety?" Clem said, frowning. He looked between the two ropes.

"Better safe than sorry," Olly said. "The main line will run between the broken ends of the pier. But in case it fails, I've set up a safety attached to the bench, and—"

"You're not going for your Boy Scout rope bridge badge," Jolie interrupted.

"I'm trying to save you all," Olly said stiffly. "You should remember that."

He knotted the loose end of the safety rope to a hook on his belt. The other end was attached to a cast-iron bench. He would tie it to the opposite end of the divide once he'd crossed. He reached for the harness, but Clem stepped on one of the straps before he could pick it up.

"We have a pact," Clem said. "We all promised. *You* better remember *that*."

Olly pulled the harness free, his mouth set. He didn't look at his friend. "Yeah. I remember."

"We can't tell the police what happened here."

"We have to tell them something."

"Scarlett invited us to a party, but the pier collapsed, and Scarlett and Teddy disappeared in the storm. We think they were swept away by the waves, but no one saw anything. That's it. That's what we tell them."

Olly nodded and set about strapping himself into the harness.

"He's going to back out of the deal," Jolie whispered. "We can't trust him."

Olly ignored her. He glanced up at Clem. "I need someone to take up the slack on the safety in case the main rope slips."

Clem stared back at him. Didn't move.

"I've got it," Noah said, picking up the rope and bracing his foot against the bench's leg.

"Get on with it already!" Jolie cried. "The sun's going down."

Ava glanced up at the sky. Jolie was right, although Ava was sure it couldn't be much past noon.

Olly sat on the edge of the broken pier. He clipped the harness to the main rope, paused, then turned back to Clem. "Secrets will eat you up," he said. "Trust me on that."

"My secrets are my own, not yours," Clem said.

Olly smiled sadly, like he wanted to say something else to Clem. But he didn't. Instead, he took hold of the rope with both hands and grinned at the seven people watching his every move. "I guess I'll see you all on the other side," he said, swinging himself out over the void.

Ava closed her eyes. She could hear the rope creaking and cracking. She imagined each fiber snapping and the frayed ends pulling apart. She saw Olly falling toward the water, where the waves dashed flotsam against the rocks before dragging it under in an eruption of foam. She thought she heard a splash and squeezed her eyes tighter.

"He's all right," Esme said, touching Ava's arm. "Look."

Ava tentatively opened one eye, then the other. Olly had already pulled himself halfway across the gap. The rope shook and swayed, and the metal girder groaned. But it held. Moments later, he anticlimactically heaved himself over the jagged edge on the opposite side and scrambled away from danger.

"Hey!" he shouted, grinning boyishly. "I made it!"

"Shit," Clem muttered. Ava couldn't work out if it was relief or disappointment making him pace anxiously.

"Fix the rope so the rest of us can come over," Jolie said. "Unless you're planning to leave us to the ghosts."

Olly's smile faded. "Of course not. But I need to tie the safety rope."

He lay flat on his stomach to attach the other end of the bench rope to an iron girder. Like on the island side, many of the boards had fallen away, but the metal skeleton still stood, patches exposed like the corpse of some vast, wood-scaled monster. The floor wobbled precariously beneath Olly, but he deftly clipped the rope into place.

Livia nudged Esme in the ribs. "See, boys aren't wholly useless."

"You can keep them. Lone wolf here." Esme tugged on

her T-shirt and pointed at the design, looking very pleased with herself. She'd changed out of her ruined clothes and into an outfit she'd found in the club lost property—jeans and a T-shirt with three wolves howling at the moon on it.

"That's three wolves, not one," Livia said. "But no one's going to hit on you in that thing, so I suppose your point stands."

"Send the harness back over," Jolie ordered. "Come on!"

Olly started to unbuckle the straps, but then he paused. Watched them all across the divide. "I can't."

"Don't you dare. Don't you fucking dare!" Jolie screamed.

"I have to tell the police what I did to Teddy, and I know you won't let me. But I'll only say he got drunk and confessed to killing my brother. I won't involve any of the rest of you or your secrets."

"Let's talk about this when we're all across," Clem said through gritted teeth.

"I'm sorry," Olly said. "I'll come back. I promise. I'll call the police from the embankment, and they'll help all of you off the island."

"Olly, don't," Clem yelled across the divide, but Olly was already walking away into the fog. Clem grabbed a piece of rock and hurled it at his friend's back. It fell short. "You'll pay for this, I swear! I'll get you for this!"

Olly's shoulders tensed, but he kept going.

"No, no, no, this isn't happening," Jolie said. "I can't stay here any longer—he can't leave us here!"

Ava was so busy watching Olly vanish down the pier that she didn't spot Jolie running toward the edge—not until it was too late. Jolie launched herself off the island, toward the rope bridge. She caught hold almost halfway across and hung there with both hands grasping the main line. Below, the waves swelled and crashed, revealing glimpses of jagged black rocks encrusted with barnacles.

The rope jerked as the grappling hook slipped. "Jolie, no!" Ava screamed.

Her cry brought Olly sprinting back. "Shit. Shit!"

He dropped onto his stomach and reached for the hook, but it was too far away. The metal creaked as the prongs slowly bent under Jolie's weight.

"Grab hold of the safety rope," Noah yelled. "You have to reach up and grab it."

"I can't stay here with those voices," Jolie said, sobbing. "I have to get out of here."

Olly lowered himself headfirst over the edge, his fingertips brushing the grappling hook. So close, but it wasn't enough. The claws bent open, and it clattered free through the girders.

The rope Jolie was dangling from fell slack. There was a moment when she seemed to hang in mid-air, and then she dropped. Ava screamed, but somehow, Jolie caught hold of the safety rope with one hand. She hung there, swinging wildly, meters above the churning sea. Millimeter by millimeter, she shuffled her hands along the rope. She was still trying to cross over.

"Please stop," Ava pleaded. "You're going to fall."

"I have to get off, I can't stay here!" Jolie cried.

"I'm coming over to you," Olly said.

"It won't hold two people," Noah said.

"I've got this." Olly clipped onto the safety line and gently lowered himself off the edge. Slowly, he pulled himself toward Jolie.

"All right, you're going to need to swing your legs up around my waist."

"Get out of my way—I don't need your help," Jolie spat. "You lied to us!"

Jolie's fingers slipped again, but Olly was there to grab her by the panda costume. He pulled her toward him, and she looped her legs around his waist. Then she punched him in the face. Olly took the punch, then began to edge them both back toward the island.

"No, no," Jolie cried, flailing again. "I won't go back."

"It's closer," Olly said, grimacing with the effort. "We can't make it all the way over; the rope is too slack."

"A few more centimeters, and I'll be able to grab you," Noah said.

He was lying on the sagging part of the pier beyond the

iron archway, despite the loose boards. Ava knew she should help, but she felt paralyzed. *Let them die*, a voice in her head taunted. *You don't care about them.*

Then something cracked, and the voice stopped. Ava didn't recognize the noise at first. It wasn't the pier giving way. Instead, it sounded like a creaky door, then burning wood. The pops and crackles of flames.

The safety rope snapped close to the bench. Ava saw it flick past her, whipping like an attacking snake.

Jolie screamed.

"No!" Ava cried, closing her eyes. No splash. Just screaming.

"Hold on!" Noah was yelling. "Can you climb?"

Ava forced herself to look down through the iron arch. They hadn't fallen. Olly had managed to grab hold of the original line hanging loose from the girder. Blood trickled down the rope where the skin had been ripped from his palm. With his other hand, he'd grabbed a fistful of Jolie's panda costume. She kicked and struggled two meters above the crashing waves and jagged rocks.

The crossbeam creaked ominously. Ava felt the boards shudder.

"Oh no," Noah said. "No, no, no."

"Give me your hand!" Ava snapped out of her inaction. She flattened herself on the ground and reached desperately toward Jolie and Olly. Esme and Livia lay beside her, their hands all grabbing at the air, too far away, too late.

"You have to climb," Noah yelled.

"I can't unless I drop her," Olly gasped.

"Then drop her," Clem ordered, his voice cracking. He looked panicked, his earlier anger at Olly gone.

"No," Ava cried. "She'll be swept out to sea."

"It's going to collapse," Clem cried. "Drop her and climb."

The beam groaned again, and Ava felt the ground beneath her drop. Below, Olly stilled. He closed his eyes and shook his head, seeming to laugh to himself.

"All right, then," he said. "If that's how you want it."

SEVENTEEN

Ava screamed, only Olly didn't drop Jolie. Instead, with a cry of exertion, he lifted her up one-handed and thrust her toward the waiting arms above. It was just enough. Hands grabbed at her panda costume and pulled her over the collapsing edge.

Boards fell away. Metal creaked and twisted; wood snapped with an awful popping sound. Ava threw herself clear as the island's welcome arch tilted and fell, catapulting lumps of concrete and rock into the air. It sounded like thunder, only a hundred times louder.

Finally, everything fell still except for the ocean.

"Olly, no," Clem whispered. He scrambled to the edge.

"Stop," Noah said, holding him back. "You can't go down there—it's not stable."

"Olly's down there!" He struggled out of Noah's grip. "Olly. Olly!"

"The beam went, and there was a rock slide. No way he…"

Noah didn't finish. There was no need. Ava stood with the others and stared down at the tons of rock and metal, dashed by the waves. No one—not even Olly, with his superhuman strength and hero complex—could have made it out alive.

Jolie's voice cut through the sound of Imogen's hysterical sobs. "*Drop her?*" She pushed past Ava to square up to Clem. "You told him to *drop me*?"

Clem wiped his eyes on his sleeve. "It was you or him, and what does it matter now? Olly's dead, and you're alive."

Ava blinked at Jolie and Clem. It felt like she wasn't really there. She could see the pair of them arguing, and Livia pacing frantically, the trails of mascara streaked down Imogen's cheeks, and Noah standing numbly next to a pale-faced Esme. But none of it was real.

She wasn't real.

"You tried to kill me!" Jolie yelled.

She went to shove him, but he swatted her hands aside and pushed her back. "He's dead because of you!" he cried. "It's all your fault—"

He was cut off by Jolie's right hook. He staggered back with his hand to his face, mouth open with shock. Blood slowly colored his bottom lip a glossy red. Ava rubbed a thumb over her own lip, only it felt like a stranger's touch. When she looked down at her hands, they didn't belong to her.

"We all heard you threaten him, so don't try to pin this on me," Jolie cried. "You wanted him dead—"

Clem swung at Jolie and knocked her down with one punch. No warning. Ava's world shrank in on itself. Sounds dulled. Colors faded. All she could smell was the sickly sweet tang of Clem's bloody lip, only maybe the smell was a memory of something else. Someone else's blood.

"Fuck you," Clem's voice said far, far away.

No one moved. Jolie lay on the ground, unconscious, a look of mild shock on her face. Ava stared from outside her own body. Clem bared his teeth, and his gums and tongue were bloodred. His eyes were wild. She'd seen the same look on Scarlett, Teddy, and Olly's faces as the voices had pushed them toward their breaking points, right before they'd confessed.

Only this time, no confession came.

Clem wiped his bloody mouth on his sleeve. "I guess I'm stronger than you all thought," he snarled. "I'm going to be the *One*, and you? You're all going to die."

He whipped his head around to look over his shoulder, as though someone had called his name. Without another word, he ran off toward the carnival.

Ava's senses reset with a rush. The volume turned up. Colors intensified. She stumbled like the world had pitched beneath her.

"What happened?" Imogen sniffled.

Noah stepped forward so his boots were millimeters from Jolie's limp hand. "She happened," he said softly. "Olly might have been the only good one among us, and now he's dead."

Ava looked up at the iciness of his voice. While Jolie's anger ran hot, Noah's was cold. She could still remember that night she'd watched him fight through the glowing screen of her camera. The way he'd taken hit after hit without defending himself. And when his looming opponent, with his wiry beard and meaty hands, had looked at the spectators with a shrug, that was when Noah had swung with everything he had.

"Don't," Ava said quietly. What she meant was *Don't be that person.*

He blinked at her but didn't move away. Ava was reminded of what Esme had said about how they each had a point of no return. Noah's was tightly clenched in his fist, nails digging into his palm. After you passed that point, there was no going back. The island won. Whispers won.

"Is Jolie all right?" Livia's voice interrupted.

Ava glanced down at Jolie. She was breathing, and there was no obvious blood except for beneath the skin, where a bruise slowly reddened on her jaw. Alive, but still unconscious. Then Jolie moaned and blinked slowly. Ava's stomach sank, but she didn't know why. She'd been so sure Jolie was going to fall from the pier and die, and her panic had washed away any bad feelings toward her friend. At that moment, Ava would have given anything to have Jolie back, mean words, accusations, and all. But now she felt torn. Jolie was alive, and Olly was dead.

"What happened?" Jolie groaned, painfully sitting up.

"Which part would you like us to recap?" Noah said. "The part where Olly died because of you? Or Clem punching you in the face because you accused him of killing his best friend?"

"Clem punched me?" she said disbelievingly. "What the hell?"

Noah's fists tightened. Then he took a slow breath and pulled himself away from the edge. "If I give in, it's not just me who gets hurt," he muttered cryptically. Then he spun around and stalked off, swearing under his breath. Sat bent over on the park bench, fighting himself and barely winning.

"Did you hear what Noah said?" Ava said quietly. "Olly's dead."

"Yeah, I heard," Jolie spat, moving her jaw from side to side and wincing. "As much as I'd like to be able to block out your whiny voice."

"You don't care, do you? Olly died because of you, and you don't even—"

Jolie jumped up. "I don't know, all right? I don't know anymore. Maybe I *don't* care! Happy now? Maybe I just *don't care.*"

Esme stepped forward and gently pulled Ava back, away from Jolie. "Ignore her. We need to work out what we're going to do next."

Voices erupted all at once. Imogen, Livia, Jolie, and Esme, everyone talking over everyone else. Imogen's voice was terrified and desperate; Jolie's, angry and sarcastic. Livia sounded resigned. Esme was trying to make the others stop talking, but she only added to the noise.

Ava took a step back. Where was *her* panic? The pounding heart, the sweat pouring off her brow, the rising fear that rooted her to the spot as her breath caught in her throat. Ava was meant to be the person who freaked out when bad things happened, but her panic had just...run out. She could see the island in rational colors rather than shades of fear, and she was clearheaded.

"The island has its hooks in us," Livia was saying. "There's no way to escape."

"There has to be," Jolie cried. "I can't stay here! Not with those voices whispering in my ear all the time!"

"You're all acting like children," Esme argued. "Shouting doesn't—"

"We're all going to die," Imogen sobbed. "I don't want to die."

"Stop!" Ava said.

The firmness of her voice silenced the group, and even Noah looked up from his spot on the bench. Jolie looked like she was about to say something, but Ava held up a hand to her. Unbelievably, Jolie closed her mouth.

"No more running," Ava said, feeling oddly detached from her words, like they weren't her own. "I've had enough."

"We just give up?" Imogen whispered.

"That's not what I'm saying. But it's time we took back some control."

"And how are we going to do that, genius?" Jolie muttered.

"We find whoever—or whatever—is behind all this, and we stop them." Even Ava was surprised by her own decisiveness; she didn't usually do decisive. She was more of a wait-and-watch kind of person. Let other people do the big things. She'd take the pictures.

"But we don't know who's doing this," Imogen said.

"Noah and I worked some of it out," Ava said, gesturing to where Noah was sitting hunched over on the bench. "There's a pattern. If someone confesses their secret, they're the next to die. Scarlett first, then Teddy. Now Olly."

"'Keep your secrets. Never speak. Whispers, Whispers. One, One, One,'" Esme said, repeating the words they'd found above Baldo's skeletal remains. "I keep hearing that word. *One*. I think the last person to confess their secret gets to be the One, whatever that means."

"Whispers only needs *one*," Livia pronounced.

Everyone stared at her. Ava wasn't ready to believe in Whispers.

"So someone, or something, is trying to make us feel so bad about ourselves that we confess?" Jolie finally said. "But if we do confess, the voices will trick someone else into murdering us. And the person who holds out the longest *wins*, while everyone else dies?"

"I think so," Ava said.

"Nobody confess to anything," Jolie said. "Problem solved."

"I'm not sure it's that simple," Noah said, the first words he'd spoken since walking away from the group. "All these mind games are designed to push us over the edge. Make us do more and more terrible things until we snap."

"Then we watch each other. Stick together. Make sure no one does anything stupid," Jolie said with no hint of irony.

"It might be too late," Noah said. He held up the end of the safety rope, where it had broken close to the bench. "The rope's been cut. The ends are hardly frayed at all."

"So it wasn't my fault," Jolie said, but she didn't sound convinced by her own words.

"One of us weakened the rope enough for it to break," Noah said.

A pause. A beat. Everyone stared at everyone else, trying to work out who had killed Olly.

"You helped Olly make the bridge," Imogen said, glaring at Noah. "You're the most obvious suspect."

"Maybe." Noah smiled weakly. "But I knew this was just the safety rope in case the primary failed. Why wouldn't I have cut the main line instead?"

"Clem," Esme said. "He didn't want Olly to go to the police."

"*None* of us wanted Olly to go to the police," Ava said. "But Olly also knew Clem's secret. They argued about it, and Olly told him he'd had enough of secrets, remember?"

No one spoke. They all knew Esme and Ava were right.

"Clem just murdered his best friend, but he still didn't confess," Ava finally said. "Scarlett, Teddy, and Olly all died because they couldn't keep a secret. They failed the test. What if Clem passed?"

"He did basically just threaten to kill us all so he could be the *One*," Esme said.

"All right, well, I guess that settles it," Noah said. "We need to find Clem before he tries anything stupid. Stupider."

"We can't go *looking* for him!" Imogen cried.

"He'll find us either way," Livia mumbled.

"Will you listen to me?" Imogen said. "This island is going to wake up. We should go back to the club and barricade ourselves inside. Try to wait out the night."

Ava stared up at the darkening sky. Imogen was right. It wouldn't be long until the pier burst into life again, and the last two times that had happened, she'd lost herself somewhere in a dream of lights and music. Awful things happened at night. People died at night.

"I say we find the bastard," Jolie said. "No more sitting on our big asses waiting to die."

"And do what with him?" Noah said.

No one answered.

Esme cleared her throat. "Let's find him first and then decide," she said.

Ava pointed at a trail of blood. The spots led toward the flooded carnival. Clem's bleeding face would show them the way. She followed the trail to the stairs down into the water. The drips vanished, but a bloody handprint on the side of the fishing for ducks booth pointed the group in the right direction.

Ava led the way through the rancid water. Every now and again, she heard splashing footsteps that she was sure didn't belong to one of the group. The slap of tent fabric as someone ducked out of sight. A thought took hold of her: Clem, stalking her through the carnival, determined to make her his next victim. The girl who'd rejected him and kicked him in the balls. In her mind, his once-beautiful face was twisted and monstrous, drooling and pointy-toothed. Coming for her.

But Clem wasn't a monster.

"What *are* we going to do when we find him?" she whispered to Esme.

"Noah can knock him out, and we'll tie him up or something."

"Noah's not knocking anyone out," Noah said wearily.

"Then I will. Big stick to the head, and he's going down." Esme armed herself with a piece of driftwood, testing its weight in her hands. She'd have looked scarier if it weren't for the ridiculous three wolves T-shirt.

"This is messed up," Livia slurred. "Seriously messed up."

"Relax, it's all good," Esme said. "Aaah-wooo!"

Livia managed a brief smile, but it didn't last long. They all stumbled to a halt. The bloody smears left by Clem's hands had stopped. Towering over them was a mirror maze, the attraction at the center of the carnival from which all the strings of lights originated. There was a drip of blood on the top step. Clem had gone inside.

Ava remembered Scarlett's last words to the group: *He's in the mirrors.*

EIGHTEEN

The face from all the portraits held court above the doorway. Even rendered in fiberglass, Whispers was beautiful, like someone had made a composite of the hottest men on earth. The bone structure of that retired Hollywood superhero, the eyes of the Saudi guy on Instagram, the lips of that boy band member who'd tried to reinvent himself as an R & B musician. He would have looked almost blandly perfect if it weren't for the greasy black makeup across his eyes, giving him a sort of Mad Max vibe. Tainted, hedonistic, wicked.

The model appeared to be holding the mirror maze sign, all lit up with a hundred light bulbs. A giant speech bubble asked WHO ARE YOU? in pink neon that fizzed and crackled in the damp air. It was so tacky, it was terrifying.

"The real question is, who are *you*, Mr. Whispers?" Ava said.

"*What* are you?" Noah muttered before trying the doors.

They opened into a room completely covered in mirrors and lit by dozens of spotlights. Even the floor and ceiling were mirrored, making Ava feel like she was stepping into a constellation of stars. She floated through infinity as the universe stretched away in every direction. She tried to tell herself it was just a plywood hut dressed up with paint and lights. Nothing to be scared of.

The doors creaked closed.

Imogen jumped around in fright and clutched a hand to her chest. "I don't like it," she said. "Something has shut us in here."

"It was the wind." Noah yanked on the door to show her it still opened.

"I think we should go back to the club," Imogen said. "What if we get lost and never find our way out?"

"Place your right hand on the wall and only turn right," Ava said.

"Is that life advice?" Jolie muttered.

Ava ignored her. She ran her fingers along the wall to feel for doors. It was physically impossible to get lost in a maze if you kept turning the same direction every single time. Unless, of course, the maze was an infinite spiral straight down into hell. Which, at that particular moment, Ava wouldn't have bet against.

She found three ways into the maze via hidden entrances that were only visible if you looked from the correct angle and noticed the distortions in the starlight. "Three doorways," she said, trying to sound less scared than she was. "Do we go in together or split up?"

"By the gibbon's tits, classic horror film mistake!" Jolie said. "But go on, then, make the moronic decision, why don't you?"

"We don't have time to go round in a group," Esme said, like she hadn't heard Jolie. "Let's do pairs."

Livia immediately took Esme's hand. "Best friends forever."

"Or until the ghosts eat you," Jolie muttered. She glanced from Ava to Imogen to Noah and smiled evilly. She smacked Noah on the back so hard he jerked forward. "You're with me, Fight Boy."

Noah shot Ava a remorseful look, then shrugged. That left Ava paired with Imogen. Brilliant. If she was about to be murdered by her ex-crush, Imogen's was not the last face she wanted to see.

"If you find Clem, make him come back to the club," Esme said.

"But I'm a pacifist," Imogen said. "And Ava's...Ava."

Esme tossed her piece of wood to Ava. "Ava's tougher

than she looks," she said. "But when in doubt, just kick him in the balls and yell for the rest of us."

"All right, let's all meet outside in fifteen minutes," Noah said. "And try to not die, if it can be helped."

"Thanks for the pep talk." Jolie strolled through one of the doorways and was gone.

Ava and Imogen's door led into a room of endless archways lit by neon lights. The floor tiles were tessellated shapes that hid whether any given archway was a door or a mirror. The whole place was designed to disorientate the senses, and Ava lost track of left, right, up, and down within moments. She felt for the wall with her right hand. As long as she didn't lose touch, she couldn't get lost.

She stepped around a corner and was surrounded by a thousand versions of herself. She moved, and all those other Avas moved too. Only she wasn't alone. There was something hiding out of sight; she could sense it. A presence. She was being watched.

Imogen stumbled around the corner behind her. Her shiny dress was disheveled to the point that Ava couldn't make out its original color. Her hair was the frizzy texture of a Barbie's, left unbrushed in the toy box.

"What are you staring at?" Imogen said.

"I was waiting for you. Unless you want to get separated and go through alone?"

"I don't want to go through at all! What if it's not

Clem we find? Have you thought about that? What if it's Whispers?"

"We don't know that he's even real."

"Something's putting all these thoughts in our heads."

Or bringing their own darkest thoughts to the surface.

Ava smiled reassuringly at Imogen. "It's each other we need to worry about, not monsters in mirrors."

"You mean Clem?" Imogen stopped walking with a sigh. "We don't know he actually cut that rope."

"What about the things he said? '*You're all going to die, and I'll be the One*,' or whatever it was?"

"We've all said things we regret."

Ava folded her arms and stared at Imogen with a raised eyebrow. "You've threatened to kill someone, then run off into a flooded carnival like a madman?"

"Um, no." She bit her lip like she couldn't decide whether to say more or not. "But this place keeps making me think about something...to do with Rachel."

Ava's stomach clenched. She tripped on a loose piece of flooring. In the distant mirrors, she thought she caught sight of a flash of blue light. "What about Rachel?" she said.

Imogen paused to examine her eyebrows in the mirror. "What you have to understand is that I'd been friends with Rachel since primary school. We were practically sisters, and that relationship came with a lot of responsibility on my part."

"Responsibility?"

"Rachel had a problem with her weight for the whole time I knew her."

Ava grimaced at Imogen's choice of words. "Rachel had an eating disorder."

"In the last few years, she did. Before that, she was... big." She shook her head, like she was clearing the thought. "But she had other problems too, and it took a lot out of me, having to deal with them."

"Imogen, does this have something to do with your secret? Because if it does—"

"Oh, no!" Imogen said a bit too quickly. "Rachel's not my secret. That's silly. I don't have a secret. But that doesn't mean I don't think about her sometimes, and lately I've been thinking about something I said that I wish I could take back."

"What did you say?"

"Nothing bad. You know what some people are like, always taking things the wrong way. When you're trying to give them some constructive criticism and they get all sensitive. People like that are so annoying, right?"

"I guess it depends on whether you're saying something mean."

"I'm never mean! How unkind."

Ava shrugged and walked on through the next hidden doorway. Imogen hurried behind, her brow furrowed with annoyance.

"And actually, before you decided to turn everything around to get at me—which, incidentally, is exactly what Mother does—I was trying to explain that Clem might not be the bad guy you think he is."

"No one's saying he's a *bad guy*," Ava said, not fully meaning it. He definitely wasn't acting like a good guy. "But we do need to find him and make sure he doesn't do anything terrible. This island is making us into people we're not."

Or maybe it was revealing their true selves. Ava thought about the sign outside: WHO ARE YOU? Ava didn't want to know who she really was. She doubted she'd like what she saw.

"I don't believe Clem actually killed Olly," Imogen continued. "There are so many people here who are much worse than Clem."

"Like?"

"Uh, Jolie? Or Noah. Or Esme. Or maybe Livia killed him in a drug-fueled rage."

Ava tried to imagine Livia in any kind of rage, drug-fueled or otherwise. She laughed at the thought. "All I know is that Clem is acting strange, like Teddy did after Scarlett's death. So let's find him and make sure he's all right."

"Yeah, he probably needs a friend," Imogen sighed. Ava rolled her eyes and rounded the next corner. "He's always seemed so sweet," Imogen continued dreamily. "We have a lot in common, actually. We're both musicians, for starters."

"You and Clem?" Ava laughed, then realized she was being cruel. "I've never seen you two talk. Ever."

Imogen pulled a face. "I think maybe he was being respectful. Treading carefully after Rachel's death. Actually, I think we'd have talked more if it wasn't for her."

"Rachel?" Ava said, pausing.

"They went out on a date. Clem and Rachel." She waved a hand. "But they weren't right for each other."

Ava shouldn't have been surprised; Clem had dated half the girls in school. But Rachel hadn't seemed like his type. Quiet, self-conscious, always dressed in a baggy men's hoodie that hid most of her face and body.

"God, it was so boring listening to her," Imogen babbled. "'*Oh, how lovely is Clem's smile? Aren't his lyrics amazing?*' It was pathetic."

"We've all had our ill-advised crushes," Ava muttered.

"I don't know why he asked her out. Maybe he thought she'd leave him alone if they went out once. Maybe it was a dare."

"That wouldn't make him a very nice person, would it?" Ava said wearily. Bring on the beautiful mirror monsters. Anything to save her from Imogen's constant bitchiness.

"I guess he felt sorry for her, then," Imogen said. "I mean, Clem's the best-looking boy at school. Everyone likes him. Even Jolie, although I don't think he likes her back. She's so… abrasive."

"I guarantee you, Jolie does *not* like Clem," Ava laughed.

"That's not what it sounded like last night."

Ava stopped again. "Jolie and Clem?"

Imogen smiled smugly. "I overheard Jolie telling Clem that she couldn't sleep and did he want to play on some Wild West gunslinger game with her."

"And then what happened?"

"I don't know. They went off for a walk and didn't come back *all night*. And then today they've seemed funny with each other. And Jolie accused you of taking photos."

Clem and Jolie together? But that didn't make sense. Jolie hated Clem.

"Do you think they kissed?" Imogen said.

Ava ignored her and took the next right turn. Imogen scurried at her heels, repeating the question like Ava hadn't heard the first time. Turn after turn—the mirrors went on forever. A never-ending parade of Avas and Imogens and Imogen's question. *Do you think they kissed? Do you think they kissed?*

Around the next corner, the maze opened up into a small room with plywood walls and a creaking floor through which rotten tufts of grass protruded. The walls were bare except for seven framed mirrors. One caught Ava's attention. Its surface was slightly warped, and it distorted her body and face into someone who wasn't quite right, wasn't quite her.

She stepped closer to take a better look, only her reflection didn't move. The girl in the mirror held one finger to her lips in a *shhh*. Ava jumped back, knocking into Imogen.

"Watch where you're going," Imogen snarled.

"I thought I saw something in the mirror," Ava said.

"Was it your own reflection?" Imogen said, laughing at her joke. "Who are you, Ava?"

"What?" Ava spun around.

Imogen pointed to a signpost. WHO ARE YOU? it read, pointing at the mirrors with seven wooden arrows.

"Oh." Ava glanced back into her mirror.

The reflection wasn't her. It was sharper around the edges, without any of the prettiness Ava possessed in real life. There was something cruel and bitter about the twist of the reflection's lips. The mirror girl stared through Ava as if seeing straight inside her. Then she grinned slowly to reveal a mouthful of splintered teeth, brown with rot.

A blinding light like the flash of a camera made Ava recoil. When she blinked the brightness away, her terrible reflection was holding a photograph. She flapped it like a Polaroid and tucked it inside her coat. Ava could feel it slip into her own pocket. She pulled it out.

It was a photo of Rachel standing on the roof of the multi-story car park. So alive in that moment, trapped in time, while in the real world, her bones were crumbling to dust beneath the ground. Ava forced the thoughts back where they'd come from and pushed the photo back into her pocket before Imogen could see it. Imogen, though, was engrossed in her own reflection.

Ava looked more closely. Standing in front of Imogen was a girl who looked a little like her but also entirely different. The girl in the reflection was a twisted ideal of 1980s glamour. Jessica Rabbit, with an impossibly small waist and swollen red lips.

"You're right, I am special," Imogen whispered. "Just look at me."

Mirroring Imogen's movements, the reflection ran her hands up and down her body. She did a little shimmy, and Ava caught sight of something on the reflection's back. A patch of rotten flesh. Bones breaking through paper-thin skin. Ava gasped, making Imogen turn in shock. When Imogen saw the horror on her reflection's back, she screamed.

"Get it off, get it off!" she cried, scratching at her shoulder blades.

"It's not real." Ava tried to pull her away from the mirror.

"What did you do?" Imogen squealed, pushing her away. "You ruined it!"

"Wait," Ava called, but Imogen had already run out of the room, heading back the way they'd come. The girl in the reflection crumbled into a pile of ash on the floor.

A choice—go back after Imogen, or continue. It wasn't really a choice, though. Not if she wanted to escape the island alive. Giving up and going back meant not finding Clem, and it meant leaving behind whatever answers the mirror maze might be hiding.

"Who are you, Ava?" she asked herself. "A coward or a survivor?"

Sighing, she reached out to touch the fingers of her right hand to the wall. She continued on through the maze. Right turn after right turn, she walked and walked and got nowhere. The mirrors all looked the same. Maybe she was going in circles—but how could she be when she hadn't broken contact?

Or perhaps she had.

The lights flickered, and a feeling of panic rose inside her. She was going to be trapped in there forever, in the darkness, alone. She lost touch with the mirrors and let her legs carry her whatever way they found first. Left, right, right, left. The lights buzzed with a low hum that seemed to pulse through her veins. The walls closed in on her.

She slapped her hands against the mirrors, searching for a doorway she couldn't see. There was nothing. She spun in circles, but she was enclosed in a small box with no entrance, no exit. Her breath burned in her chest, and her vision shrank to a narrow tunnel surrounded by blackness.

"Deep breath," a voice said behind her.

She spun around. Whispers. Watching her from inside the mirror like it was a window. Real, terrible, beautiful. The same face from all those portraits, painted again and again over hundreds—if not thousands—of years. Never aging, never changing. The monster in the mirrors.

"It's nice to finally meet you, Ava," he said, staring at her with unblinking black eyes. "I've been watching you for so long."

NINETEEN

"Who are you, really?" Whispers said, stepping between the mirrors that surrounded Ava. His voice had a singsong tone to it and a coldness that froze Ava to the core.

She turned in circles, staying as far from the mirrors as she could. Whispers followed her every movement. Real. Centimeters away from her. Her heart thumped so hard she couldn't hear her own thoughts.

"This isn't happening, this isn't happening," she repeated. Any second now, she was going to wake up in her bed and realize everything about the pier was just a nightmare. She dug her fingernails into her palms. Whispers continued to grin at her.

His face was the one constant. Hollow black eyes, perfect

features. Everything else was made up of shifting planes of light. One moment he was dressed like a circus clown in baggy striped trousers and suspenders over a tight T-shirt. The next he was in a sailor's uniform, then an outfit from ancient Rome, then a caveman's furs.

Ava spun faster, looking for a way out. There was nothing but endless versions of herself and Whispers, walking from mirror to mirror and casting no reflections of his own. There was no door. No escape. Ava tried to yell for the others, but her throat was closing up. She couldn't breathe, she couldn't breathe.

"I'll still be here when you're done," Whispers said. "I'm not going anywhere."

It was as if his words flipped a switch inside Ava's head. Calmed her. There was nowhere to run and no way to fight. Panicking was only going to make things worse.

She stopped turning and forced herself to look at him. Terror was still flooding through her, but she was the one in control, not her panic. *Think*, she told herself. *Find a way out of here. Survive.*

If he wanted to kill her, there wasn't much she could do about it. But he had yet to make a move. Maybe he was trapped in the mirrors and couldn't touch her. Maybe he was playing with her like a cat taunting its prey. Maybe she could buy herself enough time to steady her thoughts and find a way out of the maze.

"What...what are you?" she asked, her voice shaking so much the words were barely audible.

He inclined his head at her. "Some have called me a stain on this world, left behind by all humanity's guilt and shame. But I was here first. Waiting for the right *One*."

"Baldo," she managed to say. "Baldo was your *One*."

"One of thousands, yes."

He licked his teeth with a long black tongue. Ava swallowed heavily.

"What is the *One*?"

"A vessel of sorts. A human host." Whispers stepped closer to the mirror with bared teeth. She tried to back away, but he vanished and reappeared in the mirror closest to her, making her heart trip over itself.

"My physical form is...*incompatible* with your world. But with a human host, I can walk among you. Enjoy the many pleasures your world offers."

"Like a parasite."

He made a hissing noise and angrily scuttled to and fro behind the mirror, like he was looking for a way out. "I am the voice in your head, the knife in your hand, and the secret in the shadows. I am the wind and the rain and the crashing waves. Now, then, forever. Call me a parasite again, human, and I'll show you exactly what I am capable of."

Ava shrunk away from the mirrors. "If you're so powerful, then why are you playing games with us? It is you, isn't it? Putting thoughts in our heads, making us kill each other."

He forced his face into something close to a smile.

"I cannot choose just anyone as a host. My *One* must be special. After all, it is their guilt that tethers me to the human world, and I must be sure it will never break."

"What happens if it does?"

He laughed, and his laugh was like a scream trapped low in his throat. He snapped his fingers, and the image in the mirrors changed.

Ava was standing in a huge cavern. The walls, the ceiling, the ground—everything was covered with so many tangled black roots that the original surfaces couldn't be seen. The roots glistened and pulsated like they had a heartbeat.

"The center of the island," Ava whispered.

"For so long, I slept. And then one day I felt it—human guilt. Like attracts like, I suppose, and your guilt is little different from the fabric of my own world. Guilt has roots that spread and tangle themselves around places, or people, or moments in time. It was these roots that crept through the cracks into my world and sought me out like an old friend. For thousands of years, I followed the sweet stench of guilt up and up until I found a way through into your human world."

He snapped his fingers again, and the cavern rushed away. Ava felt as if she were plummeting through blackness.

Muddy walls with their slimy roots rushed past, faster and faster.

"The first time I climbed up, the host I picked was too weak, and I ventured too far from this island. When they couldn't hold on to their guilt, they confessed it out loud. My link with them snapped, and I was pulled back where I came from. It took another thousand years for me to climb back up. That second time, I knew I had to find a person who would never let go of their guilt. A person who was strong and worthy of being my *One*."

The walls stopped rushing abruptly, and Ava was back in the cavern. She stumbled and fell to her knees. Whispers pressed close against the glass. "I tell you this," he growled, "so that you know I have lived a million of your human lifespans and you will never find a way to stop me."

Ava took a shaky breath and let it out slowly. "You blackmailed us into coming here to see which one of us can withstand your tricks and still not confess our secrets."

He stepped back from the mirror. He examined his long, pointy fingernails. "Blackmail implies I want only to take from you and give nothing in return."

"What could you possibly have that we'd want?"

"Everything," he said in a syrupy voice. "You'd like it if the whole world got to see your photos, wouldn't you, Ava? You could be famous for your art…with my help."

"A steep price," she whispered.

"It would be nothing to you. Such a little thing. All I ask is that you stay with me on this island so that I might step out of the mirrors."

"You can't leave the island."

"My strength wanes more the farther I go. I've never ventured past the town you call Portgrave, but why would I want to? Here I can build an entire world, and you can be its queen. A carnival, if that's what you want, but I'm not choosy, so long as people come here."

He snapped his fingers again, and the scene behind him changed to a bustling carnival full of laughing people. Children ran past holding balloons, then vanished like smoke. Whispers watched them hungrily, licking his lips.

"Do…do you eat people?" Ava said.

"Oh, please. My kind do not need to eat. What is that analogy you humans seem to understand? Guilt is the web, and I'm the spider. I simply like a large web made of lots and lots of guilt. But of course, my real form looks nothing like a spider. Would you like to see it?"

Ava shook her head. She glanced over her shoulder, hoping a doorway might have materialized somehow. All she found was Whispers, grinning at her, flitting between the mirrors as fast as a blink of the eye.

"Who do *you* think the *One* will be, Ava? There are seven still in the running. Will it be you, perhaps?"

"Never."

He stopped smiling and bared his teeth at her. Suddenly, they were sharp and pointy, crammed together in his too-small, human mouth. Almost immediately, he calmed himself and was once again a beautiful boy.

"Then you will die," he said, sounding almost bored. "It's how the test works. Only one can live. Otherwise my story might get out, and I survive by not drawing attention to myself."

"The last person to confess passes the test?" She didn't wait for him to answer. "And what happens if they refuse to be your *One*?"

"I should admit that the test is somewhat rigged. If I don't like one of you—if I don't think you will suit—then..." He snapped his fingers, and the mirrors were mirrors again. One version of Whispers and a thousand Avas, all of them terrified, cowering at his feet. "It's easy enough to sway the competition toward my favorites. Toward someone who will appreciate my attention. Clem, for example."

Ava pushed herself off the floor and stood up to face him. "What about Clem?"

"You just missed him, I'm afraid. He was here not long ago, promising me his devotion if I'll save his life. He was quick to sell out the rest of you, I have to say."

"You're lying."

"Am I?" He jerkily ran at the mirror like it was a window, too fast for anything flesh and bone. He slammed into the other side, making Ava jump away. She collided with the mirror behind her and quickly scrambled clear. "It's hard to know what is real and what's all in your head, isn't it?" he said.

Ava moved, hoping she might spot a doorway distorting the light. She wanted to touch the mirrors and feel her way, but not with Whispers waiting on the opposite side. He seemed to sense her thoughts and smiled slowly at her.

"If someone doesn't challenge Clem, he is going to win this little game of ours."

"Challenge him? You mean murder him?"

"A confession would suffice, but killing him would be simpler. I think you'll be surprised how far you'll be willing to go when push comes to shove. When it's you or them."

"I'm not a murderer." She squared her shoulders and fixed him with a hard stare. "And we're not playing your game anymore."

He shrugged and went back to examining his claws. He ran the points against each other, making the noise of knives being sharpened. "You better tell that to Clem. He is definitely still playing."

"Someone stopped you before, forty years ago," she said, thinking of Baldo, dead in his tunnel, a screwdriver in his heart. Had someone been trying to kill the host to destroy the monster?

The change in Whispers was immediate and terrible. His

limbs and fingers seemed to lengthen; his lips tightened and stretched as his jaw grew in size, row upon row of splintered fangs erupting from his gums.

"I can be your worst nightmare," he growled, leaning so close to the mirror that his teeth scraped against the glass with an awful noise. "I can destroy you from the inside out, and it won't matter if you survive. You'll spend the rest of your life thinking of me and dreaming of me, and when you forget everything else, my face will remain."

Ava stood rooted to the spot, not breathing, not moving.

Scrack, scrack, scrack went his teeth against the mirror, like a monster trying to bite its own reflection. Ava watched as a hairline crack spread slowly down toward her feet and across the mirrored floor. She took a single gasping breath. It burned all the way down, deep into her lungs, like the air was poison.

Then Whispers was a boy again, smiling like nothing had happened. "Decide who you are soon, because only one will survive."

And he was gone.

Ava waited, gasping her burning breaths and feeling her heart trip over itself with every beat. But nothing happened. The mirrors were empty. She was alone, standing in a slightly grubby box of a room surrounded by tarnished mirrors. It smelled of mold and stale air. Whatever magic Whispers had conjured had vanished with him.

"Move," she told herself.

She forced her fingers to touch the surface of the mirror. She trailed them along the wall until she found the doorway, and then she kept on turning right. Moments later, she shoved her way through a rotting fire door. She didn't think she'd been in the maze for longer than half an hour, yet night had fallen outside. The others were gone.

She ran through the attractions, quickening her pace as the shadows lengthened around her. She jumped at a rumble behind her, but it was just an approaching storm. The first raindrops fell, heavy and cold. Within seconds, she was soaked through, water running from her hair, down her face, into her mouth.

She tripped up the steps, into the main square. The arcade was all lit up. Lights flashed with promises of prizes and cash. The slot machines played electronic music interspersed with the sound of coins falling into trays and deafening applause. She heard champagne corks popping and a woman moaning in ecstasy. Ava threw herself at the doors and rattled the handles. It didn't budge.

Footsteps scuttled across the main square, then stopped. She spun around. Nothing but gleaming puddles and sheets of rain.

Something moved in the shadows. A dark shape. She hammered on the door, screamed at the others to let her in. Kicked the glass until a spiderweb of cracks spread from the center. Called each person's name—Jolie, Esme, Livia, Imogen, Noah.

"Let me in, let me in!"

Voices. The screech of something heavy being moved. The door opened, and she hurled herself inside, skidding on a puddle of rainwater and falling heavily to the floor. "You were meant to wait. You didn't wait for me!" she sobbed. "I saw him, and none of you waited."

Noah and Esme closed the doors and barricaded them with one of the machines. The sound of the storm was lost under the electronic beeps and music of the arcade games. The five others stood in a semicircle around Ava, frowning, exchanging looks. Jolie and Imogen had bottles of alcohol they'd brought down from the club like it was a party.

"Why didn't you wait?" Ava said.

"We forgot," Noah said slowly. "We thought everyone was out."

Jolie laughed abruptly. "Shit, we forgot about Ava."

"It's like you didn't even exist," Imogen said wonderingly.

Esme bent down in front of her. Her knees cracked. "What do you mean, you saw him?"

"Whispers."

"Whispers?" Livia said, her voice trembling. "What did he say?"

Ava tried to catch her breath long enough to speak, but her voice came out in short, sharp gasps. "Clem has volunteered to be his *One.*" She lifted her head. "I think Clem's going to try to kill us all."

TWENTY

A jackpot machine exploded with cackling laughter. CLOWN AROUND, it read in lights. Above the wheels, there was a clown's face with a round red nose. His tongue protruded through oversize teeth. The lights making an arch over his head flashed so that it looked like he was juggling seven numbered balls.

Seven balls, seven survivors.

The machine's sequence skipped and got stuck on repeat. A single note sounded again and again. *One, one, one, one, one*, the lights flashed. Ava jumped up and yanked the plug from the wall.

The power took a few seconds to drain from the machine. With the last sparks of electricity, YOU LOSE flashed up, and then the clown's laughter distorted and faded. Ava kicked the machine. A heavy thud sent pain blooming through her toes. She kicked it again and again—*thud, thud, thud*—and didn't stop.

"I think it's suffered enough." Esme pulled her back.

Ava shrugged Esme off. Too much nervous energy made her feel jittery and wired. She'd have run if she could, but every door was barricaded, and outside, the island was alive.

Alive, alive, alive. Coming for her. The noise of the arcade drummed into her from every direction.

"You're safe now," Esme said. "Chill."

"Safe? Of course we're not safe! There's an ancient *thing* pitting us against each other, and the only way to survive is to make sure nobody else does!"

"This isn't the Hunger Games," Esme said.

"He's going to keep whispering to us until we either confess or agree to murder each other!"

Esme's smile faded. "No one's making me do anything."

For some reason, this enraged Ava. "Who are you, really?" she cried. "How do you think you'll break?"

Esme said something, but Ava couldn't hear her. The noise of the arcade drowned out everything else. Laughter, clattering coins, gunshots and explosions from the video games. The sounds closed in on her, making it impossible to hear even her own thoughts.

Ava clapped her hands to her ears. "I just want all the noise to stop," she begged.

"*I can make it stop*," a voice taunted. "*Confess, and it will all go away.*"

"Confess?" she said, dropping her arms limply to her sides.

"*Confess, and you'll be free. Tell me what happened at the Oracle. Tell me what you did.*"

Rachel. The car park. Blue flashing lights. All she had to do was confess. It would be so easy. Speak the words out loud, and it would all be over. No more noise, no more whispers, no more mind games. It was like that feeling before you vomit, rising inside her, tipping over the edge. The point of no return. She had to let it go.

"I wanted my photos to mean something," she said, her voice slurred. "To capture something that mattered. Rachel, she…"

She took a shaky breath. Opened her mouth to continue.

But then she saw something and stopped. There was someone reflected in the windows of the arcade—darkness outside, bright lights within. Someone who wasn't there. A smiling boy with black smudged across his eyes.

Whispers. Waiting for her confession with his hollow eyes and hollow belly.

He wasn't going to get it. He wasn't going to get *her*. She snatched up a green plastic golf club from the ticket exchange. Swung it at Whispers's face. Smashed it against the unyielding window until all that was left was the bent handle. She hurled what remained of the club at the doors. It bounced off pathetically.

"Go to hell!" she screamed.

Whispers was already gone. The window was empty apart from her own reflection and the five others watching her with worried expressions—worried for themselves, not for her. She knew what they were thinking. That maybe they should have left her outside in the dark.

"Do you feel better now?" Jolie's reflection asked.

Ava turned around to face her. She couldn't catch her breath enough to speak.

"I don't want her in here with us," Imogen whispered, not very quietly. "She's crazy."

"*See, they're not your friends*," the voice came from behind her. "*They don't care about you.*"

Ava screamed wordlessly and spun back to the window, but Whispers was nowhere to be seen. Her own reflection stared back at her, wild-eyed like an animal, all tensed muscles and bared teeth. Whispers was still watching her, just out of sight. She could feel him there. Laughing at her.

She spotted a pile of yellowed flyers and posters on the counter. Snatching Jolie's bottle of vodka, she sloshed it at the windows and slapped paper after paper on the glass.

"Help me," she cried. "We need to get rid of the reflections."

"Ava, stop. It's not real." Noah stepped forward and tried to take the bottle from her hand. She clung on.

"He's in the mirrors. The windows, the glass. We need to cover it all, and then he won't be able to see us."

She tried to yank the bottle free of his grip, but he was stronger than her. Fine. Let him have it. She'd find something else. She let go abruptly. The bottle smacked him in the mouth.

The sounds of the arcade stopped ringing in Ava's ears. The blood on Noah's lip shocked her into stillness. Whispers's voice in her head shrank back and vanished, and she felt like Ava again.

Noah was still too. So still the hairs on Ava's arms prickled. He touched his bleeding lip.

"Noah, I'm sorry," she said. "That was an accident."

"The thing with anger is that it hurts everyone who gets too close. That's why I have to stay strong." He gently placed the vodka bottle down on the counter. Walked away into the maze of fruit machines and video games without another word.

"Damn it," Ava said.

She clasped a hand to her mouth. Nausea caught in her throat. She saw the windows, half plastered with her makeshift wallpaper. Vodka dripped down the glass like the rain outside. One of the flyers peeled away to reveal a sliver of night. No Whispers. Had he ever been there?

Ava pulled the loose flyer off the window. It was a copy of Clem's invite, damp now. The silhouette of a naked woman, her head thrown back in ecstasy. APPEARING LIVE TONIGHT: WHITE FLAG. Clem's stage name. Everywhere she went, everything she did, Whispers was one step ahead, taunting her.

"Why are we here?" she said. When none of the others answered, she faced them. "Why are we in the arcade and not the club? What made you come here?"

"We're following my plan now," Imogen said smugly. "Lock the doors and wait out the night."

"The club has only one exit leading outside. If something happened, we'd be trapped," Livia said. "So we came down here instead."

Ava glanced at her surroundings, nodding slowly. There were half a dozen entrances to the arcade and a staircase up to the club, all of them blocked off by fruit machines. But she couldn't help but think Whispers had been the one who'd put the idea in their heads. No decision they made was safe, not when he was pulling their strings from every mirror.

"We'll hear it if Clem smashes one of the windows to get in," Jolie said. "We'll be ready for the wank badger."

"As long as we hold it together, we'll be fine," Esme said.

"Hold it together and stick together," Livia added.

"Yeah." Ava brushed her hair back from her forehead.

They needed to stick together. Only she'd driven Noah

away. Pushed him closer to his own event horizon. "I'm going to say sorry to Noah."

She trailed through rows of arcade games as pixelated spaceships were shot into oblivion. The screens flashed through looped sequences, ending on their leader boards. She stopped to watch. Clem topped every board. Clem, then Noah, Imogen, Jolie, Livia, Esme, and finally Ava. Was that Whispers ranking his favorites or another of his mind games?

And why was Noah second after Clem? Did that mean he too was close to reaching his breaking point?

She spotted Noah watching a Pac-Man demo screen.

She walked over.

"Poor Pac-Man. It's like he's trapped in an infinite nightmare," Noah said without turning around. "He runs through maze after maze until his ghosts finally catch him."

"Or maybe he wins this time," Ava said.

"It's literally not possible." Noah leaned back against the machine. The blood had dried on his swollen lip. "These original gaming machines only have so much memory. The final level is half a maze, and then a jumble of numbers and letters. No escape."

Ava tried to think of something hopeful to say. She came up empty. "Sorry about your face," she said instead.

"Yeah, me too," he sighed. "Every day, I curse the gods. *Why did you give me this face, gods?*"

She laughed despite herself. "You're not wholly awful. Don't be too hard on yourself."

His mouth twitched at the corner. Half a smile. "You're not wholly awful either."

"I'm losing my shit at every opportunity," she muttered.

"We're *all* losing our shit," he said.

"Yeah, but you're all doing it with some class and mystery." She gestured over her shoulder. "We should get back to the others. Safety in numbers."

He nodded, but before they could move, lightning cracked outside. He frowned. "Is it me, or is the weather on this island particularly bad at night?"

"I think the storms are Whispers's doing. Maybe he's nocturnal."

"You really saw him? Because a few hours ago, you were convinced this was all in our heads."

"It *is* all in our heads. Because he put it there." Ava tapped her lips, thinking. "Clem going over to the dark side has made the storms worse."

His *One* was his link to the real world. The stronger the link, the easier it was for Whispers to mess with their reality. And as long as Clem was in line to become the *One*—as long as Clem kept his secret inside—the storms would make escaping the island much, much harder.

The closest fruit machine spun its wheels with a sudden whirring sound. The lights flashed to the noise of rapturous applause, and discontinued pound coins bounced out of the tray. They flew out so fast and forcefully that they ricocheted at Ava like bullets. She cried out and shielded her face with her arms. The coins ran out, but the mechanism continued to whir.

"What the hell?" Ava glared at the fruit machine. A reflection in the shiny surface flitted away. Whispers, watching her coldly, no longer laughing.

"Let's get back," Noah said. "At the very least, we can use the others as human shields."

They found the rest of the group close to where they'd left them, surrounded by a ring of unplugged machines that shielded them from the noise of the arcade. Drinking. Laughing. Forgetting. The night had cast its spell over them once again, and they'd started to lose all their fear. Livia, Esme, Jolie, and Imogen were sitting on the floor, four points of a compass. Livia was scratching letters into the linoleum with the screwdriver they'd found in Baldo.

Imogen glanced up as Ava and Noah approached. "Livia's making a Ouija board," she said, giggling shrilly. "Tell her it's dangerous and she needs to stop."

"It's only dangerous if she slips and cuts a finger off," Noah said, squeezing into the circle between Livia and Jolie.

"Got ten," Livia mumbled around her roll-up. She scratched a yes and a no, then paused to admire her work.

"This isn't a game," Ava said, glancing at the darkness

outside. "The ghosts are another one of Whispers's tricks; they're not going to help us."

"My granddad will," Livia said firmly.

"Whispers will use this as a way to manipulate you. We can't trust anything or anyone, not even our own thoughts. Definitely not a Ouija board."

"Says you," Imogen said. "But none of *us* have seen this Whispers. Why would he appear only to you and not us? Why are you so special?"

"It's easier to find a way into Ava's head," Jolie muttered, "through all those cracks."

"This is ridiculous," Ava said. "We're in danger, and you won't listen."

They barely seemed to hear her; they were too engrossed in the Ouija board. With an irritated hiss, Ava stomped over to sit against a fruit machine. She sulkily watched the group from a few meters away while they all laughed and joked like nothing mattered. If they didn't wake up soon, someone else was going to end up dying. They were going to keep on dying until Whispers had his *One*.

"Helloooo, spirits," Livia intoned in a low voice.

The five people sitting on the floor had all placed their fingers on the screwdriver in the center of their circle.

"We'd like to talk to my granddad, Alfred Quentin Holt," Livia continued.

Alfred? Ava's gaze jumped from Livia to Noah. His dark

eyes were on hers. Noah had called out to someone called Alfred while he lay on the rocks beneath the broken pier. Alfred was Noah's secret.

As he watched the realization cross Ava's face, Noah's expression hardened. He shook his head almost imperceptibly.

"Is there anyone there?" Livia said.

The screwdriver twitched, then dragged noisily across the floor. It stopped again. Ava stepped closer.

"Who did that?" Imogen whispered.

The screwdriver slid toward the letters *a*, *q*, then *h*. Ava leaned forward to look at the initials engraved in the screwdriver's handle, the weapon that had killed Baldo: AQH.

"It's him," Livia said. "Crap, what should we ask?"

"How do we escape?" Esme said.

The screwdriver moved. It shot around the board, turning on its handle to point at letters, then jerking over to the next. It moved so fast that Ava could barely keep up with the words it was spelling out. And then it stopped.

Livia took her fingers off the screwdriver. "Okay," she said slowly. "That was weird."

"What was the message?" Imogen whispered.

"Umm, I kind of didn't keep track," Livia said, wincing. "I forgot about that part."

"'Kill the One,'" Ava said. "Which is exactly what Whispers wants you to do. He wants us to kill each other until only one remains."

"I'm totally up for killing Clem," Jolie muttered.

"No one's listening to me!" Ava cried. She could feel the night's magic creeping into her head, trying to convince her that she was safe right up until it was too late. But she wasn't going to let it trick her again.

She stood up. Her anger was making her jittery, and she stormed down the aisle toward the far end of the arcade. The video games seemed to laugh at her as she passed, so she kicked one for good measure. Then she rested her forehead against the wall and tried to get her breathing back under control.

After a few minutes, she became aware of a cold breeze. All the doors were barricaded, so where was it coming from? She padded past a long row of games lined up against the back wall. Space-themed shoot-'em-ups, an Old West gunfight game, *Pong*. All were lit up but one. A faded OUT OF ORDER sign was taped to its screen, and the machine had been pulled away from the wall.

She approached slowly, the breeze catching her hair. A secret tunnel was cut into the wall behind the game, leading off into darkness. Someone could have gotten inside the arcade without anyone noticing.

A rush of fear hit her too late. Then a hand clamped over her mouth and yanked her backward.

"Don't even think about screaming; I have a gun," Clem hissed in her ear.

TWENTY-ONE

"I only want to talk to you," Clem pleaded.

The gun was plastic, snapped off an arcade shooter game. A trick, and she'd fallen for it. But the gun being fake didn't do anything to make Ava less scared. Clem kept glancing at the reflections in the shiny machines, shifting his weight from foot to foot. Erratic. Unpredictable. Dangerous.

He had dragged her into the over-eighteens area. She sat against the leg of a pool table and tried to make herself as small as possible. Behind Clem, steps led up into the main arcade. But all the noise meant no one would be able to hear Ava even if she screamed.

"Stop looking over there. Listen to me for once in your life. I just want to talk."

"What do you want to talk about?" she said, forcing herself to meet his eyes.

"I saw you with him just now. What were you doing?"

Her mouth was dry. "Noah? Talking, I guess—"

"But you won't talk to me?" He paced toward her but stopped a meter away. "Are you sleeping with him behind my back? Is that what you're doing?"

"What? No! And given what I've heard about you and Jolie, you don't get to accuse me of anything!"

Bad move. Clem slammed a fist against the pool table's tattered velvet. Ava flinched away from him.

"It meant nothing! And if you hadn't been ignoring me, I never would have gone with her. It was your fault."

So her hunch had been right. Jolie and Clem. It was true.

Behind him, one of the fruit machines briefly flared to life. *Magic Bomb*, it was called. There was a countdown next to the wheels: THREE, TWO, ONE, in big lit-up numbers. They flashed brightly, and then number three went out. Clem spun around, but the machine instantly went dark.

"Stop it," he yelled. "Just stop!"

"I didn't do any—"

He angrily interrupted her. "Is Jolie why you rejected me? Have you been talking to her about me?"

Ava numbly shook her head.

"Stop looking at me like that. Like you're scared of me. You have no reason to be scared of me! Why are you scared of me?"

Ava opened and shut her mouth. “It’s only that...we found the cut rope, Clem.”

Behind him, *Magic Bomb* lit up again. The number two flashed. It meant something, Ava was sure of it. It was counting down. What had number three represented?

“I had no choice,” Clem cried. “We can’t leave. You know that, don’t you? We have to stay here and play the game.”

The number two flashed faster and faster.

“So you killed your best friend?”

“Not on purpose!” Clem clasped his hand to his mouth. “Shit, Olly. I didn’t mean for you to get hurt. I just wanted to stop you from escaping. I had to do it, don’t you see? You left me no choice.”

The number two light went out, and Clem sagged back against the machine, holding back sobs. The number one light waited expectantly. The lights were Clem’s confessions, Ava realized. Two down, one to go. Clem had admitted to spending the night with Jolie and killing Olly. That left his secret.

She thought of the club flyer that had brought him to the pier with its seedy image of a woman and Clem’s stage name: WHITE FLAG.

Ava remembered Whispers’s warning. Clem would be his *One* unless he confessed. But Ava knew what his final confession would mean. Clem would no longer be useful, and he’d die. Tricking him into confessing would save Ava, but it would also doom Clem.

That wasn't who she was.

"We can get out of this," she said. "We can beat Whispers if we all work together instead of turning on each other."

He shook his head slowly, again and again. There were tears in his eyes. "That's not the game. We have no choice but to play it his way."

"His way means all but one of us will die! Is that what you want?"

"There's a way." He rushed to kneel in front of her, leaning in close. "He'll let us be together. He said so."

She forced herself to keep her expression in check. He'd killed his best friend. Ava didn't know what else he was capable of.

"Your photos and my music, together, with his help. We could make something beautiful on this island, Ava."

"I..."

His expression changed. "If you don't want to be with me, then I can't help you."

He glanced at the gun and angrily threw it aside. Snatched up an empty bottle that had rolled down the steps. A weapon. Ava held her breath. Was he really capable of cold-blooded murder?

"Stop looking at me like that!" he yelled, brandishing the bottle like a club.

"Like what?"

"Like you're scared of me. I'm a nice guy. I don't hurt girls."

The number one on the fruit machine seemed to pulse. If he confessed his last secret, he'd no longer be dangerous.

It was him or Ava.

Whispers's words: *I think you'll be surprised how far you'll be willing to go when push comes to shove. When it's you or them.* But there was a difference, she told herself, between her and Clem. She wasn't playing Whispers's game; she was trying to survive.

She had no choice. She had to make him confess.

She thought about his invite with the naked woman's silhouette and the way he'd said *I don't hurt girls.*

"I…I know that," she stammered. "That you're a nice guy, I mean. But I don't want you to think I'm like the others." She tried to remember the names of the girls he'd dated over the years. "Girls like…Scarlett. Or Jolie, or Rachel, or…"

A flicker of pain crossed his face when she mentioned Rachel's name. The number one flared and brightened. Clem's secret had something to do with Rachel. Something that had happened at Black Box.

"None of those girls were good enough for you," she said. "Rachel wasn't good enough for you."

"You were jealous?" he said.

"Of course I was."

He scratched his head, muttering to himself. Paced like he didn't know what to do. He still held the bottle, but it dangled at his side, briefly forgotten. "Girls and their stupid games," he mumbled. "Saying one thing, doing another."

"Did Rachel hurt you?" she asked tentatively.

He rounded on her, angry again. "What do you know about Rachel? Why are you asking me that?"

She held up both palms as if that might calm him down. "I just got the impression she wasn't a nice person."

"She was a mess. Always staring at me, trying to talk to me. So I thought, why not? One date won't hurt, and it might be a laugh. But she led me on."

Ava's heart skipped a beat. *She led me on.* Four words that no nice guy in the history of nice guys had ever said. She bit down her revulsion.

"I hate girls like that," she said.

"We both had a few drinks. But the next morning, she blamed me. Said I took advantage of her being drunk."

The number one light burned so bright Ava thought the bulb might explode.

"She led you on," Ava forced herself to say.

"She agreed to a date, she came out with me, she flirted with me. And she never said no, so I went with the moment. Even though…" He paused, frowning. Closed his eyes. "Even though I knew she didn't want to."

The number one on the fruit machine blinked out.

TWENTY-TWO

The glaring lights went dark. Clem let the bottle drop to the carpet, all his anger and aggression gone. He opened and shut his mouth. "What's going on?"

Ava felt no relief at his confession, only a thick nausea that clogged up her throat, making her mouth feel woolly. Standing in the distance, unlit by the brightness of the arcade games, Rachel's ghost watched her with an accusation in its hollow eyes. And then it flickered back into oblivion.

"No, no, no. I've failed the test, and now I'm marked," Clem cried. He ran for the stairs. A smack, and he fell backward and landed with the sound of breath forced from his lungs.

Noah and Jolie stood at the stop of the steps. Noah was

staring at his own fist like he didn't recognize it. Jolie was staring at Ava like she didn't recognize *her*. The look was close to disgust, but that was too mild a word for it.

Jolie called to the others. "We found her. And Clem."

Esme rushed over, followed by Imogen and Livia. "Are you all right?" Livia said. "We realized you'd disappeared and came to look for you."

Esme removed a piece of plastic twine from a cellophane bag of forty-year-old sweets. She tied Clem's hands together. When he stirred slightly, she pulled the string tighter. He groaned, slowly coming to.

"I don't think he's dangerous anymore," Ava said, so softly she doubted Esme heard. "He already confessed."

"I'll take him up to the club." Esme heaved him upright, and Clem let himself be led up the steps. He turned and looked at Ava. Gave a slow shake of his head. Then he was gone.

"What happened?" Livia took Ava's arm and pulled her upright, hugged her around the waist, then released her. "We were worried about you. Once we remembered you existed. Sorry, we forgot again."

"Did you know?" Ava said, looking past her to Imogen. "About Clem and Rachel?"

Imogen shrugged, avoiding her gaze. "They went on a date. I already told you."

"But he..." Ava couldn't bring herself to say the word. "That night at Black Box, he..."

Imogen rolled her eyes. "Oh, please. The thing about Clem *forcing himself on her*? Rachel lied all the time, and that was just another way for her to get attention after he dumped her. Obviously, I told her to stop saying such malicious things. Poor Clem."

"He admitted it was true. He confessed."

Imogen paled and swallowed heavily. "That's nonsense," she said. "Clem could have any girl he wanted."

She hurried after the others. Jolie watched her go with a slow shake of her head. With one final glower at Ava, she climbed the steps two at a time, leaving Ava alone with Noah and Livia.

"Wow, that's just..." Noah ran a hand through his hair. "Clem. Shit."

"Poor Rachel," Livia said. "Do you think that's part of the reason she jumped?"

Ava shrugged. She felt like throwing up, only there was nothing in her stomach. She was empty, apart from the butterflies that spread from her jaw down to her groin. If she could have torn off her own skin and scrubbed its insides clean, she would have.

She needed to be alone. But on the way out of the over-eighteens area, she saw Jolie angrily bashing a pop-up rat game with a padded mallet.

"Are you okay?" Ava asked.

Jolie slammed the mallet onto another rat's grinning snout. "Why wouldn't I be?"

"I don't know what happened between you and Clem, but—"

"But what?" She rounded on Ava with her hands on her hips. "You thought Rachel led him on? Did *I* lead him on?"

"I had to say that," Ava said. "I had to make him confess."

"Do you know what the stupid thing is?" Jolie went on, her voice cracking. "I don't even remember anything from that night. Nothing after we went to play the target range game. I know *something* happened, because you took those goddamn pictures, but I don't remember it!"

"It's Whispers," Ava said, "playing mind games with us. It probably never even happened."

Ava knew this was the wrong thing to say before the words left her mouth.

"We both know what kind of man Clem is, and you're still siding with him?" Jolie cried. "But I don't remember saying no—I don't remember saying anything! So I guess I have no right to be upset, do I?"

Ava could feel the panic rising inside her. She had to get away—from the shouting, from the feelings, from everything. She ran for the back of the arcade and stopped at the broken game. Rested her head on its dark screen. In the background, she could hear the others making their way upstairs. They were talking about what they were going to do with Clem and how they needed a plan. Then came silence. She lifted her head. Her reflection watched her from the screen. Reflections.

"We need to talk without you watching us," she said. She didn't expect Whispers to reply, and he didn't.

She climbed the staff stairs to the club. Most of the others had found booths to sleep in, but Clem and Esme were still awake. Clem was sitting in the middle of the room with his hands tied. Esme was watching him silently and coldly. Ava ignored them and made her way through to the dance floor. She yanked on the heavy curtains until they pulled away from the rails. The stink of old smoke caught in her throat. She heaved them through the bar.

"Making a nest?" Esme said.

"Getting rid of reflections," she said. "Tomorrow morning, we're going to talk without Whispers listening in."

Esme shrugged and went back to staring at Clem.

Ava dragged the curtains up the stairs to the roof. It took more effort than she'd expected, but after several trips, she managed to toss a curtain over each of the metal ventilation units and all of the duct work. Then she sat and stared out at the lights of the island, waiting for morning.

Ava hadn't thought she'd sleep, but she did, leaning against one of the covered ventilation units, the kind of dreamless, heavy sleep that left you disorientated and confused when you awoke. With aching limbs, she blinked into glaringly bright sunlight. Footsteps and voices announced the arrival of the others. Clem shuffled along between Esme and Noah, his hands still tied.

They all sat in a quiet circle. Ava took a deep breath of sea air. For the first time in days, they were alone with their own thoughts. Time ticked by slowly and steadily.

The group didn't speak. Jolie sat and scowled, more black bear now than panda. Noah systematically crushed lumps of rust in his fist. Esme dipped a finger into the orange powder he dropped and painted stripes on her cheeks. Imogen brushed at her dress, managing only to spread the dirt further. Livia lay on her back to watch the clouds pass by with her hands knitted behind her head. Clem stared at Ava and nothing else.

A drop of rain fell on Ava's cheek. She brushed it aside. "We don't have long," she said.

"Can't we stay here?" Imogen sighed. "I like it here."

"Puddles mean reflections," Ava said. "We need to make a plan while he can't get in our heads. He may be quiet during the day, but he's still here. Watching."

Esme dusted off her hands. "All right. The cavern in the rock. There'll be something there that can help us—there has to be."

"The cavern where you nearly died?" Noah said.

Esme fired finger guns at him and grinned. "Exactly."

"I'm more bothered by what we're going to do with that piece of crap," Jolie said, glaring at Clem. "When do we get to throw him off the roof?"

"Depends on whether you actually want to escape or

not." Clem's voice and demeanor seemed resigned and heavy, but not particularly scared.

"Ha! Like we need you," Jolie retorted.

"We can't let Whispers in," Livia said quietly. It was the first time she'd spoken since coming up to the roof. "My grandfather made that mistake." She took something out of her pocket, cradled it in her hands. "He tried to stop Whispers, and in the process, he gave him enough guilt to hold him in our world."

"All right, back up." Noah raised his hands. "Alfred?"

"I'm not sure he even knew that Whispers was in his head," Livia said. "He thought he'd left him behind."

"How do you know this?" Imogen said.

"I worked it out." Livia opened her hands to reveal the screwdriver. "He was the one who killed Baldo. He was trying to stop Whispers, but his guilt over becoming a murderer ended up keeping Whispers with him."

"No confessions," Esme said.

"It's not mine. It's his. And he's dead now."

"Um, I'm missing something," Jolie said. "Can someone explain what the weasels you're wittering on about?"

"A few of us found Baldo's skeleton," Esme said, watching Livia with narrowed eyes. "He'd been stabbed in the heart with that screwdriver."

"Like the Ouija board told us. '*Kill the One*,'" Noah said. "I remember Alfred crying when he was drunk. He'd repeat the same things over and over about how the pier was destroyed. How he'd ended it all. How he'd had no choice. I didn't understand what any of it meant until now."

Livia spun the screwdriver in the dirt, watching it clear a scuffed patch.

"He set the fire too?" It all fell into place for Ava.

"I think so. The fire started in the funfair. He was the one responsible for looking after the rides."

"He killed Baldo to destroy Whispers. And he tried to destroy the island so no one would come back here. So Whispers couldn't replace his human host."

Livia nodded slowly. "But killing someone—even when they deserve it—leaves a mark on you. And his guilt was enough to stop Whispers from falling back into his own world."

No one spoke. Ava tried to stop thinking about how she'd tricked Clem into confessing to save herself. At the time, it had felt like her only choice. But the guilt still raged in her belly like a storm. Guilt that Whispers could cling on to.

"We need to keep Whispers out of our heads. Otherwise, we'll either take him with us to the mainland like Alfred did or he'll trick someone into sabotaging the escape plan. Does everyone understand?" Ava said.

"Got it." Jolie threw her a contemptuous salute.

Esme cracked her knuckles. "I don't think you do. Olly died because Clem cut that rope and you tried to cross over when it wasn't safe. Because you both let the whispers get the better of you."

"Olly broke the pact," Clem said. "Don't forget that part."

The pact. Ava chewed her lip. Everyone was so concerned with escaping that they hadn't stopped to think about what would happen if they did manage to get home. They couldn't tell the police the truth. No one would believe them, and they'd all end up accused of murder.

"Clem has a point. We need to stick together," Ava said. She hesitated, not quite believing what she was about to say. "And we have to stick to the pact we made the other day."

Frowns and confused glances. Only Clem was smiling. "What do you mean?" Imogen asked.

Ava stared into her lap. She couldn't stand to see Clem's smug face. "I mean, we have to stick to the original plan. Scarlett, Teddy, and Olly all died in an accident when the pier collapsed."

Jolie jumped to her feet and pointed furiously at Clem. "And what about him?"

"Nothing," Ava said softly.

"He gets away with everything? Rachel, Olly...*everything*? He wanted to kill us all, remember?"

"At least I tried to survive," Clem said, still not looking away from Ava. "At least I was willing to admit to myself *who I really am*."

"A murdering rapist, that's what you are," Jolie said.

"And I'll still be those things back on the mainland. And you know what? There's nothing you can do about it."

"I can give in to Whispers," Jolie said defiantly. "If I do, then you're the next to die. It's sounding more and more appealing by the second."

His smile faded. "You're not going to do that," he said, although he didn't sound convinced.

Jolie rounded on the rest of the group. "And you're all on board with this?"

Ava stood up and stepped toward Jolie. "We can't turn on each other if we want to escape. We have to be able to trust each other."

"We can't trust Clem!" Something in Jolie's expression broke, shifting from anger to horrified disgust in a split second. Her voice went quiet—dangerously quiet. "How much of this is you trying to protect that secret of yours?"

"That has nothing to do with it," Ava said. Her throat went dry. Lies always tasted like sand.

"Who are you?" Jolie said, shaking her head. "You're turning into someone I don't even recognize."

"Well, that makes two of us, doesn't it?" Ava retorted.

"At least I'm not about to forgive a rapist so I can go back to my nice, fake little life."

"At least I have a life worth fighting for. What do you have, Jolie?"

"Sit down. Both of you," Esme ordered.

Ava and Jolie continued to stare at each other, neither backing down. In the end, it was Ava who looked away. She rejoined the circle and sat pulling threads out of one of the curtains from the club. Anything to avoid meeting Clem's jubilant gaze. Jolie was right. Ava didn't even recognize herself these days.

"We're done here," Jolie said. "Let's find a way to escape already."

"Wait. We go together," Esme said. "And we don't let anyone out of our sight. *Anyone.*"

Jolie saluted again and rolled her eyes. The other members of the group prepared to leave. Everyone except for Livia.

"This is my fault," Livia said quietly. "We're all here because of me."

"That's not true," Noah said.

"My grandfather brought Whispers to the mainland, but how did he find all of you?"

No one replied.

"I'll tell you! My guilt let him in, and then I spread him like an infection. I did something awful, and it was enough for him to hold on to."

"It's not your fault," Esme said.

"My granddad died more than a year ago, but it didn't banish Whispers back to his realm. He survived because he was inside *me.*" She pulled a twenty-pound note out of her pocket. There were familiar typed words on one side. "You wanted to see *my* invitation? This is it. I stole this money from my mum, and she blamed him. It was the last straw, and she kicked him out. Six months later, he died, and it was my fault."

"Don't," Esme said.

Livia had stopped listening. "He kept Whispers suppressed for forty years only for me to lead him to all of you," she said. "Taking this money killed my granddad, and now it's going to kill all of us too."

No one spoke.

"Was that a confession?" Imogen whispered.

The group exchanged looks. Another confession meant another person Whispers no longer wanted.

"He can't hear us," Esme said. "It's all right, he wasn't listening."

Livia started crying. "Esme, I—"

Esme ground her teeth. "Hold it together. It's time to go."

She marched toward the stairs without looking back. The rest of the group followed, Livia with tears streaming down her face, everyone else grim and determined. Clem walked close to Ava. He winked at her, grinning. "I never thought you had it in you."

"What?" she said.

He nodded at the camera round her neck. "Selfie? For posterity? No? Oh well."

Ava glanced down at the camera around her neck. Her reflection stared back at her, cold and silent. A shape flitted past, but maybe it was just the shifting light behind the clouds. She looked up with a slow shake of her head.

"I didn't mean to—" she started to say, but it tasted like sand.

"I'm not judging," Clem said. "But will you warn them? That's the question."

He walked on ahead with a chuckle, leaving Ava alone with her reflection. All the things she'd said, all the things they'd agreed on—how much had been real, and how much had been another one of Whispers's games?

And Livia…Whispers had heard Livia.

TWENTY-THREE

The sea churned, and crashing waves lifted a haze of freezing droplets into the air. Ava wondered if it was her guilt giving the water its strength. Because of her, Clem and Livia were both marked for death.

They'd be off the island within hours, she told herself. None of it would matter once they escaped. Keeping quiet was the right thing. Ava chewed on the side of her fingernail and ripped a strip of skin free. *Stop*, she told her spiraling thoughts, but they didn't listen.

"I bet you're trying to convince yourself you have no choice," Clem whispered, sidling up close. He rubbed his wrists where the twine had left behind red rings. They'd untied his hands. Clean slate and all that.

"It's the truth," Ava said.

He edged even closer. Too close. "Really? Because it's not too late to tell her—"

"No!" She dropped her voice to a whisper. "Stop it."

"You two all right?" Noah said, glancing over his shoulder.

"We're good." Clem grinned triumphantly.

"Keep your mouth shut," Ava hissed, walking on ahead.

"Now you're getting the hang of this game," Clem called after her.

"Do you remember where the entrance to the tunnel is?" Ava asked Esme, blocking out Clem's taunts.

Esme stood with her hands on her hips, chin high, and surveyed the beach. Ava wished she had Esme's presence and confidence. Even in her awful wolf T-shirt and lost property boot cut jeans, she was effortlessly cool. And how come she wasn't scared? She'd nearly died in that tunnel, and here she was, suggesting they go back inside.

"Somewhere among those rocks." Esme pointed toward the piles of stones that had fallen from the cliffs.

They climbed over the rocks until they found the entrance to the cave. It was narrower than Ava remembered, and she had to duck so that roots didn't tangle in her hair. Esme retrieved one of the old lanterns from its hook on the wall. She lit it with Livia's lighter and headed off down the tunnel without waiting for the rest of them.

"Slow down," Ava called after her.

"No time like the present," Esme replied.

"You're in a rush to fall in a hole and die?" Noah joked.

"I'm in a rush to get off this island," Esme retorted. "I've had enough."

"So you're running straight into danger," Ava muttered. "Makes perfect sense."

"I won't let a creepy cavern have any power over me," Esme said. "I'm too tough for that."

"You're also full of crap," Livia whispered.

"I heard that," Esme said, venturing deeper into the tunnel.

The stench hit Ava after a few steps. Rotting meat and dead leaves. She recoiled with a hand over her nose and mouth. Esme, in comparison, took a chest-stretching deep breath and kept walking. Ava had a sudden memory from school of Scarlett picking on Esme for living in a dilapidated home with no running water. In response to every mean comment, Esme had said, *Yes. And?* with a defiant stare. Scarlett had backed down.

Ava couldn't imagine the cavern doing the same. Facing off against hundreds of tons of rock, mud, and ancient magic didn't seem entirely sensible. But then again, Ava had met the creature living in the holes and knew to be scared.

"Did something die in here?" Jolie complained. "Many somethings?"

"Don't say that," Ava said.

They reached the hole that had nearly swallowed Esme. Livia paused. "Maybe he takes the bodies down there," she mused.

"The bodies?" Imogen said, her eyes widening in horror.

Livia fought a smile. "Hundreds, maybe thousands of people must have died on this island, but no one in town ever mentions it."

"Because there's some kind of weird spell on this place," Noah said. "You can sit on the beach and stare at it for hours. Then you look away, and the memories…" He mimed the thoughts floating out of his head and dissipating with a puff.

"Have any bodies washed up on the beach?" Livia said.

"Not that I know of."

"Exactly." Livia tapped the side of her nose.

Imogen edged closer to the hole. "You think there're dead people down there? Do you think *Scarlett's* down there?"

Livia smiled slowly. Without warning, she jumped at Imogen with a sudden growl, making Imogen shriek and leap back. She knocked into the wall. Roots tangled themselves in her hair. She scrabbled to free herself, then rounded furiously on Livia.

"That was very, very unkind!"

"But funny," Livia laughed.

"You pretend you're a good person, but you're not," Imogen said in a low voice. "I bet *he* would like to know what you said on the roof."

Livia's smile faltered. "I know all about you too, Imogen, so don't try to threaten me."

"And don't you threaten me, or...or..." Imogen bustled on ahead without finishing.

Ava waited until she was out of sight. She raised an eyebrow at Livia. "What's going on between you two?"

"She's annoying," Livia said, as if that explained everything. "Besides, I'm grouchy because I quit."

"Quit what?"

Livia grinned wickedly. "Everything."

"Are you a-holes coming or what?" Esme yelled back through the tunnel.

Reluctantly, they circled the hole and stepped out of the tunnel and into the cavern. Ava was once again taken aback by its vastness. The ceiling stretched overhead like a dark sky. The walls were supported by knotted roots. The entire history of the island was stacked up in jumbled piles all across the floor, some of them taller than Ava.

"It's just junk." Clem played a funeral march until Esme threw a pewter plate at him and knocked the harmonica out of his hands.

"There could be something useful here," Esme said.

"Personal catharsis, you mean?" he muttered, dusting off the harmonica. He sat cross-legged on the floor. "You're going to watch us all get crushed by ancient artifacts so you can prove you're not scared."

"Here's hoping," Esme said, looking him up and down.

Ava tossed aside musty carnival costumes and rubbed dust from her eyes. Deeper into the pile, there were broken chairs and a noticeboard listing steamship departure times. It was all just a heap of mementos from the many incarnations of the island that had existed over the millennia. Nothing useful.

She wandered through the cavern. She could hear the others' voices and the sounds of rummaging. A low whisper caught her attention. She rounded a pile of Roman armor and saw Imogen crouched next to a shield, her face inches from the shiny metal. She was saying something in a quiet voice punctuated by giggles.

"You're right. I *am* special," she whispered. "Rachel never understood that, and neither do they."

"Imogen, who are you talking to?" Ava said.

Imogen whipped her head around so violently Ava was surprised her neck didn't snap. Her expression was *wrong*, like a possessed china doll. Her eyes were too wide and her smile too stretched. Her hair was matted into thick black tendrils that hung over her face.

"He only needs *One*," she said.

"Snap out of it," Ava said. She shook Imogen's shoulder, but Imogen lunged for her. Teeth grazed skin, and Ava snatched her hand back.

Her cry summoned the rest of the group. "She tried to bite me!"

"Uh, no I didn't," Imogen said. Her expression was calm. "You're being even weirder than usual."

"You did!" Ava held up her hand to show everyone the red marks close to her thumb.

"You probably did that yourself," Imogen said. "You're trying to distract everyone from the fact that you're losing it."

"I'm not losing it." Although Ava wasn't sure this was strictly true.

"I believe Ava," Livia said, eyeing Imogen with suspicion. "You were talking in your sleep last night, and it was as creepy as fuck."

"What? No, I wasn't." She straightened up and twisted her hair over one shoulder. "This place sucks. I'm out of here."

"We're meant to be sticking together," Noah said.

"I'm safe. I've not confessed to anything," Imogen said. She glanced back over her shoulder at the shield. "Because I've not done anything, by the way."

"If she's going, I'm going." Clem got to his feet and dusted off his trousers.

"So you can plot behind our backs? I don't think so," Jolie said.

"Why would I do that? Like you all keep reminding me, I'm the one who's in the most danger. I confessed, so I'm a marked man." He gave Noah a measured look. "And my money's on you snapping next, Park."

The group glanced over at Noah. Surprisingly, he didn't

argue. His expression was cold and closed off, like it had been when Ava had first bumped into him on the carousel. He looked like a stranger again.

"See you losers later," Clem said. He followed Imogen out of the cavern.

"Let them go," Esme sighed. "If Imogen's losing it, we're better off without her."

"And if she kills Clem?" Noah said.

Esme replied with a shrug and went back to digging through all the junk.

Ava turned to Livia. "What was Imogen saying in her sleep?"

Livia put on a high-pitched voice. "'I'm special, Mother. I'm going to be famous one day. I need to just do it.'"

Ava laughed. Once upon a time, she and Livia had laughed together a lot. Her brief flash of nostalgia was quickly washed away by a wave of guilt. Livia had once been Ava's friend, and yet Ava was letting her walk around oblivious to the fact she was marked for death. She took a deep breath.

"Liv, about this morning. There's something I have to tell you—"

They were interrupted by a shout from Jolie. "Looks like I've saved all your asses. Get over here."

They hurried over. Jolie had found what looked like an ancient canoe made of wood and woven reeds. How it was still holding together, Ava didn't know. Something so old should surely have been dust. But other than a few holes, the boat was in one piece. It wouldn't take much to fix it up. Without speaking, Noah heaved the canoe onto his shoulder and carried it out of the cavern.

Ava was glad to get back outside, away from the stench and the dusty air and those darker-than-dark holes. She helped Noah lower the canoe onto the launch ramp outside the boathouse and followed him inside for supplies. He set about collecting tools and nails and a jar of some kind of thick, tarry sealant. He studiously avoided Ava's eye.

"Are you all right?" she asked. "You've been quiet since what happened in the arcade."

"Yeah. No. I don't know." He leaned against the doors with a sigh. "It felt good, you know? Hitting that bastard."

"I don't think that makes you a bad person."

He laughed bitterly. "Pretty sure we're all bad people here, Ava."

"Stop," she said. "Don't let him in."

"Don't worry. I'm not going to let my anger hurt anyone else. I made that mistake before." He raised a can of nails at her like he was toasting her health. Before Ava could ask what he meant, he stepped outside. Ava followed and walked straight into him when he stopped abruptly.

In the brief time they'd been in the boathouse, the sky had turned an ominous gray, and the sea had become tar. The day was slipping away from them, and their chance of escape with it. Esme, Jolie, and Livia could have warned them. Instead, Esme and Livia were arguing in the boxing ring while Jolie watched with amusement.

"I don't get it," Livia cried. "We were so happy."

"Clearly not," Esme said.

"You left me because you were scared, not because you didn't want to be with me. I know you, Esme—"

"No, you don't! I don't need you, Livia. I don't want you. Everything I need is right here." She drummed on her own chest with a fist.

"We were good together, and you threw it all away. Love isn't a weakness, Esme."

"Love? What we had wasn't love. It was me holding your hand while you looked for yet another way to self-destruct."

"One day, you're going to need someone, and I won't be there." Livia ducked under the ropes and ran up the stairs toward the main square.

"Livia, wait," Ava called after her. She angrily rounded on the others. "Come on, we can't let her go off by herself."

Esme said nothing. She climbed out of the ring and joined Noah by the boat. Jolie held up both hands. "I'm not taking sides!"

"She's in danger by herself. Damn it."

Realizing that no one was listening, Ava took off after Livia. But when she reached the top of the steps, there was no sign of her. In the short time it had taken to run up the stairs, the sun had sunk lower in the sky and the shadows had lengthened into unrecognizable shapes.

Ava ran to the signpost in the center of the square. "Livia?" she called, but there was no answer. She glanced at the club. The front door was slightly ajar, and the lights were on inside. It made sense that Livia had gone to wait in the bar. But before she could reach the doors, a flash of light caught Ava's attention. The photo booth.

It lit up a second time, then a third and a fourth. Ava approached slowly. There was someone behind the filthy curtain. She could hear the *thud*, *thud*, *thud* of feet swinging against the seat. Shapes moved inside.

"Livia?"

No reply, only a strange wet noise like someone was eating a pear. A column of photos dropped into the tray. The same photos that Ava still had in her pocket. Scarlett and her kissing. The shuffling and slurping sounds continued. Ava backed away, but a gust of wind caught the curtain. It billowed open, revealing the whole booth. Scarlett and Teddy were inside, locked in an embrace, hands groping, tongues searching. Scarlett's hair was wet with blood. Teddy's skin was charred by lightning. He looked up with a sudden snap of his neck.

"Who will be the *One*?" he said.

"Will it be you, Ava?" Scarlett said.

Ava stumbled backward and fell over her own feet,

landing heavily on the ground. The curtain flapped closed on the ghosts. When it billowed open a second time, Scarlett and Teddy were gone. She tried to scramble upright, but her feet kept skidding out from under her.

Bare feet paced toward her. She stopped moving, every inch of her turning to stone. The feet were completely coated in dust, as were the legs above, and their owner's bare chest, and his head. Olly, only not Olly. Ava could remember Olly's smile. This was all wrong.

"Four down, six to go," he said.

"Olly," Ava whispered, shuffling away from him.

He followed, smiling that awful smile. "You've forgotten me already," he said.

"That's not true. No one's forgotten you."

"All the dead are forgotten. Only *One* will be remembered. Six survivors, but there can only be *One*."

Ava frowned. There were seven survivors, not six. Ava, Jolie, Livia, Esme, Noah, Clem, and Imogen.

Olly's smile spread wider. "You'll be too late," he laughed.

TWENTY-FOUR

Ava ran. Time juddered past. The sun fell into the ocean, and the fog rolled in. Lights flickered on, and in the distance, music slowly rose in pitch and tempo. Night chased at Ava's heels. She threw open the doors of the club and raced upstairs into the mirrored bar. She skidded to a halt.

Livia.

She was lying flat on her back like she was fast asleep, except her skin was ashen and her lips tinged blue. Still. Not breathing. A half-empty vodka bottle was beside her. Noah, Esme, and Jolie knelt around her. The disheveled look of Livia's clothes made Ava think they'd been trying to resuscitate her, but not anymore. Esme was crying, Jolie shook her head again and again, and Noah's brow was dotted with sweat.

"She's gone," Noah finally said.

Ava couldn't move. Livia—the most alive person Ava knew. It wasn't possible for her to die. Ava felt like all her insides were trying to escape in opposite directions, but her skin wouldn't let them go. It was all her fault that Livia was dead.

Esme traced her little finger against Livia's, like she couldn't bring herself to fully hold her hand. She looked up at Ava with panicked eyes. "Where were you?"

"I don't know," Ava whispered. "I was just a few seconds behind her, I'm sure of it. But there were…I saw something in the photo booth."

"It's been more than an hour," Noah said quietly. "We got started on the boat repairs."

"An hour? No. That can't be true." She clasped a hand over her mouth. "What happened to her?"

"Someone poisoned her, that's what," Esme said, staring at Ava with suspicion.

"Why would anyone want to kill Liv?" Jolie said. "She never did anything."

"Well, she did call me creepy, sooo…" Imogen said.

Ava forced her eyes away from Livia. Imogen was sitting at the bar, examining her penciled-in eyebrows in Scarlett's compact mirror, stroking them from start to tip.

"What?" Ava said softly.

"It's true," Imogen replied without looking away from her reflection. "Just saying."

Anger like nothing Ava had ever experienced flared in her gut. She crossed the room in four strides and stood far too close to Imogen. "Just. Saying?" she said slowly.

"She did," Imogen said weakly. "And what about what she did to her granddad?"

"And that means she deserved to die?" Ava said, digging her nails into the bar until one gave and bent back at the tip.

"That's not what I said," Imogen sighed. "But she chose to take drugs. She knew the risks, so it was her fault if she overdosed—hey!"

Esme appeared at Ava's side and snatched the compact from Imogen. She hurled it against the mirror behind the bar. It smashed a crumbling white patch in the center, like a snowflake.

"My Tiffany!" Imogen said. "What did you do that for?"

"Livia is dead," Esme said very, very softly. Every muscle in her body was tensed. Her eyes were unblinking and steady. Imogen nervously glanced at the others. When no support was forthcoming, she swallowed heavily and looked back at Esme.

"We all have our ways of coping," she said stiffly.

"Coping," Esme repeated.

Imogen looked at Noah. "What's wrong with her? Why's she staring at me like that?"

Noah folded his arms. "We all have our ways of coping," he said.

Imogen slipped off her seat. "Well, I'm not staying here if you're all going to be aggressive. Thanks to Mother, I struggle horribly with any sort of confrontation. She has always—"

"Shut up about your mother," Ava screamed, lashing out with a suddenness that took even her by surprise. Spittle dotted Imogen's face.

Jolie circled Livia's body to join them at the bar. "You want to talk about aggressive? Because I *love* aggressive."

"She really does," Noah said.

"That's because I'm the angry hothead," Jolie said. "A volcano ready to erupt. And Noah here, he's all repressed rage and stone-cold violence."

"Are you threatening me?" Imogen said.

Jolie's smile widened. "And Ava? She's all about self-hatred, like a storm cloud. You never know when that lightning is going to strike."

"What are you talking about?" Imogen whispered.

"Esme, though? Esme is ice, and I have no idea what happens when she gets really, really angry."

"You can't talk to me like this," Imogen said, moving to leave.

Noah instantly stepped forward and picked her up under the arms. Placed her back on the stool and stepped back.

"Please. Stay," he growled.

"Let's talk about what you said," Jolie continued. "You were telling us all how Livia deserved to die?"

"Stop putting words in my mouth," Imogen sobbed. "All I said was that she was a drug addict, and sometimes drug addicts overdose."

"She told me this morning that she was quitting," said Esme.

"Then maybe it was Clem. I don't know."

"Clem had no reason to hurt Livia," Ava said.

"Livia was a skanky drug addict!" Imogen cried. "She probably had a heart attack."

"Imogen?" Noah said like he was talking to a child. "What did you do?"

"Did you spike her drink?" Jolie said. "Crush up some of her pills and slip them into the bottle?"

"I've done nothing wrong," Imogen pleaded, squirming in her seat.

Esme walked to Livia's body and retrieved the vodka bottle next to her. She slammed it down on the bar.

"Drink it, and we'll believe you."

"I don't actually like vod—"

"Drink it!" Esme said. She leaned forward and smiled at Imogen. "Pretty please?"

Imogen picked up the bottle with a shaky hand and slowly raised it to her lips. At the last moment, she threw it at Esme and ran.

She went for the main exit, but Noah was too fast. He leapt for the doors and blocked her way. Imogen skidded to a halt and made a dash for the emergency stairs instead. Ava was a few steps behind, taking them two at a time.

Imogen burst out onto the roof of the club. She tried to slam the door behind her, but Ava shoved it back open and stumbled out into the wind, the others following. Fog hung low in the dark sky. It had been dusk when she'd entered the club. Now it was nighttime, and the pier was awake.

They found Imogen standing at the edge of the roof, staring down. The wind caught in her long hair, turning it into Medusa's snakes.

She spun around to face her four accusers. "You don't understand!"

Behind her, the carnival hummed with lights and life. The carousel played its eerie tune, a slow parade of fire-melted monsters. Spotlights swept through thick fog. Ava shielded her eyes as the brightness flared, recasting the island as a sepia photograph. Whispers was stronger than he'd ever been. Imogen had let him in, feeding him with her guilt. But she'd not confessed.

"What did Livia ever do to you?" Esme said.

"I had no choice!"

"There's always a choice," Noah said.

"Livia confessed, and so she had to die. That's how the game works," Imogen pleaded.

"Whispers didn't hear her confession," Esme said. "She should have been safe."

"Oh, but he did." Imogen's expression contorted into a pleased little smirk. "Isn't that right, Ava?"

Ava shook her head. "Why, Imogen? We were going to escape."

"What's the point?" Imogen said. "You think I want to go back home? Back to watching all your pathetic little lives, knowing that somehow you're all going to get everything I want, while I'll be left with nothing? You're all like leeches, sucking the world dry while I get no reward."

"You think Whispers is going to fix that for you?" Noah said.

"He can make me famous. He wants me to be his *One*. He recognizes my potential."

"Only that's not going to happen," Esme said, stepping closer to Imogen. "I'm not going to let you win."

Imogen stepped back. Glanced over her shoulder at the precipice. There was nowhere for her to go but down.

"Confess," Ava said.

"He won't want me if I confess!"

"Exactly," Noah said. "You'll be out of the game and no longer a danger to the rest of us."

"Your choice," Esme said. "But you're not getting away with this."

Imogen gulped heavily. "Okay, fine. I put the pills in Livia's drink. She knew my secret, and she was going to tell. Happy now?"

"Happy?" Esme whispered.

"Your secret," Ava said urgently. "What's your secret?"

"Nothing! All you people did such terrible things, and I don't know why I'm stuck here with you. It makes no sense."

"Rachel," Ava said. "I know that your secret is something to do with Rachel."

"Yes, it has to do with Rachel! But I did nothing wrong. Rachel was so needy the whole time we were friends. It was disgusting, the way she'd cry and stuff her fat, ugly face with food and then puke it all up. Her breath smelled of vomit!"

"You rancid bitch," Jolie said.

"Oh, shut up. You have no idea how hard it was for me. Listening to her go on about how fat she was. Listening to her obsess about Clem, then cry because she finally got what she wanted and didn't want it anymore. Talking to her on the phone at two in the morning because she wanted to end it all and needed me to talk her down. Constant attention-seeking."

"Attention-seeking? Rachel killed herself," Esme said.

"And I told her to do it. *Just do it*, I said, and I was glad that she did."

"You…told her to kill herself?" Ava breathed.

"They were just words," Imogen spat. "It's not my fault if Rachel decided to act on them."

Behind her, the pier brightened like the flash of an exploding bomb. The music blurred into a tuneless noise, getting faster and faster.

"*Let her fall*," Whispers taunted. His breath was smoke against Ava's neck. "*You've done it before, you can do it again.*"

"You're a monster," Esme said, stepping closer.

"I'm a good person," Imogen cried, snot bubbling from her nose. She backed up so her kitten heels skidded on the edge of the roof.

"You're not," Ava spat. "You think you get to judge other people, but you're worse than all of us."

Imogen laughed then, and kept on laughing like she couldn't stop. Ava raised her camera and watched her through the screen. *Click*. The flash lit up Imogen and plunged the rest of the carnival into darkness. There was nothing but Imogen teetering on the precipice.

A scream. Feet slipping on crumbling bricks. "Mother!" Imogen cried out.

Then she was gone.

A heavy thud shook the broken fire escape, and the fog cleared from Ava's mind. The carousel stilled and went silent. Ava lowered the camera and slowly looked over the edge. A broken doll flopped over the metal. Black hair. A puddle spreading beneath her, dripping from the stairs.

"What have we done?" Noah whispered.

"She fell," Jolie said quietly. "No one touched her. Right?"

Esme stared down at Imogen's body, her expression hard and unforgiving. "They were just words," she spat. "Isn't that right, Imogen?"

TWENTY-FIVE

Ava slept fitfully on the club's grimy linoleum, next to Noah, Esme, and Jolie. Livia lay beside them with her purple coat covering her lifeless face. Ava kept falling asleep only for a sudden twist in her stomach to jolt her fully awake. When she tried to close her eyes again, it felt like she was free-falling through empty space. In this manner, the hours dragged by until the sun rose and it was time to go.

Time to go home. But even if they made it, Ava had no idea how to go back to her old life.

They stepped outside into the bright light of the morning. Esme cradled Livia's curtain-wrapped body in her arms. Everything was calm and quiet. Perhaps Whispers was asleep, full to bursting with guilt. Most of it was Ava's.

Four people were dead, and she'd played a part in two of the murders.

"Where is she?" Noah said, snapping Ava out of her thoughts.

He stood in front of the crumpled fire escape, staring at the spot where Imogen's body should have been. A clump of black hair was twisted around the sharp end of a bolt, but there was no Imogen.

"Maybe he really does take them," Jolie said.

"He's not having Livia," Esme said, tightening her hold on the body. Livia was going home with them, and that was the end of the argument, according to Esme. Never mind that a dead girl would raise questions, especially when it became clear that a fatal cocktail of drugs had flooded her system.

"What are we going to do?" Jolie said as Esme walked on ahead. "We need to dispose of the body. Weigh her down and bury her at sea. Otherwise the party-gone-wrong story will fall apart, and no one's going to believe the truth."

"Esme's too upset," Noah said. "She's not going to listen to us."

"Let's fix the boat and see if she calms down later," Ava said.

"People don't just *calm down* when they lose someone they love!" Noah cried. He closed his eyes and squeezed the bridge of his nose. "Sorry, I...sorry."

He hurried after Esme toward the boathouse. Clem

stepped out from behind a drinks stand, smirking. "Sounds like someone's falling apart," he sang, rolling his harmonica over his fingers. "Someone's going to break."

"Esme's not falling apart," Ava snapped. "And neither is Noah."

Part of this statement was true. Esme wasn't showing any signs of letting Whispers in. When it came to Noah, Ava was less sure.

Clem pointed between Jolie and Ava. Jolie, Ava, Jolie, Ava. "Who's going to be next, I wonder?"

"No one," Ava said. "None of us are going to let Whispers in, because we're better than you."

"Keep telling yourself that."

"And you keep telling yourself that your face doesn't look like a surprised chipmunk's," Jolie said.

"Shut up. Are we escaping today or killing some more people?" Clem said. He stalked off, feeling his face like he was checking for fur.

They all caught up with Noah and Esme outside the boathouse. Noah had dragged the canoe into the light and was checking on the repairs he'd made the previous night while Livia lay dying in the club. Esme had laid Livia down on the deck of the huge lifeboat inside the hut and was now drawing swirling tattoos on her arms with a Sharpie. Ava raised her camera to take a picture but stopped herself. She was done taking photos of other people's pain.

"Wow. Ava without a camera in front of her face," Noah teased.

She blinked at him. "Yeah. I know."

"You'll be back at it in no time. Don't worry."

She nodded, but her heart wasn't in it. Portgrave felt tainted, and she wasn't sure she could photograph it anymore without seeing Whispers's face in every reflection. "What about you? What will you do?"

He sat back on his heels. "I'm leaving town, never looking back."

"That sounds tempting."

"Maybe I'll see you on the bus," he said.

"Have a wonderful life together," Jolie muttered.

Part of Ava wanted to tell Jolie to come too. First bus out of town—they could start over. But too much had passed between them. Too much had changed.

Noah glanced past Ava. "What about the rest of you? Where are you going next?"

Jolie shrugged. "Probably nowhere," she muttered.

Esme returned Noah's gaze. "I suppose I'll go back to school and apply for university. That was always my plan."

"Smart ass. To study what?" Jolie said.

"I used to want to be a lawyer. For the big bucks. But I'm not so sure I can surround myself with evil and not end up tainted by it." Clem snorted. "What?" she said.

"What you call *evil* is human nature, and it's in all of

us. We only stick to the rules because we don't want to get caught. At the end of the day, it's every man for himself."

"That's borderline psychopathic," Noah said.

Clem shrugged. "It's you alone with a girl you fancy"—he glanced over at Ava—"and you know you could get away with doing anything you wanted. You're telling me you wouldn't?"

Noah shook his head. "Nah. Because I have this tiny thing called a conscience."

"Social conditioning makes you think that," Clem said, "but it's not real."

"Have fun when you end up in prison, mate."

"But I won't," Clem said wearily. "I'll be rich. Famous. Popular. And I'll be able to do anything I want, and no one will care. They'll see who they want to see."

"The only reason you're still alive is because the rest of us have more self-control than you," Jolie said. "If this were a movie, you'd totally be the next person to die, and everyone would cheer."

"Only it's the real world, and the bad boys always win," he said, winking at her.

"I'm not sure they get to be happy, though," Noah said.

"Ha! Keep telling yourself that while you're living your meaningless life. *But at least I'm happy.* Loser."

The two boys stared at each other. Neither spoke.

Noah's fists were tightening.

"Forget not letting Whispers in," Jolie muttered. "I say we kill him."

"No one cares what you think," Clem said. He wandered over to the rocks by the boxing ring with his hat carefully perched on top of his side-swept bangs. Ava was struck by the urge to run at him and launch him into the waves. She dug her nails into her palms. It was Whispers who wanted that, not her. She wasn't a murderer.

"*Not you, maybe*," Whispers taunted.

Jolie brushed past her. It took Ava a moment to understand it, the way her shoulders were tight and her face not quite her own.

She reached Clem. Lifted her arms.

"Jolie, no!" Ava cried.

She jumped up at the same moment as Noah and Esme.

They ran, closing in on Jolie. Not fast enough.

But Jolie hesitated. And that second's hesitation was enough. Ava and Esme each grabbed a handful of her panda costume and yanked her away from Clem. Jolie didn't resist. She was too busy staring at her raised hands with a frown. Turning them over to examine her palms.

Clem turned, fear flashing quickly across his face. He tried to mask it. "Coward," he spat, curling his lip at Jolie.

"Yeah," Jolie said, laughing to herself. "Yeah, I am."

"I thought we were too late," Noah said, breathing out heavily.

Jolie grinned at him. "Got to keep you all on your toes."

"You stopped," Ava said, smiling at Jolie. "You've made it into my top three most awesome moments."

"Ahead of the seagull who swallowed that whole rat?" Jolie said, clutching her chest in mock awe.

"Mr. Seagull still beats you." Ava took a step toward Jolie and almost moved to hug her, but she wasn't quite ready for that. She stepped back again and cleared her throat. "Only just, though," she added.

Jolie smoothed down her panda costume. Pretended like she didn't care. The flush to her cheeks said otherwise. "He's not worth the sweat."

"He really isn't," Ava said. "And he has stupid hair."

"Screw you," Clem muttered.

"Let's finish this boat," Esme said. "Come on."

A noise made Ava hang back. There was something in the water. Something churning below the surface that no one else had noticed. She squinted at it. It looked like pieces of debris from the broken pier swirling together, snapping as they slotted into place. The thing had a shape now. A body and a tail. A head. Monstrous jaws.

It began to move through the water toward Clem, stalking him like a shark. Ava glanced at him; he hadn't seen it. He was too busy looking at Portgrave, barely visible through the fog. She knew she should warn him. Shout for him to run. She didn't.

There was no line, just a slippery slope. She had tricked him into confessing. She had failed to admit her mistake to Livia. Then she'd stood back and let Imogen fall from that roof. And now she once again did nothing as the thing swam closer and closer, a dark shadow beneath the surface. She didn't shout at him to run. *She hoped that he'd stay exactly where he was.*

The thunder of a hundred waves breaking all at once shook the boathouse. The *thing*—wood, metal, broken bottles—launched itself up, up into the air, two stories high, propelled by a swirling column of water that rained down and drenched Ava from head to toe.

She shielded her face as it slammed down on the rocks. Debris exploded in every direction, sending her tumbling to the ground. Laughter, whispers in her ear.

"*If you won't, then I will*," the voice said, and then it was gone. Thunder rumbled overhead.

Ava slowly lowered her hands. They were bleeding where she'd been hit. Her head throbbed. There was a gash across her calf where something had ripped straight through her trousers. Blood pooled around the toe of her boot, but it wasn't hers.

She followed the thin red river back to its source. Clem. A two-meter shard of wood had impaled him through the heart.

TWENTY-SIX

Ava could hear Esme, Jolie, and Noah shouting, but she wasn't really listening. Instead, she stared and stared at Clem's body, at the pool of blood widening around him. It ran off the rocks and made rivers in the sand.

"He only needs *One*." Noah stumbled away from the others. "Clem lost the game, and now he's dead. We have to play the game."

"Calm down," Jolie said.

"Clem's dead!" Noah backed up against the rope of the boxing ring. He startled as if hearing a voice. "What's the point trying to fight it? We can't change a thing. We can't escape."

Jolie and Esme moved toward him. He ducked under the ropes and paced from one side of the ring to the other.

"The boat's undamaged. We can still escape," Esme said.

"Not from ourselves!" He pointed angrily at Clem's body. "In the end, we all have to pay our debts. There's no running away."

"Yeah, there is," Esme said. "We're not going to let Whispers have us."

"You're right, you're right," Noah said. "He doesn't get to have me. I'm not going to be part of his game."

"Great," Jolie said. "Then stop ranting and get down here."

"There can be only *One*," Noah said, his voice shaking. "He won't stop, not until all of us break."

"Shut up," Esme screamed, suddenly furious. "Just stop it!"

Ava put her hands over her ears. She couldn't move from her spot, even though Clem's blood was trickling around her feet. The smell of all that blood pulled her back into her memories, and it wasn't just Clem who'd died, but Rachel as well.

She watched Jolie and Esme arguing with Noah, their voices muffled. Jolie joined him in the ring, but he kept pushing her away. She shoved him back, her face contorted with anger. Her words were lost to the sound of the waves. The water churned in vicious whirlpools and slammed pieces of driftwood up against the rocks. Overhead, a storm rolled in. The first drops of rain fell on Ava's cheeks. One of

Whispers's storms, jubilant in its dark clouds and rumbling thunder.

Ava lowered her hands from her ears, and the world rushed in, noisy and unforgiving.

"I wanted him to die, and I'm glad he's gone," Noah cried.

"Damn right. He was a piece of crap," Jolie said. "He's not worth losing your head over."

"I've spent the past year trying to be a better person than I used to be. But it was all a lie. I like the violence; I like the pain."

"Stop." Esme pointed at the ocean. "You're feeding the storm with your guilt, and we can't escape in this."

"There's no escape, not from our secrets."

Esme muttered something under her breath. Then she ducked beneath the ropes to face Noah in the ring. "So tell us what it is. Your secret. Confess."

Ava was shocked back into the moment. She scrambled over rocks to reach the ring.

"Esme, stop," she said. "What are you doing?"

"Getting Livia and myself out of here." Her eyes were on Noah.

"Livia died believing it was her fault that Alfred died." Noah took an unsteady breath. "But it was my fault."

"What happened?" Esme said.

"Esme!" Ava stepped between then. "Noah, don't."

He didn't hear her. "Alfred was my friend. I met him on the beach, and he was the one who got me into the fights. But after I got arrested, I lost my nerve. I thought I could just quit with no consequences."

"What does this have to do with Alfred dying?" Esme said.

"There'd been this big match lined up for weeks, and a lot of money had changed hands in bets. I refused to go and left Alfred to tell the organizers. They were furious and demanded he fight in my place. I guess they figured humiliating an old man would send me a message."

"But Alfred died of natural causes," Jolie said. "Didn't he?"

"Will you all just stop talking?" Ava pleaded.

"That's what everyone said. But after that fight, he was never the same again. A month later, he was dead." Noah closed his eyes. "If it wasn't for me, he would still be alive. We can't escape our mistakes. Someone always has to pay, and it was Alfred who paid for me."

Noah's secret hung in the air, then fell to the ground with the last of the raindrops. The storm calmed with a sigh. But overhead, the clouds rumbled ominously, and the waves still crashed.

Say something to him, Ava thought. But for some reason, she couldn't find the words.

"I don't want to be part of his game," Noah said quietly. "I don't want to hurt anyone else."

Distant laughter made Ava glance over her shoulder, but there was nothing there. When she turned back, Noah was already running up the steps toward the main square.

"Wait, Noah," she called after him. He didn't stop.

She ran. Jolie and Esme yelled after her, but she ignored them. She needed to catch up with Noah. She needed to tell him that what he'd done didn't matter. She knew exactly who he was, and he wasn't a bad guy.

She ran into the square, but there was no sign of him. She rushed around the side of the arcade to the carousel where she'd first found him. Nothing. Then she ran back and peered down the steps into the carnival. The water stood still and undisturbed. She turned around. Spotted something at the edge of the broken pier.

Black boots. A hole in one of the toes.

She walked over with legs made of lead and looked off the edge of the island. There was nothing there but the rocks that had killed Olly and water. Endless, churning water. She picked up one of the boots and numbly clutched it to her chest.

Noah Park, the mystery. The first time he'd vanished from Portgrave, Ava had hoped he would never come back. This time, she knew that he was gone forever, just like that. She was seconds too late.

With a sudden flare of rage, she hurled the boot into the ocean.

"You monster!" she screamed. "Why can't you just leave us alone?"

"*Confess and you'll be free*," a voice laughed.

Ava screamed wordlessly and ran. She sprinted across the main square toward the steps down into the carnival, between the rotting attractions. She didn't know where she was going, just that she had to get away from the feelings boiling up inside her. But the feelings followed her, growing and growing and growing.

She burst out from between the tents and onto the beach. She paused, gasping for breath. The sea sucked hungrily against the shingle. Rain splashed into the swash. She swept her hair out of her face and stared through the already failing light at the portrait hut, sitting haphazardly at the water's edge. This was where it had all started. Where she'd first seen Whispers.

She flung herself through the door. Snatching up the jar of worms or tongues or plastic props, she hurled it at the mirror as hard as she could. It missed. The jar shattered into a thousand pieces, and the stench of formaldehyde filled the air. The contents flopped wetly to the ground. She grabbed the edge of the table and flipped it over. It slammed against the wall. A few of the portraits dropped, and the mirror wobbled but didn't fall. Ava scrambled over the table and swung a punch at the glass. A spiderweb of cracks spread out from the point of impact.

"You broke the rules of your own game. You killed Clem just to push Noah over the edge."

"There are no rules." Whispers's image appeared behind the cracks. It briefly guttered and faded, then returned.

"You're not meant to be able to touch us!"

"Of course I can touch you," he said. "I can take possession of inanimate objects, although I confess it is hard work to maintain. People are much more fun, if they let me in."

"I'll never let you in. You hear me? Never."

He disappeared again. Manifesting the shark had weakened him. It had taken all his strength to kill Clem.

But Whispers wasn't dead. Ava could still feel him.

Watching, waiting.

Guilt. Guilt strengthened him. She forced herself to think about Noah. His smile, his laugh, the way he'd held them all together even when he was falling apart. He shouldn't have died. He was meant to live. And she could have saved him, if only she had been a bit quicker. The guilt welled up inside her until she felt like she might burst.

Whispers flashed back, bright and terrible. Buoyed by the waves of guilt rolling off her, he was no longer flickering in and out of existence. He observed her with interest, like a bird might look at a brightly colored bug before devouring it.

"Killing Clem must have used nearly everything you had," she said.

"It was worth it," he said, baring pointy teeth. "To see

you all fall apart again. Did you honestly think *friendship* could defeat me?"

"And yet here you are, struggling to muster up a reflection."

"It won't be long before I recover. Not now that I've pushed you all closer to your true selves. Tell me, how did it feel to watch Clem die? Did you like it?"

"I'm not going to let you in," she said.

"You stupid human. Every bad thing you do, every surge of guilt you feel lets me inside. How do you think I whisper my suggestions into your ears? I can come and go as I please, so long as you have something to feel guilty about."

"But it doesn't last, does it? You need your *One* to tether you to the real world permanently, and that can't happen unless someone breaks like Clem did. You can't force someone to be your *One*; otherwise, you wouldn't have spent all those years as Alfred's passenger."

Whispers's face darkened; his edges hardened. "You know nothing."

"What happens if you don't find someone? How long can you hold on for?"

"Longer than you'll live," he muttered. "But if all of you prove disappointing, I'll bring some new candidates to the pier. You are nothing special."

Ava knew a lie when she heard one. She could hear the desperation in his voice. "That's not true, is it? It took you forty years to find a way into someone's head. I reckon we're your last chance. You need one of us to become your *One*; otherwise, it's another thousand years in that lonely cave for you."

"I will live forever," he hissed. "I have been here longer than you can ever imagine, and I will survive long after Noah's bones crumble on the ocean floor."

Something inside her shattered. She slammed her fist into the cracked mirror, sending shards of glass scattering across the floor. Whisper's reflection laughed at her from each piece.

"Noah died because of you. Because he didn't want you to have to kill him. How does that make you feel?"

"Let me go," she cried, sagging to the floor.

"Confess, and you'll be free," all the versions of Whispers said.

"Never," Ava said.

His smile widened further. "Perfect."

TWENTY-SEVEN

Ava rested her head on the floor as sobs shook her body. She'd never felt so empty or so alone. She must have sat there for close to an hour, unable to stop crying. Part of her thought maybe she'd stay there forever.

But in the end, someone came to find her: Jolie the panda, silently helping Ava to her feet and leading her outside.

They sat on the beach, and Ava tried to catch her breath, but it was no good. The tears kept coming, and she couldn't make them stop.

"No rush," Jolie said, and for once, it didn't sound like she was taking the piss.

Ava buried her face in Jolie's filthy costume and clung on like it was all that was keeping her from floating away into smoke. Jolie rested her chin on Ava's head and waited. Seconds, minutes, hours—Ava wasn't sure. But eventually it stopped hurting to breathe, and her sobs turned into hiccups. She removed her face from the smelly fur and sat up.

"So, this party kind of sucks, right?" said Jolie.

Ava laughed despite herself. "It really does."

"Why did we come here again?"

"Secrets," Ava said quietly.

"Oh yeah. I'm beginning to think that no secret is worth all this."

"Where's Esme?" Ava asked.

"She's taken our boat," Jolie sighed. "Every woman for herself and all that."

"I thought she'd stay," Ava said sadly.

"You're kidding, right? How is it possible that you manage to see good in every person except for yourself, Ava?"

"Well, you think everyone's out to get you, so I guess we balance out."

"When we're together."

Ava hesitated. "Yeah. Maybe," she admitted.

"Look, Ava, I'm sorry," Jolie said, the words rushing out of her. "I know I've been a nightmare since my brother's accident. I took it out on you because you've always been the one who would never give up on me, no matter what. At least, that's what I used to think."

"I guess we all have our limits," Ava said, but she couldn't muster up all that much anger anymore. She shuffled around to face Jolie. "I didn't take any pictures of you and Clem. I wasn't lying. I've always been on your side."

Jolie nodded. "I believe you. I was just so...confused. I still don't know what parts were real and what parts Whispers put into my head. It was easier to be mad at you than to try and pick apart whose fault it all really was."

"I wish I could have helped," Ava said.

"I wish I'd let you. But you know me. Got to act tough so no one realizes how scared I really am. I have it on good authority that giant pandas are meant to be fearsome."

"Fifth-strongest bite of any carnivore."

They both laughed, but it was a bittersweet reconciliation.

The tide crept up the beach—Ava had to move her feet back to stop them from getting wet. Soon it would get dark, and then it would be just the two of them and Whispers, using his mind games to tear them apart again.

"I understand why Noah did it," she said quietly. "I don't want to turn on you, Jolie. I don't want him to win."

Jolie nodded slowly. She glanced up at Teddy's cage on the outcrop. Neither of them spoke. They didn't need to. Ava and Jolie came as a pair, like salt and pepper or macaroni and cheese.

"Come on," Jolie said, pulling Ava to her feet.

It took a while to climb the outcrop. Ava's injured leg made her slow, and the rain had left the rocks slippery. But eventually they stood at the top and stared at Portgrave in the distance.

"I reckon we can swim for it," Jolie said, her shaky voice giving away the lie.

"No problem," Ava said, squeezing Jolie's hand.

"Just so long as he doesn't win, right?"

Ava opened her mouth to agree, but then she saw something. A canoe bobbing against the lifeboat launch ramp. A girl in soaked clothes crawling out of the water, coughing and retching—Esme. And, washed up on the shore, Livia's curtain-wrapped body.

"The ocean must have pushed them back," Ava said. "Come on!"

They scrambled down the opposite side of the outcrop. By the time they stepped onto concrete, Esme was carrying Livia back into the boathouse. She placed her on the deck of the boat again and blew her a kiss.

"The waves are too strong," Esme said quietly. She gently closed the doors and sat down at the edge of the water.

"Too much guilt," Ava said, sitting on her left.

Jolie sat on her opposite side. "I was thinking about that."

"What about it?" Esme said.

Jolie flicked her lighter on, then snapped it closed. "We all have to confess. If we all do, then none of us can be his *One*."

Ava and Esme didn't say anything. Confessing wasn't

something Ava wanted to consider. Confessing her secret out loud meant confessing it to herself and admitting she was someone she didn't want to be.

"Jolie has a point. He needs someone who holds on to their guilt," Esme said. "And everything we're feeling right now is making him too strong."

"Confessing won't banish him, though," Ava said. "He only needs a little guilt to hang on to. Like how he clung to Livia's granddad."

"We don't have any choice," said Jolie. "And we can run, can't we? Skip town. Maybe we can run so far that he can't follow us."

Esme nodded slowly, agreeing.

"Are we really doing this?" Ava whispered.

"I know I'm not strong enough to resist him forever," Jolie said. "Are you?"

"It's not like we have much left to lose," Esme said.

Ava chewed her lip. "He could kill us all."

"He can't," Jolie said, laughing. "We're the only thing holding him in the human world. He needs someone to survive, or he'll fall back into his hole."

"But he only needs one," Ava said. "And there are three of us."

"We'll tie ourselves together in the boat," Jolie said. "Then he can't destroy the boat without killing us all."

"He'll still be in our heads like he was Alfred's."

"Alfred was a killer. We can be better people," Jolie said. "We have to try."

Esme nodded. "No judgments. We confess, and that's it."

Jolie flicked on her lighter again and stared at the flame. "I'll go first. A little over a year ago, my brother was badly burned in a fire. That I started. On purpose."

Ava's heart skipped a beat. She tried to keep her expression neutral and not give away her surprise.

"I didn't mean for him to get hurt," Jolie said. "I had these horrible curtains in my room, and whenever I got angry, I'd burn little round holes in the lining. Sounds weird, I know, but it helped me deal."

"I don't think any of us are in a position to judge you." Ava sighed.

Jolie smiled ruefully. "I was upset. And instead of burning a little hole, I held the lighter to the fabric until the whole curtain went up. It felt good for a second. And then I was trapped in my room, surrounded by flames and smoke. I thought I was going to die."

"When Noah tried to breathe fire," Esme said, closing her eyes, "you got so upset..."

"Yeah," Jolie said. "It took me back. I could see my brother bursting in through the door and pushing me out the window even though his clothes had caught and he was on fire, head to toe. Stupid bastard."

"Does he remember what happened?" Ava whispered.

"Of course he bloody does," Jolie snapped. Her expression softened. "He never told anyone, and I never said I was sorry. That's the part I feel guilty about. Not saying sorry."

"You can tell him when you get home," Ava said. At least there was still a chance for Jolie to make amends. Ava, not so much.

Rachel's ghost flickered in and out of existence. On the rocks. Behind the boathouse. Neck-deep in the ocean. Each time, Ava blinked and forced the image away. But it kept returning.

"Whatever," Jolie said. She quickly wiped her eyes on her grubby sleeve to disguise her tears. When she spoke again, she sounded like the old Jolie. "It feels good, you know? Offloading all that guilt. So, who's next?"

Ava's mouth dried up. She wasn't ready, not by a long shot.

"Come on, Ava," Jolie said. "You better not be backing out on me."

"No, I—" Ava started to say.

"Shoplifting," Esme interrupted. "A packet of hair dye. That was why my invitation was typed on a coupon."

"Shoplifting?" Jolie said, raising an eyebrow. "That's your big secret?"

"My whole life, I've worked my ass off to get out of this town. No university will take a law student with a police record. If anyone had found out, it would have ruined everything."

"You've been withstanding all of Whispers's tricks to keep *that* a secret?" Ava said.

Esme shrugged. "I don't like anyone having control over me. I wasn't about to let him win."

More believable, Ava supposed.

"Two down, one to go," Jolie said. They both turned to Ava.

She fiddled with the buttons on her camera. She knew the other two were waiting for her confession. No, not two. Three. Rachel was there too, silently staring from the roof of the boathouse.

Ava closed her eyes. She had to do it. It was now or never. She couldn't. But she had to.

"I was there when Rachel died," she forced herself to say.

"The photo of the Oracle on your invite," Jolie said.

Ava nodded but didn't open her eyes. "I took photos of her on the roof. Then she jumped."

Silence. Ava tentatively opened her eyes. Rachel's ghost was still there, slowly shaking its head. *Not the whole story.* Ava looked away.

"Is that all?" Esme said.

"You don't think that's bad enough?" Ava said quickly, spinning to face her.

"No, it's pretty bad," Jolie said.

"No judgment," Esme said quietly.

Jolie shrugged. Flicked her lighter on and off. "I thought

something might happen once we all confessed. That the island would cave in on itself or explode or something."

An uneasy pause.

"Nothing changes," Esme said very quietly. "No matter what we do, the world stays the same terrible place it always was."

"It's going to get better," Ava said, standing up. She moved toward the boat, and for the briefest of moments, she caught sight of Rachel standing high on the rocks. She blinked, and the ghost was gone again, leaving behind the faintest echo of laughter. Ava tried to pretend it had never been there. In minutes, they'd be off the island, with her real secret still unspoken.

"Let's go," Jolie said.

Esme scratched at her dirty hair, messing it up. "I need to..." She stopped, like a thought had gotten tangled between her brain and her tongue. "We can't take Livia with us, can we?"

Ava shook her head. "There will already be so many questions. We can't run the risk that they'll keep us in Portgrave long enough for us to pass Whispers on to someone else. We have to get away."

Esme nodded slowly. "I'm going to say goodbye."

"Do you want some company?" Ava said.

"No. I want to be alone." Esme walked off toward the boathouse. She closed the doors behind her.

Jolie watched the hut. "Ava, you think we'll be okay?"

Ava hesitated. Whispers had done a good job of breaking their friendship into little pieces, but only because the cracks had already been there.

"I don't know what I'll do without you," Jolie said. "I don't know what I'll do, full stop."

"You could come with me?" Ava said. "I mean, I don't know *where* to, but we can work it out."

Jolie narrowed her eyes and fought a smile. "You're going to want to take my picture, aren't you?"

"Someone needs to document you doing the stupid shit everyone else is too scared to try."

"So does this mean we're good?" Jolie said hopefully.

Ava didn't answer. Esme had opened the door of the boathouse, and in her hand was a can. She was sloshing liquid onto the floor. Ava remembered the oil drums inside, marked with their peeling highly flammable labels. Petrol, Ava realized.

"Don't you even think about it," Jolie cried, racing toward Esme.

Esme flicked on Livia's lighter. She lit her invite and lifted it high. She stood with her arms spread wide like an avenging angel. As Jolie lunged for her, Esme let the invite fall.

"Get back!" Jolie yelled. She shoved Esme away from the door as the spilled petrol whooshed into a blanket of flames. The fire spread across the floor, hungrily climbing up the sides of the first oil drum.

Ava skidded to a halt, shielding her face from the heat of the fire. "The petrol," she screamed. "Get away from there!"

"I'm doing my best." Jolie was dragging Esme behind her. "She's not exactly helping."

The two of them pulled Esme past the boxing ring, over to the rocks. They dropped her on the ground, where she sat silently crying.

"How much petrol did you pour in there?" Jolie said.

"All of it," Esme said.

"You mega-blockhead," Jolie said. "What the hell were you thinking?"

"It's what Livia would have wanted. A Viking pyre."

"Livia would have wanted a parade of unicorns and—" Jolie started to say.

She was interrupted by the explosion. A wave of noise and heat and light knocked Ava back against the canoe. The hut burned and burned and burned. Ava's ears rang so loudly she could hardly hear anything at all. Just the sound of crackling flames and something like music in the distance.

"Go big or go home," Jolie said, almost laughing.

For the first time since Livia's death, Esme's face cracked into a smile. Ava smiled too. It was all going to be okay, she thought. She imagined sitting on a distant beach with Jolie, laughing around a campfire, taking photos of the stars. One day, none of this was going to matter.

Then came a second explosion, this one sending the

doors of the boathouse flying open. Fire surged out like a monster's tentacles, throwing burning lumps of wood as far as the boxing ring. Ava remembered Noah's fire-breathing trick, how the flames had taken on lives of their own thanks to Whispers's trickery.

She suspected this display of anger had taken almost everything Whispers had left. A last burst of fury from a dying monster. She watched the tongues of fire twist into the screaming faces of everyone who'd died on the pier, and then they were gone. The doors slammed closed on the flames.

But the screaming continued.

TWENTY-EIGHT

Something streaked past with flames trailing in its wake. Screaming, screaming. It took Ava a second to understand what she was seeing. Jolie was the one screaming. She was running, fire swallowing her up as the panda costume sizzled and melted. Screaming as the fabric melted to her skin and her hair singed and crackled.

Within moments, Ava was on her, slapping out the flames with her coat, rolling her over and over in the swash until the fire fizzled into smoke. She smelled of sulfur and charcoal and plastic fumes.

Ava turned Jolie onto her back. Brushed fried hair off her face. It crumbled at her touch. "It's all right," she said. "You're all right. We're going to be all right."

"Took your bloody time to answer me," Jolie rasped, trying to laugh. She blinked sleepily and closed her eyes.

"Jolie?" Ava said. "Jolie!"

But she wasn't listening. Her chest heaved with short, sharp breaths, but she wasn't conscious. The fire had engulfed more than half her body—her back and chest, her right arm and left shoulder. It was hard to tell how bad her injuries were. The fabric of her costume had melted onto her, but the burns Ava could see just looked red and slightly shiny.

"You'll be okay," Ava said. "You'll be okay."

Esme stumbled upright. Stared down at Jolie. Slowly backed away. "He tricked me. It was his voice, his idea to light the fire. I let him get in my head."

"It's all right," Ava said. "Come on, let's stay calm. We have to get away now. We have to get Jolie to a hospital."

But dark clouds were gathering overhead. The light of the day dimmed and darkened into night as the fog blew across the sea, thick with smoke from the fire. Shaking her head, Esme ran for the cliff face and started the climb toward Teddy's cage. Lightning struck overhead.

Whispers's laughter rolled in on the storm.

The first drops of rain sizzled in the smoky air. Darkness swallowed Ava and Jolie, and then, one by one, the distant lights of the pier came on. It felt like time had fast-forwarded into night. If the sun was still hiding behind the clouds, Ava couldn't see any sign of it. She struggled to believe it had been there moments ago.

More rain landed on Jolie's heaving chest. Her face was untouched by the fire, but the rosy pink of her cheeks was gone. Her expression had lost all of its character—the sneers and smirks and smiles that made Jolie who she was. She could've been any sixteen-year-old girl, young and soft around the edges. Jolie was a lot of things. Soft wasn't meant to be one of them.

"I'm going to get you to a hospital," Ava said, but she already knew it was impossible. The storm was raging. The boat would be smashed in seconds. She clasped her hands into fists. "This is Esme's fault."

Jolie murmured something but didn't open her eyes.

"She didn't confess," Ava said, the truth hitting her in the gut. "And then she let him in."

She knew that Esme had lied because she'd lied as well, and it took a liar to know a liar. Jolie's confession had been the only real one, and now she was dying on the sand. If Esme had agreed to be the *One*—if she'd let Whispers all the way inside—then he would be too strong for them to escape by boat. Jolie would never make it to a hospital. There was nothing Ava could do to help her.

Except maybe one thing.

She tipped the boat over to shelter Jolie from the coming storm, then knelt down to take Jolie's hand. "I'll be right back, okay? There's something I have to do, and then we'll get you some help."

Jolie's face showed no indication that she'd heard, but Ava was sure her fingers squeezed her hand. She squeezed back, then took off at a run for the cliffs.

It was a slippery slope; Ava knew that. She'd tricked Clem into making his confession. Failed to warn Livia. Watched Imogen fall from the roof without trying to save her. Been too late to stop Noah from vanishing into the sea. Stayed silent as Whispers had stalked Clem along the shore. She hadn't killed anyone herself, but she hadn't had a good reason to yet. Now that Jolie was dying, she knew exactly who she was. If she had to throw Esme into the ocean to weaken Whispers and save Jolie, then that was what she'd do.

She climbed down the other side of the outcrop and raced across the beach. She stepped into the writhing shadows and guttering lights of the carnival. Laughter followed her at every turn, but Ava felt immune to Whispers's stupid games. None of them were real—not the distant voices of carnival merriment or the fog that swirled at her ankles. Jolie was real, and she was all that mattered.

The high striker bell sounded. Cheers filled the air, as if a hundred people were watching. Ava stopped. Three people, not a hundred. Three ghosts, translucent against the darkness, barely holding their forms. They flickered as they slowly turned to face Ava.

Scarlett, Teddy, and Olly.

Ava backed away as the ghosts advanced. Scarlett came first, her hair red with blood. She was wearing the fur coat she'd worn in the club, only it was made from sewn-together roadkill: a mangled fox, a rabbit with bulging eyes and a bleeding mouth. With a sudden movement, the fox struggled against the stitches, snapping its broken jaw at the rabbit.

Ava held her ground. They weren't real, she told herself. They were another trick.

"Confess," Scarlett groaned, and so did the dead animals.

"They're not real," Ava said. "You're not real!"

The Scarlett creature looked at her with a curl of her lip that was undeniably Scarlett.

"Confess," she repeated, rolling her eyes. "Free us already."

Teddy's ghost was wrapped in chains worn over one of Baldo's black suits. Mottled skin, fish-eaten eyes, a fernlike burn on one side of his face. Water bubbled from his mouth when he tried to speak, and his words came out as a horrible rasping gurgle.

"Your guilt traps us," he said.

"Confess," Scarlett said again.

"No." Ava forced herself to take a step toward the ghosts.

Olly came forward, dressed in an old-fashioned strong-man costume. The fairy lights caught his features, throwing shadows across bruises and cuts. The scariest thing was that, for the first time ever, he wasn't smiling.

"Confess," Olly said. "Your guilt made us."

"We are your guilt," Scarlett's dead coat barked.

"Confess." Teddy vomited black water down his chin and shirt. "Free us."

Ava bent down to yank a tent stake from the ground. It was a heavy metal thing, like a giant blunted screw, with mud in the thread. She moved to throw it. "I'm not playing his game anymore. You hear me?"

The three ghosts watched her, swaying and flickering. One by one, they guttered and faded. Olly's voice trailed in his wake. "The mirror maze," it said.

Ava walked on as the lights strobed around her, illuminating everything and then nothing. With every other flash, Ava thought she saw Rachel's ghost, jerkily appearing and disappearing in hidden corners, on rooftops, dangling upside down from the fairy lights with her ankles tied and her long hair trailing in the water. Ava blinked her away and kept moving toward the center of the carnival.

She rounded a corner, and there was Livia. Sitting on the counter of one of the attractions, a cigarette between her blue lips. She was wearing a carnival jester's outfit, and every centimeter of exposed skin—her face, neck, arms, bare feet—was marred with rootlike black veins that seemed to throb and pulse. She blew out smoke and stared at Ava. "He heard my confession because of you," she said. "And now I'm dead."

"You're dead because Imogen killed you. It wasn't my fault."

Livia cocked her head. "That's what you're going with? I thought you were better than that, Ava."

"I'm really not."

"Then I guess you're not who I thought you were." She pulled the tatty friendship bracelet off her wrist. Flickered. Vanished.

Ava breathed out slowly. "They can't touch me," she reassured herself, walking on. "They're not real."

"Nothing touches you," a voice said.

Imogen. She was wearing the slinky outfit Ava remembered from the mirror maze. Her head lolled at a horrible angle, and a shattered thighbone protruded through the fabric of her dress. Even still, she was managing to pose with the broken leg carefully crossed in front of the other.

"Who are you, really?" Imogen said.

Ava didn't know anymore. Maybe she really was that ugly girl in the mirror with hard lines and a sneering mouth, laughing at everyone else but feeling nothing inside.

"Who are you?" Imogen repeated. She scratched at her skin, and her long nails tore away a strip. Underneath, her flesh was gray.

"I'm still alive," Ava said. "And you're not."

Ava closed her eyes and forced herself to walk straight through Imogen. A warm, foul-smelling breeze hit her, but that was it. When she looked back, the ghost was gone.

She could do this.

She stepped out into an open space. The mirror maze stood in front of her, and sitting on the top step was Clem. There was a hole where his heart should have been, through which Ava could see the dark sky. He swung his feet against the wood. *Thud, thud, thud.*

"Confess," he said.

"Go to hell." She went to walk past him.

Clem raised his harmonica to his mouth and played a chord. Major seven.

Ava stopped. "Why would I feel bad that you're dead?" she said.

He lowered the harmonica. "Confess," he said more coldly.

"After what you did, you think I'm going to feel sorry for you?"

A mistake—she wasn't supposed to engage with Whispers's games. She wasn't supposed to let Clem goad her into feeling anything, especially guilt.

"Confess," he said, smiling his half smile.

The music of the carnival thrummed through Ava's head, making it difficult to think. "There wasn't time to warn you," she found herself saying. Pleading, even. "And if I had, what then?"

"You wanted me to die," Clem said, twirling the harmonica faster and faster. "Confess."

Ava swallowed the dry lump in her throat. She couldn't confess. Confessing would mean Esme became the *One*. Ava could only help Jolie if no one let Whispers in. She weighed the metal stake in her hand.

"You're the worst of all of us," Clem taunted, grinning evilly. "But he'll still break you in the end."

"You're right," she said, swinging the stake at his head. The ghost dissolved. "But not all of us break in the same way."

TWENTY-NINE

Twinkling LEDs reflected from every mirrored surface. Ava walked through the constellations with one hand on the wall and the other gripping the metal stake. She couldn't trust her own eyes or her ears. But then, she was used to navigating the world with her thoughts held at arm's length. She could do this.

And then Noah's ghost stepped out of the mirrors. He didn't look like the others. He looked too real to be a ghost, but his skin was too bloodless to be alive. Water streamed down his face and dripped into a puddle at his feet. He walked toward her, bare feet trailing seaweed.

"Noah," she said. "Why did you have to go?"

Thunder crashed outside. Lights flickered. The smell of damp wood smoldering. Sulfur.

Noah grinned at her. "Vanishing is my thing."

"Yeah." She moved to reach out for him but stopped herself. "You're not really here."

His smile disappeared. "Because you were too late to save me. Or maybe you didn't want to, just like you didn't want to help Rachel."

Ava watched him closely. He looked so much like the real Noah, right down to the curiosity sparkling in his eyes. But Noah was dead.

She stood on tiptoe and leaned forward to kiss the empty place where his lips should have been. "Goodbye, Noah," she whispered. When she opened her eyes again, he was gone.

A slow clap caught her attention from inside the mirror. Whispers was watching her with something close to a smirk.

"You're doing so well," he purred.

"Let Jolie go," Ava snarled. When he only smiled in reply, she swung her weapon at the mirror. It exploded into a thousand gleaming shards.

Whispers rematerialized in the next mirror, looking less than pleased. "You still don't understand, do you? I make the rules of the game, not you. You don't get to ask things of me."

"I wasn't asking," she said.

"This is getting tedious. You won't be the first *One* to lose their tongue."

"I will never be your *One*."

"Then Esme will, and you won't be able to help Jolie. I'll

make sure of that. The only way to save Jolie is to *let me in*. It's you or Esme. Make your choice."

"I choose the third option: neither of us."

"Alfred was like you. He refused to be my *One*, but he couldn't stop me from clinging to his guilt. All I had to do was wait for Livia to come along, opened up by her own secrets. And an immortal being like me doesn't care about waiting forty years."

"You'll wait forever. Trapped in your world, all by yourself."

"You think you're strong, but everyone breaks in the end," he sighed. "It's your choice. Kill Esme and save Jolie, or save your own soul and let Jolie die."

"Go to hell!" Ava swung the stake at his mirror, but he vanished before the glass smashed. He didn't return. Ava supposed he'd said his piece. He'd pushed the players into the arena, and now he got to sit back and watch. Ava had no choice but to continue on the path she'd chosen.

She passed through the doorway into the endless archways of the maze. A hundred arches in every direction, only one of them real. Ava's reflection watched her a thousand times over. And then, movement. Esme stepped into the mirrors. One thousand Esmes, three thousand howling wolves. Her white hair was disheveled, and her eyes burned feverishly.

"You shouldn't have come," the thousand Esmes said.

"The storm didn't give me much choice," Ava said. She

tried to work out which Esme was the real one, but it was impossible to tell. She swung at the first. A mirror. Shards of glass crunched underfoot as she moved on to the next.

"Confess to the rest of your secret, and I won't have to hurt you," Esme said. "I don't want to hurt you."

"Can't say that makes two of us." Ava swung again. She tried to not think too hard about how it would feel to break a person rather than a mirror. There was no line, not anymore. She concentrated on the weight of the metal in her hands and the memory of Jolie's burnt skin. Shallow breaths. The smell of smoke.

Another mirror shattered.

"Jolie's dying because you let Whispers in! But you can still confess and end all of this." Although Ava already knew Esme wouldn't, just like Ava wouldn't.

"What would be the point of that?" Esme sighed. "Why would I sacrifice myself to save you? I told you I would kill to save my own life, Ava. I told you that friendship is a weakness."

"You don't really feel that way. I saw how you looked at Livia. You loved her—"

"And she's dead!"

"But you can still save Jolie. If you won't confess, then you leave me no choice."

"That's it then," Esme said, smiling the briefest of smiles. She took out a penknife and flicked it open.

"That's it."

The two girls circled each other through the maze. Esme would disappear for a second, only to reappear from another direction. Ava trailed her fingers along the walls. Tried to memorize the layout of the doorways.

She swung again but smashed only another reflection. Ava eyed the spiderweb of cracks spreading across the nearest mirror. It crept downward, onto the floor tiles. Ava stopped focusing on Esme and focused on the cracks instead. They cut through each of Esme's reflections except for one.

Ava swung the stake and connected with real flesh and bone. Esme dropped to the ground in a fine red mist of blood from her broken nose. Pieces of mirror fell around her. Blood streamed down her face. Ava dropped the stake. Slowly bent down to pick up a shard of mirror. Held it like a dagger, feeling it slice into her hand.

Whispers appeared in the mirrors, clapping enthusiastically. Ava glanced at him, with his eager expression and black eyes.

"What are you waiting for?" he taunted, his voice echoing in the small space. "Don't you want to save Jolie?"

Ava took a single step toward Esme, but it felt like wading through treacle. She couldn't go any further. Even with Jolie's life at stake, she was still too weak to act. Too much of a coward.

"Would you like an audience?" Whispers said, snapping his fingers. A roomful of ghosts appeared to watch: Scarlett,

Teddy, Olly, Livia, Imogen, Clem, Noah. They all stared with hollow eyes. And Rachel, standing at Whispers's side, broken and twisted.

"Kill her," they rasped, an awful discordant noise that belonged to no one and everyone at the same time. "This is who you are."

"I don't know if it is," Ava said softly. She loosened her grip on the mirror shard.

Whispers grinned slowly. "If you won't kill her to save your friend, then how about for revenge?"

He snapped his fingers again, and another ghost appeared in the mirrors—Jolie in her sooty panda suit, crackling and smoking, eyes like embers. She stared straight through Ava with no trace of friendship left in her expression. Just anger, always anger.

"Jolie," Ava said, her legs giving way beneath her. The shard of glass clinked to the floor.

Whispers was behind her, breathing in her ear. She could feel him, and not just in her head, but creeping into the rest of her like a wrongness that prickled beneath her skin and made her mouth taste of rust. This was what it would feel like to let him in and become his *One*.

"She died all alone," he taunted. "You couldn't save her. But you can avenge her."

"Make her pay," Jolie's ghost groaned, breathing out smoke and sparks. "A real friend would make her pay."

THIRTY

Ava's guilt was a chain reaction of implosions. Her entire friendship with Jolie burned white-hot. Summers spent throwing bread at seagulls, and stealing menthol cigarettes from Jolie's brother, and jumping off the seawall with screams and laughter. Lying on Jolie's bed and dreaming of their future, back when their dreams felt close enough to touch but distant enough to chase.

Everything swallowed itself with fiery belches until all that remained was a single black point.

"You killed her," Ava choked, groping on the floor for the shard of broken mirror.

Esme sat up. She didn't appear to notice the pieces of glass embedded in her hands, the glass that made her hair gleam like it was full of diamonds. She wiped her bleeding nose with the back of her hand, smearing blood across her cheek and into her hair. She stared defiantly at Ava, as if daring her to do it.

Ava staggered to her feet. She brandished the mirror with a shaking hand. "Get up," she spat.

Esme heaved herself upright, leaving bloody handprints on the mirrors. The ghosts stretched their jaws into large grins, far too wide for anything human.

"Kill her," they hissed, clasping and unclasping their hands in anticipation.

Esme wiped her face again. There were tears this time. Ava didn't care.

"A real friend would kill her," Jolie's ghost said.

Ava tightened her grip on the glass dagger. She stepped toward Esme. Lifted the shard of mirror. Then she caught sight of her own reflection in its gleaming surface. Sharp around the edges. Cruel and bitter. A mouthful of splintered teeth, brown with rot. Something inside her sagged.

She hesitated. "Jolie?" she said. "Do you remember when we were thirteen and a seagull broke its neck on my patio door?"

Jolie bared her teeth. "Of course. Now kill her."

"When I couldn't stop crying, do you remember what you told me?"

She turned away from Esme to watch Jolie's reaction. The ghost snarled at her, eyes flashing with flames.

"You told me that the reason you loved me was because I *cared about shit*, even *diseased, food-stealing flying rats*, as you put it. You said I always reminded you that the world could still be beautiful if you just looked at it from the right angle. That was the moment I decided to become a photographer. Because I wanted you to see what I saw."

"So?" the ghost said.

"The Jolie I know has spent the last six months furious with me because I was acting like someone I'm not. She wouldn't want me to become a killer, because she'd know it isn't who I am."

"Do it!" the ghost screamed, but it was no longer Jolie's voice.

"No." She dropped the mirror. Blood coated her palm.

"You're not my friend," Jolie's ghost spat.

"And you're not Jolie," Ava said, her voice cracking into a sob. "I'm so sorry. For everything that's happened. For trying to be someone I wasn't and forgetting about our friendship. For not saving you. But I know who I want to be now."

Jolie growled. Ava stepped toward her and held out her hand. Jolie reached out like she was going to take it, but she dissolved into smoke at the first touch. Whispers rushed out of Ava, back into the mirrors.

"No," he screamed. "You're not following the rules!"

"The rules you've been making up to suit yourself?"

Ava wiped a tear away and forced herself to meet his black-eyed stare.

"I can still get inside your head," a voice whispered.

"But you can't stay," she said. "I won't let you in. You won't turn me into a killer."

He smiled slowly. "I don't need you," he said. "I have Esme."

Esme had pressed herself into a corner, tears dripping off her chin.

"Pick it up," Whispers ordered.

Esme bent down to retrieve the penknife she'd dropped.

"It's *her* fault Livia died," Whispers said, his voice all sugary. "Ava took her camera to the roof, and I heard everything Livia said. I heard her confession."

Esme looked up at Ava, hurt and confusion making her look lost.

"Ava knew, and she never told anyone. She could have warned Livia she was in danger, but she chose not to."

"He's messing with your head," Ava said.

"Is it true?" Esme said.

Ava couldn't lie. She stayed silent.

"Kill her," Whispers growled. "Together we'll make something beautiful, Esme."

Esme's hair hung across her bloodied face, making her look not quite human.

"It was his game that killed Livia." Ava backed away as Esme advanced. "Just like it was him who killed Jolie, not you."

"You killed Livia," Esme whispered. "You took her from me."

"No, I didn't." She stumbled back around another corner over a carpet of broken glass.

Esme appeared in the mirrors, her eyes wild. "She was everything to me."

"Is this what Livia would want?" Ava said.

"Don't you talk about her. Don't you dare!"

"She was my friend too."

"Shut up, shut up!"

"Esme, please. Look." Ava gestured to the walls, where Livia's ghost flitted between distant mirrors, black veins marring her face. "That's not Livia."

"It's all I have left of her."

Ava took a deep breath. She stopped retreating and stepped toward Esme. Let her press the knife against the side of her neck.

"Livia's here," she said, touching her palm to Esme's chest. "Remember her here."

"I can't," Esme sobbed. "It's all gone."

"Kill her," Whispers hissed from the mirrors. "Prove your devotion to me, and you will never go hungry again. I will give you everything you could ever dream of."

Ava ignored him and focused on Esme. "Do you remember how you met Livia for the first time? I can. It was the day you moved to Portgrave. A few of us came by on our bikes to see the new family. Do you remember what happened?"

She nodded slowly. "I hit my head on the moving van door waving to all of you, and Livia ran over to help me."

"I watched her run through traffic to get to you. Do you think that girl would have wanted you to become a murderer in her name?"

"She's not here to answer that," Esme said softly.

"And do you think she'd have wanted you to give up your freedom in the name of revenge? Because if you take Whispers's deal, you'll never be free again."

Tears ran down Esme's face. "She'd have wanted me to do the right thing, but she was a better person than I am. I'm not sure I have it in me to be like her."

"The whole time we've been on this island, you've told me that you don't care about anyone except yourself. But I don't believe it. I've seen the real you, and I'm pretty sure you're one of the good guys. Livia knew it too. She never gave up on you."

"You'll ruin my image," Esme said, managing a smile.

Ava reached up and gently took the knife from her hand.

In the mirrors, Livia's ghost vanished into nothing. Ava breathed out slowly and wrapped her arms around Esme's neck.

"No, no, no," Whispers cried, sounding more like a petulant child than a monster. His image guttered and flashed in and out of existence, like he was struggling to hold on.

"It wasn't the shoplifting that brought me to the pier," Esme said. "It was Livia. I found her invite and knew she was coming, so I did too. Livia was my secret. We split up six months ago because I was too scared to admit that I loved her. Now it's too late to tell her."

"I wanted Rachel to die," Ava admitted, the words pouring from her mouth. "At least, I thought I did. And then I didn't."

Esme frowned. Stepped back. Rachel's ghost stepped forward.

"I was bored, I suppose. I wanted something to happen. A story for me to tell. I watched her standing on the Oracle for half an hour. I took a dozen shots from different angles and waited for her to jump."

"And then she did?"

"It took a few seconds for her to fall, and the whole time, I wished I could go back and do something to help. She was suddenly this living person—and then she was dead."

"You didn't know me," Rachel's ghost said, sounding young and scared.

"I wish I had," Ava said. "I wish I'd put the camera down and found out who you really were."

The ghost nodded, and then it was gone.

Esme reached out to take Ava's hand. "I kind of think regret and guilt aren't such terrible things. Not if they make us into better people."

"They don't make you better people," Whispers growled. He was no longer in the closest mirror. He'd jumped back several layers. Small. Weakened. Fading. "They won't save you."

"Then we'll spend the rest of our lives learning how to be better," Ava said.

"We'll save ourselves," Esme said, "and there won't be enough guilt left to hold you here."

"You can't do this!" Whispers's form flashed between a thousand different iterations, none of them sticking.

Esme snatched up the metal stake Ava had brought into the maze. She swung it at the wall with a scream and smashed a hole through the mirror. A long fissure spread downward, snaking across to where Ava stood. Like lightning, it branched and grew until every wall was a fractal of cracks.

Whispers bellowed in fury. Esme swung the weapon again, and broken mirrors rained down like falling stars. The pieces tinkled onto the floor to make a gleaming carpet. Ava and Esme found themselves standing in the center of an empty black box with twinkling lights shining down from the ceiling. A green sign read FIRE ESCAPE. A door with a push bar. Clear night sky.

"Is he gone?" Esme whispered.

Ava glanced up at the flickering fairy lights overhead. "Sleeping. Falling," she said. "Either way, let's get the hell out of here."

Supporting Esme with one arm, Ava stumbled through the floodwaters as the lights of the carnival guttered and faded. The moon burst free of the clouds and lit the island in a bright, otherworldly light.

"Where do we go?" Esme said.

"Anywhere but here. Far away from Portgrave. Far away from all of this. We have to leave it all behind."

Esme glanced up at the smoke and sparks rising from behind the outcrop, where the boathouse burned. "I can do better," she said. "I have to be better."

"Come with me," Ava said. "Travel the world and never look back."

"And ruin my whole lone wolf image?" She side-eyed Ava, and her face cracked into a grin. "Yeah, why not."

Ava guided her through the tents. They hurried past Whispers's portrait hut at the edge of the island. The sea crashed darkly against the shore. As Ava watched, the hut collapsed into the water and drifted apart as if it had never been.

"I hope he never finds his way back up to our world," Ava said.

"Alone forever feels kind of fitting for him," Esme agreed.

"Forgotten," Ava added.

It felt like the end. It should have been the end. Then Ava heard the snap of wood and the sound of waves sucking back from the shore. Something rose from the water, a dark shadow against the night sky. It was shaped like a man, but as tall as the cliffs and wrongly proportioned. Its legs were broken debris that had washed up on the rocks. Its arms were braids of seaweed and stinking dead jellyfish with leathery skin. Tiny pieces of mirror gleamed where a face should be, reminding Ava of the compound eyes of a fly.

"No one escapes," it said, wood and metal grinding together to make the words.

It brought a huge fist down toward them. It smashed through Baldo's stage and exploded shards of wood into the air.

"The tunnel!" Ava cried, running for the hidden entrance between the rocks.

They ducked inside as the monster stamped its foot down where they'd been standing seconds earlier.

"Go, go," Ava gasped. Her feet pounded against the mud. She jumped the first of the funnel-shaped holes, now full of dead roots. She weaved past the one that had nearly swallowed Esme. The roots on the walls were withering and peeling away. Ava slapped the stringy curtains out of her face. Everything was dying.

They made it to the cavern. But smoke from the boathouse was billowing in through the tunnel. There was nowhere else to go. The cavern shook. The piles of old objects vibrated and fell. An impossibly loud noise knocked them off their feet. A crack spread across the ceiling, snaked down the walls, crept across the floor. Clods of earth and rock rained down. Another bang. Ava tried to stand but lost her balance and fell to her knees.

"He's breaking through to get to us," Esme cried. "Run!"

Too late. With a rush of dust and noise and exploding rock, the ceiling fell. Ava couldn't see or hear or even tell which way was up. She scrambled blindly away from the chaos as the cavern collapsed around her. The air was thick and choking. It stung her lungs when she tried to scream.

"You can't escape me," a voice boomed.

The monster emerged through the dust, trampling what was left of the cavern. The whole cliff had split in half. Baldo's cage lay on top of the rubble. The wind picked up debris and swirled it around Whispers like a tornado. The ground rumbled like the whole island was collapsing in on itself. Long fingers grabbed Ava around the throat. *It's not real, it's not real*, she told herself. *He can't touch you.* Only she couldn't breathe. The fingers tightened and tightened. Her feet kicked helplessly.

"No one escapes," Whispers laughed. "I have destroyed thousands upon thousands of you humans, and I will not be beaten by *children*."

He snatched her up, high into the air. She could see the whole island, from the broken pier to the burning hut to the carnival as tents fell into a spreading chasm. Behind Whispers, the cracked ground revealed a network of black holes filled with dying roots. Beyond, darkness stretched downward forever, toward the heart of the island.

"Would you like to see where I came from?" Whispers taunted.

Ava could feel the world closing in on her. Her chest burned like it was on fire. She clawed at the seaweed fingers encircling her neck, but it was no use. She was going to die. This was what it felt like to know you were going to die. He was going to throw her into the pit, and she'd fall and fall, just like Rachel had.

But as everything slipped away, she saw something—a figure emerging from the dust, climbing to the top of the rubble mountain. Bleeding and filthy but as defiant as ever.

"Let her go!" Esme ordered.

"You can't save her," Whispers laughed.

"I'll let you in on a secret. I just want to save myself." Esme winked at Ava, and then she jumped.

Esme collided with the monster and wrapped her arms tightly around its neck. Ava felt its grip loosen enough for her to fall away. She landed heavily at the edge of the crevasse, millimeters from oblivion. The monster teetered and stumbled, pieces of wood and mirror falling away as it struggled to cling to their world. And then it was gone, tumbling into the hole with a terrible howl, taking Esme with it.

"No!" Ava screamed, but it was too late. She scrambled toward the edge, arms outstretched as if she might stop Esme from falling and somehow catch Rachel too. But both of them fell. Esme and Whispers were swallowed by darkness. It was over.

THIRTY-ONE

Ava pushed the canoe away from the island. It rocked on the waves, sloshing icy water over her legs. A current caught hold of the boat and spun it away from the rocks and through the fog, faster and faster. Ava let the boat find its own course.

Once she was clear of the island, she pushed Jolie's carefully wrapped body overboard. The rocks inside the tent fabric pulled her down to the bottom of the ocean. A pirate burial. Jolie would have approved.

"I should have saved you," Ava said.

Jolie's ghost flickered in and out of existence, her eyes no longer glowing and her skin no longer burning. "Leave it behind. All the guilt, all the regrets. Leave me behind."

Ava shook her head. "I'm not sure I can."

"Then there's a chance he'll follow you like he did Alfred."

Ava shielded her face from a wave that threatened to drag them under. For a second, the nose of the boat dipped beneath the surface. But then it righted itself somehow. Ava watched the pier disappearing. The smoke seemed to clear long enough that she thought she saw figures watching from the rocks. Rachel, Scarlett, Teddy, Olly, Imogen, Clem. Noah, waving. Esme and Livia, holding hands.

"Leave it all behind," she repeated, and the ghosts melted into the fog. Jolie smiled, and then she was gone. The empty space inside Ava had never felt more full of grief.

A current spun her in a circle. She rested the paddle on her knees and gave in to the dizziness.

The boat's spinning eventually slowed by itself. Ava spotted Portgrave in the distance, getting farther and farther away. She was reminded of some documentary she'd watched at school, only half paying attention because she was too busy sharing a packet of sweets with Jolie.

"The thing about riptides is that they always circle around eventually and bring you back to shore," she said. Trying to escape seemed pointless.

From the current, the island, herself. But she was going to keep fighting. She had to keep fighting.

Picking up the paddle, she dipped it into the water and tried to get her bearings. She squinted through the fog, but there was nothing to see. No shoreline, no ocean, no island, no pier. All she had was herself. Ava hoped on the ghosts of her friends that she could be enough.

ACKNOWLEDGMENTS

This book started out as a love letter to Agatha Christie, the Point Horror books, and all the scary films I probably shouldn't have watched as a child. I am forever thankful to a lot of lovely people for helping me turn it into an actual book.

If it wasn't for the Write Mentor Children's Novel Award, its Jedi Master, Stuart White, and all the competition readers, I would have given up. The competition not only gave me a glimmer of confidence in my writing but also introduced me to my amazing agent.

Thanks to Chloe Seager for your insight, support, and all-around cleverness. You helped make this a far better story than I ever could have hoped for and sent it out into the world on my behalf.

To my UK editor, Lauren Fortune, thank you for seeing straight to the heart of this book and for being its most enthusiastic advocate. And to everyone else at Scholastic UK who has played a part in this journey so far.

To my US editor, Steve Geck, for bringing my book over to the States, Cassie Gutman and Alison Cherry, for their editing greatness, Nicole Hower and Kelly Lawler for the beautiful cover, and Beth Oleniczak and Jackie Douglass for all things marketing and publicity. I'm so happy that I get to introduce this book to a new continent of readers.

I owe a glass of wine to my earliest readers, including Ailsa Stuart, who saw potential in the manuscript back when it quite literally didn't make any sense, and Fiona Longmuir, whose love for evil little Whispers warmed my heart.

To Phill, Eliza, and Max, who all make my writing dreams possible. I will never be able to thank you enough.

ABOUT THE AUTHOR

© Alexis Knight Photography

Kathryn Foxfield writes dark books about characters who aren't afraid to fight back, but she wouldn't last five minutes in one of her own stories. Kathryn is an ex-microbiologist, a onetime popular science author, and a parent. She lives in rural Oxfordshire in the UK, but her heart belongs to London.